Mrs. Jane West

A Tale of the Times

Vol. I.

Mrs. Jane West

A Tale of the Times
Vol. I.

ISBN/EAN: 9783337137397

Printed in Europe, USA, Canada, Australia, Japan

Cover: Foto ©Andreas Hilbeck / pixelio.de

More available books at **www.hansebooks.com**

TALE

OF THE

TIMES.

BY THE AUTHOR OF A GOSSIP'S STORY.

DEDICATED, BY PERMISSION, TO MRS. CARTER.

IN TWO VOLUMES.

VOL. I.

While Hope pictures to us a flattering scene of future blifs,
let us deny its pencil thofe colours which are too bright
to be lafting.—When hearts deferving happinefs would
unite their fortune, Virtue would crown them with an
unfading garland of modeft, hurtlefs flowers; but ill-
judging paffion will force the gaudier rofe into the wreath,
whofe thorn offends them when its leaves are dropt.

SHERIDAN'S *Rivals.*

Dublin:

PRINTED BY WILLIAM PORTER, GRAFTON-STREET.

1799.

ADVERTISEMENT.

SOME recent publications may, perhaps, make it neceſſary for the Author of the preſent Work, in order to evade the cenſure of plagiariſm, to ſtate, that ſhe could, if neceſſary, produce the teſtimony of ſeveral reſpectable witneſſes, to prove the entire plot of the following ſtory, and nearly three parts of the writing, were finiſhed previouſly to the appearance of the play called "The Stranger" at Drury-lane Theatre; and that ſhe is not conſcious of having borrowed one idea from that much-admired performance.

She has ſeen two works advertiſed, which ſhe has been informed bear a reſemblance to her own plan: "Letters "from an Hindoo Rajah;" and "Waldroff; or, the Dangers of Philoſophy." As ſhe has never met with either, ſhe cannot tell how far her ſentiments may be ſimilar to theirs.

There

There is a clafs of writers to whom fhe owns herfelf under fome obligations, as they not only fuggefted to her the portrait of her complete villain, but alfo furnifhed her with feveral fpecious paffages, which fhe has appropriated, unaltered, to the character of Fitzofborne. She could fpecify the quotations, with the names of the authors; but perhaps their *liberality* will be better pleafed with a general acknowledgment.

A

TALE

OF THE

TIMES.

CHAP. I.

Forth fteps the fpruce philofopher, and tells
Of homogeneal, and difcordant, fprings
And principles; of caufes, how they work
By neceffary laws their fure effects;
Of action and re-action. He has found
The fource of the difeafe that nature feels,
And bids the world take heart, and banifh fear.
COWPER.

MRS. PRUDENTIA HOMESPUN again begs
leave to return thanks to the world for its very
favourable reception of her lucubrations. She
is now firmly convinced, that the clamours
which are circulated againft the injuftice and
bad tafte of the times, may be confidered either
as the declamations of difappointed ambition,
or the ebullitions of malevolent fpleen, foured
by the fuccefs of fome happier rival. She con-
ceives herfelf to be particularly fortunate in ex-
ifting at a period more favourable to mental exertions than thofe which have been commonly
deemed the golden ages of literature. Contemplating from her eafy chair the vaft extent
of

of modern difcoveries, not only in the fciences,
but in morals and government, and extending
her meditations from reflection on what her
learned co-adjutors have done, to fpeculation on
what they propofe doing, fhe is compelled to
acknowlege, that the clofe of the eighteenth
century claims diftinguifhed pre-eminence for
thofe indubitable marks of genius, originality in enterprife, and boldnefs of invention
over the colder ærás of Pericles, Auguftus, and
the Medicis. Nay, fhe will go fo far as to affirm, that the labours of the " New Philofophy" will be remembered by their effects, when
the theories of all former fchools fhall be forgotten.

It muft be very gratifying to a retired old woman, to confider that her productions may fail
down this fwelling ftream of fame with thofe
of her immortal contemporaries. She confeffes
that her ideas differ in fome refpects from
theirs; but as every one profeffes the fame end,
namely, the improvement of the univerfe, fhe
rejoices that fhe is permitted, by the liberality
of the times, to diffeminate her own peculiar
fentiments. If fhe be of opinion, that Morality appeared to better advantage when fhe was
contented to be the handmaid of Piety, than
fince fhe has fet up for an independent character; if fhe be convinced, that the abilities and
attainments of man are in this life fo limited,
that he will never be able to " wield thofe elements," to endow a machine with intellectual
powers, or to array himfelf with a felf-invefted
immortality; if fhe be perfuaded, that the filial
and conjugal ties are no remnants of feudal bar-
barifm, but happy inftitutions, calculated to
promote domeftic peace; if fhe has been taught,
that

that religion is more than fentiment, and female
virtue fomething ftronger than exterior decorum; if fhe fhudder at the eloquence which
extenuates impiety, terms feduction an amiable
frailty, and gaming an elegant amufement con-
demned by the infane morality of the law;
furely fhe may hope for that celebrity which a
bold oppofition to received opinions generally
enfures. Nay, fhould fhe even prefer the
Gothic ruff and pinner, as better adapted to
Britifh wives and mothers than the loofe drapery
of Grecian Bacchanals, or the more offenfive
appearance of uncivilifed favages, though recommended by the fanction of Parifian enthu-
fiafts, when, with more than Pagan infatuation or cannibal infenfibility, they meet to
commemorate in their feftive dances—not the
triumphs of their Gods, nor the death of their
enemies—but the murder of their parents, their
hufbands, and their children; may fhe not
plead a clofe attention to the coftume of manners, and reproach the fenfual copyifts of a
Cleopatra or an Afpafia with want of energy,
who adopt all the characteriftics of the archetype, of which they exhibit a degrading model?

Her intention in refuming the pen is to en-
force her opinions by argument, and to illuftrate them by example; and fhe reveals thofe
intentions thus early, that the lover of the wonderful, and the admirer of the horrific, may
not complain of having been cheated into the
perufal of a performance that has not only a
plan for its conduct, but alfo a moral tendency
in its defign. Mrs. Prudentia intends to lead
her readers through no other labyrinth than the
wiles

wiles of fyftematic depravity, nor to prefent any object more foul-harrowing than a deceived and entangled, but ultimately penitent heart.

While fhe confefles that the ground-work of her ftory has a remote analogy to fome well-known facts, fhe ftrongly reprobates the idea of perfonality. The incidents are all her own, and it is only in one portrait that fhe has attempted to fketch a likenefs from nature. She affures the cenforious, that, even in that portrait, fhe has fo adjufted the drapery and varied the colours, that it will be impoffible for the moft curious eye to difcover who fat for the outline.

Though regardlefs whether the fafhionable inftructors of the day record her as one of their kindred fpirits, or condemn her for being a fervile admirer of prefcribed forms and reprobated reftrictions, there is a numerous clafs of readers, whofe favour Mrs. Prudentia is anxioufly folicitous to obtain—the truly liberal, and the fincerely good. With candour to forgive fmall faults, they unite difcernment to difcover good intentions, and courage to defend the caufe of principle againft the farcafms of wit, and the cool contempt of piqued infidelity. To fuch readers, and fuch critics, fhe fubmits the following pages; and as a proper reprefentative of the illuftrious order, fhe intreats

Mrs. CARTER

to accept her public thanks for the invaluable honour of her approbation of the Writer's former efforts, and her permiffion to infcribe thefe pages with her refpected name. If the prefent attempt fhould appear favourable to the caufe

of

of morality and religion, fhe humbly hopes, that the lenity infeparable from fuperior talents will pardon thofe errors in the compofition, which an accurate tafte muft difcover and difapprove.

———————

CHAP. II.

The faireft anceftry on earth,
  Without defert, is poor ;
And every deed of lofty worth
  Is but a claim for more.
          SIR ELDRED OF THE BOWER.

SOME reafons, which are not neceffary to be developed in the following pages, made me wifh to take a little excurfion from Danbury in the courfe of laft autumn. A generous public having fupplied the means, I hired a one-horfe chaife, and taking with me my whole family, confifting of my maid Betty and my favourite old tabby cat, fet out for Brighton. I there heard a narrative which made a very deep impreffion upon my mind ; and, as the communicativenefs of my difpofition will not allow me to conceal any thing which I imagine capable of conveying inftruction, or even innocent amufement, to that worthy fet of beings, whom, in common with my fifter authors, I term candid readers, I have determined to prefer publifhing the Hiftory of the Countefs of Monteith to a particular defcription of my own travels. To this refolution I may, perhaps, have been influenced by a culpable degree of modefty. The

A 3   public

public, no doubt, are very anxious to know
how many miles a day Betty and I journeyed; at
what inns we flopped, and what we had for
fupper. Could not a florid defcription beftow
fome fprigs of fame on the chalky cliffs of Dun-
ftable? Might not the horrors of Woburn
fands be rendered more gloomy by a convenient
whirlwind, hurrying into the air the arid foil?
Is there no old decayed manor houfe, where I
could call forth the " fheeted dead to fquenk
and gibber;" or, fuppofing we were benighted
on Finchley-common, could either Rhætian or
Carpathian Alps fix a more appropriate ftation
for the haunts of a banditti? Though in a
former publication I have unwarily announced
my age and order, Betty, for aught the world
knows, may be young and beautiful; nay, fhe
may be an orphan foundling, the heirefs of
fome diftinguifhed family; and I may, if I
choofe, after a long feries of adventures, unite
her in the hymeneal bond with fome all accomplifhed youth, who had previoufly refcued us
from the robbers after a moft bloody engagement. I begin to fufpect that I have chofen the
lefs promifing, or rather the lefs lucrative plan;
but I entreat my readers to believe, that it is
not becaufe I want powers for the terrific and
the romantic, that I continue to purfue the
moral and the probable. Something muft be
allowed to my defire of fupporting that character of firmnefs afcribed to my fifterhood, and
which, though it fimply confifts in choofing to
have our own way, the wits are apt to call pertinacity. I will alfo candidly own, that, fince
the fuperior ftation in this walk is already occupied by real genius, I have too much prudence to enter into a competition, where I fhall
be

be fure to meet with a defeat; and too much pride to enlift among a herd of fervile imitators, who miftake confufion for defcription, and fancy that what is horribly impoffible, muft be interefting and grand. But, as my days of dotage are not far diftant, if lady Monteith fhould be unfortunate in her appeal for attention, I and Betty may appear upon the fcene; even my cat too may be introduced in an epifode. I have feen a fubject equally unpromifing worked up to an aftonifhing effect, and really admired by readers who had been fome years out of the nurfery:—But, inftead of terrifying the world with a denunciation of what I may do, let me haften to fulfil my prefent promife.

IT is now more than ten years fince Powerfcourt Houfe exhibited a fcene of feftivity and hofpitality unrivalled in modern times, and which might ferve to recal to the mind of the fpectator the fplendid fêtes of Kenilworth, where the lady of the lake welcomed the approach of majefty, and the cruel diffolute earl of Leicefter fought to divert general attention from his vices by a captivating difplay of elegance and amufement. The motives of the venerable baronet who inhabited Powerfcourt were widely different from thofe of the haughty favourite of Elizabeth. His wife was too inoffenfive to fear cenfure; his heart never panted for court-favour; and the praife of magnificence or refined tafte prefented no attractions to his unobtrufive and benevolent mind. He called all the country together, and ftrove to make them very happy, becaufe he was very happy himfelf; and the occafion of this exuberant joy was the union of his only daughter and heirefs, Geraldine Powerfcourt, with James earl

earl of Monteith, a young Nobleman who had just attained complete majority, and acceded to all the splendid titles and fortune of the house of Macdonald.

Beside all the beauty and fashion of North Wales, these distinguished nuptials were honoured by the presence of two deities, generally supposed to be absolutely inimical to each other. Cupid and Plutus, forgetting ancient enmity, agreed jointly to light the Hymeneal torch. It was impossible to suppose a union contracted under a more perfect coincidence of harmonious equality. The families on both sides might be said to lose themselves in the clouds ;. for their claims to pre-eminence, advancing far beyond the limit of authentic history, soared into regions which no prudent antiquary would dare to explore. The lineal honours of these illustrious families rested upon a surer basis than mere oral tradition. Sir William Powerscourt could point out the spot of ground where his Ordovician ancestor harangued his vassals before he mounted his scythe-armed car, and led them to join the British forces assembled at Caradoc: and an aunt of lord Monteith's preserved the beak of the galley, which conveyed Donald king of the Isles from Illa, when he paid a visit of ceremony to his contemporary Fergus, some hundred years prior to the invasion of the Romans. It is true, that some incredulous critics, whom nothing can convince, doubted whether the feudal customs, with which Sir William embellished his narrative, existed at that remote period; and I have heard a whisper, that the venerable relic which lady Madelina so carefully preserved was nothing more than the remains of a great gilded dragon, originally suspended over

over a Chinese temple belonging to her ladyship's *maternal* great-grandfather, though so happily executed, that, like Hamlet's cloud, you
might say it was equally like a " camel, or an
ousel, or a whale."

But though these vestiges of remote superiority might rather excite the doubts than fix
the conviction of the observer of costume, the
Macdonalds and Powerscourts preferred indubitable claims to the honours of antiquity,—extensive influence and ample possessions. It sometimes happens, that close attention to adventitious or fantastic appendages induces us to overlook inherent permanent qualities. Lady Madelina's zeal for the dignity of her family was so
warmly exercised in the defence of old Donald's
galley, that she had no leisure to advert to the
fearless intrepidity and the generous liberality
with which her ancestors defended the rights
of their clan, and succoured their oppressed dependants during the period that the house of
Stuart sate upon the Scottish throne. " They
shone the glory of the north" till after the
restoration ; but the reign of Charles the second,
so fatal to principle and morality, first conta-
minated the house of Monteith, and sapped
the foundations of its feudal greatness. In the
voluptuous court of that dissipated monarch, the
then earl forgot the wild shores of Loch Lomond, and the " flowery borders of the ancient
Forth ;" and abandoning his castle to ruin, and
his dependants to despair, glittered a faint
satellite in the train of tinsel greatness. His
extravagance and prodigality were in some degree repaired by the alliance of his successor
with the heiress of a rich Blackwell-hall factor ;
but the archives of the family are rather silent
upon

upon that head, and Lady Madelina could never relate a fingle anecdote explanatory of the event of thofe difgraceful nuptials. Since that period, the Macdonalds had perfevered in the plan of leaving the family eftate, clear from incumbrances, to the eldeft fon. The younger fons either fell in the defence of their country, or ftarved in fome obfcure corner, while the daughters had only their high birth to add to the perfonal qualifications of merit and beauty, advantages not always fufficient to attract the mercenary heart of man. With no other portion Lady Madelina herfelf beftowed on the fortunate head of the houfe of Frazer, the ineftimable treafure of her hand. He was indeed far advanced into the vale of years, and his title was only fimple Sir Simon; but her ladyfhip preferred him to all the dukes, marquiffes, and earls, who, according to the indubitable teftimony of herfelf and her maid Peggy, had for more than twenty years unremittingly implored her compaffion.

The father of the young earl, whofe nuptials with the heirefs of Powerfcourt have been announced in the beginning of this chapter, fell a victim to the demon of modern honour, about the fame time that the pale orgies of diffipation had made a vifible inroad in his lady's health. The fhock at the dreadful circumftances of his exit haftened the cruel attacks of difeafe, and fhe expired a few months after her lord. The noble pair had ever found each other's fociety too vapid to difpel the gloom of one domeftic evening; yet his lordfhip conceived himfelf obliged to refent the intrufion of a young officer, who entered her ladyfhip's box at the opera at a time when the earl was of her party. He fell at the firft fire, and the countefs

found

found it impoffible to furvive him. The fcandal-ous chronicles of the age afferted, that the colo-nel's appearance was neither unexpected nor un-welcome to any but the earl, and that difappoint-ment, and the neceffity of feclufion and œcono-mical retrenchment, barbed the mortal dart of woe in the bofom of the fair inconfolable. Till I am convinced that jealoufy is the only motive which can direct the attention of a hufband to his own wife, and that connubial forrow wants energy to break the fragile thread of female ex-iftence, I fhall adhere to my own reprefentation of this cataftrophe.

Lord Monteith, following the example of his progenitors, left his eftate totally unincumbered to his only fon James. His beautiful daughter Arabella found a protectrefs in the friendfhip of her aunt, lady Madelina, who adopted her as her own daughter, and publicly declared her refolution, in cafe fhe fhould produce no heir to the houfe of Frazer, to bequeath to her all the ample poffeffions with which Sir Simon's tender gratitude had endowed his beloved bride. At the age of feventeen, after having experi-enced the adulation and the luxury of two London winters, the lovely Arabella fet out for her aunt''s caftle fituated in the wilds of Loch-aber, now reduced to a ftate bordering upon fecond childhood, fhe had the melancholy prof-pect of being perfectly immured.

Her brother's plans were more eligible and agreeable. His guardians infifted that in his education he fhould purfue the routine ufually adopted by young men of his elevated rank. He had been entered at one of our public fchools, and thence removed to the Univerfity. To counteract a dangerous propenfity to the

fatal

fatal allurements of Newmarket, it was propofed immediately after his father's death, that he fhould make the tour of Europe. He returned when of age, affumed the fortunes of his family, and with them the reprefentation of the ancient peerage of Scotland in the Britifh Parliament, an honour which had been for fome time enjoyed by his anceftors.

Since the forms of his election rendered neceffary his prefence at Holyrood Houfe, he could not avoid paying a vifit to the feat of his family. His manners were popular, his countenance ftrikingly prepoffeffing, and his perfon dignified, athletic, and graceful. The Highlanders recognized in the " bonny Lad" the true reprefentative of the houfe of Macdonald; and the ancient dependants, who, fince their Lairds had deferted Monteith, vegetated on the fpot which the attachments of their youth rendered eminently dear to them, led their young mafter the tour of his domain, and pointed out to him its local advantages. They endeavoured to direct his attention to the maffy grandeur of his caftle walls, the extenfive profpects enjoyed from its turrets, and the faded magnificence of its mouldering furniture. They repeatedly affured him that in his grandfather's time Monteith boafted a diftinguifhed preference over the abode of any other Highland chieftain. The young Nobleman was not paffionately attached to ruins; the ftormy winds, howling through the long galleries, difturbed his repofe, and he wifhed for no nearer acquaintance with the genius of the tempeft. He beftowed with a liberal hand fuch relief as would afford poverty a temporary aid; but, without exerting fufficient patience to inveftigate the caufe of the calamity, or fufficient

courage

courage to redrefs the evils which even a curfory glance difcovered, he haftened to Kinloch Caftle, to pay his dutiful refpects to lady Madelina.

Neither the manners nor the refidence of her ladyfhip were calculated to remove the difguft with which "Scot and Scotland had infpired him." The houfe was fituated on a bare precipice, the foot of which was wafhed by the ftormy fea that feparated the main land from the Hebrides. When its amiable miftrefs removed from the deferted walls of Monteith, fhe carried with her all her "Houfehold Gods," I mean the venerable inhabitants of the picture gallery, and the fcreens, chairs, and tapeftry hangings, with which the white-armed fpinfters of Macdonald had fucceffively decorated their family-feat. Sir Simon, doubtlefs, felt fincere exultation at this valuable acquifition; he only ftipulated that the remains of his progenitors fhould not yield their places to the new comers. A coalition was therefore formed, and every wall and apartment in the caftle was crowded with multiplied garniture. Screen concealed fcreen, chair fupported chair; a ftripe of Jacob meeting Efau repaired the difaftrous rents too vifible in the taking of Troy, and puzzled the Ciceroni who attempted to unravel the confufed hiftory; while Frazers and Macdonalds, placed in full oppofition, frowned fierce defiance upon each other, regardlefs of the bond which now united the once rival families, and ungrateful to lady Madelina's eloquence, who gratuitoufly performed the part of eulogift to them all.

On the third day after her nephew's arrival, when fhe had explained the family exploits to the eleventh century, he unluckily recollected a moft prefling engagement which called him

instantly

inſtantly to London. The occaſion was ſo urgent, that he could not poſſibly ſtay to hear the fate of ſome collateral branches which were then divided from the parent ſtock. Lord Monteith threw himſelf into his poſt-chaiſe, and ſo ſtrongly did the connections of his anceſtors rouſe his do-meſtic feelings, that he could think of nothing but getting a good huſband for his ſiſter, to free from her confinement, till different ſcenes ex-cited gayer ideas.

CHAP. III.

In this calm ſeat he drew the healthful gale,
The happy monarch of his ſilvan train;
Here, lided by the guardians of his fold,
He walk'd his rounds, and cheer'd his bleſt domain;
His days, the days of unſtain'd nature, roll'd,
Replete with peace and joy, like patriarchs of old.

THOMSON,

IN the preceding chapter I introduced my readers to the family of the bride-groom; but I muſt beſtow ſeveral on that of the bride.

Sir William Powerſcourt's was certainly a moſt ſingular character, and in one particular he widely differed from many gentlemen of his rank in ſociety. His ſtrong attachment to the ſeat of his anceſtors was more the reſult of ge-nerous philanthropy than of any lucrative con-ſideration. 'Tis true, he conſidered Powerſcourt-houſe as circumſcribing within its domain all the beauties that fancy ever feigned; but as he rode round his eſtate, his feelings reſembled

thoſe

those of a conscientious guardian rather than of
a self-accountable owner, and the landlord and
master were in his beneficent bosom ever sunk
in the milder qualities of the protector and the
friend. His hospitable doors were open to indigence; his delicacy was never hurt by the simplicity of rustic manners; and though the indolence of his temper sometimes prevented him
from taking an active part in restraining oppres-
sion, or introducing merit to its deserved reward,
his liberal purse was always ready to remedy the
defect. "My good neighbour Jones," said he
one day, "I certainly might write to the lord
" lieutenant, and get that rogue of an adjutant
" broke, who would not admit that your son
" David was of a proper size for the militia,
" though he swore in other substitutes two
" inches shorter; but perhaps the man has
" nothing to live upon but his commission, and
" being very poor is forced to do dirty actions.
" Here; remember me to David; tell him that
" I like a lad of spirit; and there are the ten
" guineas he was disappointed of." A little
time afterward, in consequence of some nefa-
rious proceedings being discovered, the adjutant
waited upon Sir William to entreat his interces-
sion with lord W. in his behalf. He pleaded long
service and the hurry of business in his defence,
and hinted at the wants of a large family.
" Sir," said Sir William, " I dare say that
" what you tell me is very true; but as it is not
" my own affair, I don't like to write to my
" kinsman or trouble him about it. But as you
" seem to have puzzled yourself a little in these
" army matters, I think you had better try some
" other plan of life. I can put you into a farm,
" and make you game keeper of one of my
" manors;

" manors; and I hope you won't think it an
" employ beneath you, for I shall always be
" glad to see you at Powerscourt." The offer
was accepted; and Sir William afterwards owned
that, beside two years' rent, he lost a consider-
able sum with which he had entrusted him, to
enable him to set up; but his benevolent heart
never suffered him to wish the deed undone:
" for," said he, " though I believe the man was
" no better than a cheat, his wife appeared to
" be a very notable woman, and brought up her
" family very well."

Sir William did not marry till he was much
on the wrong side of forty; and even then that
event proceeded from the same principles which
governed all his actions. The wife of a neighbouring gentleman delicately hinted, that one
of her daughters was deeply in love with him,
that death must be the inevitable consequence of
his obduracy. The good baronet was thunderstruck; he had no predilection for marriage, and
certainly no preference for the young lady thus
obtruded upon his choice. His conscience entirely vindicated him from any wicked design of
stealing the fair one's affections; neither his
glass nor his flatterers had ever attributed to him
the most distance resemblance to an Adonis, and
he wondered much that any body should fall in
love with his brown bob and Kevenhuller hat;
but since it was so, (and the lady's mother pro-
tested she did not exaggerate,) he never should
enjoy any peace of mind, if he could think
himself the cause of making a fellow creature
miserable (for Sir William could not give entire
credit to the dying part of the story). Rather
than have such a weight upon his conscience,
he would marry.

Lady

Lady Powerfcourt, however, very foon after her marriage, difcovered that fhe had made a great miftake, and was incautious enough to difclofe the fecret to her hufband. It was not from the brown bob nor Kevenhuller hat that the god of love took aim when he pierced her tender bofom, nor was the mortal fhaft barbed by the virtues which adorned the refpeclable character to which they were appendages. Like Hudibras's Cupid, he certainly

 "——Fix'd his ftand
 " Upon a wealthy jointure land."

Powerfcourt-houfe poffeffed irrefiftible attractions, and fhe had heard her papa and mamma frequently affert, that if Sir William would but marry a woman of tafte, it might be made one of the fweeteft places in all North Wales. She knew that Sir Ralph Morgan's lady fpent all the winter at Bath, the fpring in London, the fummer at her country-feat, and in the autumn took a tour; that fhe drove four in hand, gave balls, kept a groom of the chambers, and a French waiting-maid, had twelve new dreffes a-year, and fet the fafhions for all the country; yet Sir Ralph's eftate was not half fo large as Sir William's. What heart could refift fuch invincible attractions? She immediately fell very deeply in love.

I have in a former publication ventured to give my opinion, that the two faces of Hymen are not exact counter-parts to each other. The fmiling countenance which fronts the long vifta leading to his temple, has few traits of fimilitude to the auftere phyfiognomy which is defcried by thofe who, after they have offered
        facrifice,

sacrifice, retire behind his altar. The discussion of preliminaries might have convinced the lady that the nuptial cup contained some drops of an acid quality. To the charms of Powerscourt she had annexed one grand ingredient, which unhappily did not exist, at least not in its supposed magnitude. I mean, the easiness of Sir William's disposition. Though, "gentle as zephyr blowing underneath a violet" upon most occasions, he had upon others a little of the old bachelor's tenacity about him. He would keep lady Powerscourt a coach and six with all his heart, but he did not like ladies driving four in hand. She might have half a dozen English waiting-women if she pleased, and as many Welch ones, but he did not approve of French filles de chambre. He had no objection to hergiving balls to the neighbouring young ladies, and she might make them as happy as she could; but he thought that married ladies ought not to be jigging about themselves; and as to dress, she might be clothed every day in silver brocade; but his wife should never wear feathers and flowers in her head-dress, like a stage-player.

The grand point of dispute, however, was the occupation of the four seasons. He was willing to take her to town for three months, because the country must be rather dull to women in winter, as they could neither shoot nor hunt; and if she were not well, he would accompany her to Bath or any where that would do her service; but to live at Powerscourt only three months, what would all his neighbours say, and how would his tenants go on without him! My lady strove to convince him that their opinions were not worth regarding; but Sir William was firm. He had long considered them

as rational creatures, and he could not hastily renounce that opinion; beside, he was fond of farming, and deeply engaged in schemes of agricultural improvement; and if he stayed so little at home, he must either be the dupe of imposition, or renounce those pursuits. Here his obliging consort hinted, that, since he was so engaged in rural pursuits, business allowed him a fair excuse for absence, and she would be willing occasionally to dispense with his attendance. Sir William was not remarkably quick of apprehension; and, certainly, most bridegrooms in his situation would have been inclined to refer the lady's proposal rather to the exuberant desire of gratifying his peculiar inclination, than to any latent wish of being deprived of his society. He saw it quite in that point of view; and though he made no answer at the time, yet a retrospective consideration of the ineffable condescension which prompted her to give up what she had repeatedly declared to be the greatest blessing of her existence, his dear conversation, rather than tear him from scenes to which he was attached, convinced him that he ought to make some sacrifice to reward such self-denying complacency. One journey to Bath was therefore promised, an annual visit to London had been before tacitly agreed to, and I am not certain whether the overflowings of gratitude might not have compelled the good baronet to submit to be whirled about eighty miles a-day along rough roads by way of taking an autumnal tour, had not his lady, instead of rewarding his compliance by a gentle smile, assumed something of a mortified aspect when he announced his design of accompanying her. He was willing to
attribute

attribute this fudden change to her defire of having the magnificent plans that fhe had juft formed for the improvement of Powerfcourt caaried into execution under her own infpection; and this hope reconciled him to fchemes which had at firft met with fome oppofition. He had objected to her defign of cutting down the long avenue of oaks which led to the houfe, and converting the ground into a fweeping lawn, dotted with lilacs and laburnums, interfperfed with Chinefe temples and leaden ftatues. He was equally averfe to the removal of his ftraight yew hedges; for, though all the world was againft him, he conceived them more natural than the fharp angles of that modern embellifhment, a ferpentine walk. He thought too that the ftags horns and crofs-bows were as proper internal ornaments as papier-machee decorations; and many a bitter figh did it coft him, when his lady's mama and fifters joined in protefting, that, unlefs the dark Gothic windows and hideous tapeftry-hangings were removed from the drawing-room, and light fafhes and India paper fubftituted in their ftead, they fhould fall into hyfterics every time they went into the room; but his tranfport at the idea that thefe propofed alterations had tended to attach his wife to a fpot which would be honoured with fuch indubitable proofs of her tafte and genius, determined him to be a paffive fpectator of every propofed alteration.

It was in the month of September that Sir William was the happieft of men. Two months were allotted to ceremonious vifitings, during which the nuptial retinue moved over every mountain, dale, foreft, and glen, which the temerity of the coachman pronounced pafs-
able

able. Sir William had the gallantry always to accompany his lady; he heard all her wedding paraphernalia univerfally admired, and his own brown and gold pronounced immenfely becoming, while his point ruffles were cried up as the very fummit of elegance. Unaccuftomed, however, to the duties of the toilet, he grew weary of white gloves and powdered perukes; and recollecting with pleafure that all his vifits were paid, he refumed his drab frock and brown bob with fingular complacency. He was meditating a quiet ride round his farm, when my lady, entering, interrupted his agreeable reverie by informing him, that fhe had received a letter from lady Morgan, who was then at Bath, and infifted upon it that they muft come there immediately. The moft divine actor was juft come out, who infinitely tranfcended Garrick when in the meridian of his powers; befide, all the world was there, and her numerous acquaintance were anxious to be introduced to a lady of whofe beauty and accomplifhments they heard fo much. To her ladyfhip's intimation that they muft fet off immediately, Sir William replied, that it certainly was impoffible; there were more than 50 workmen employed in embellifhing the houfe and gardens: but the provident forecaft of lady Powerfcourt had provided an unanfwerable refutation of this objection. She had engaged a moft capital improver to come down, and find out all the capabilities which the houfe and local fcenery poffeffed. Sir William might rely implicitly upon the tafte and judgment of this gentleman, who had given fatisfaction to moft of the nobility and gentry in the kingdom, by exercifing what might almoft be called the magic power of turning every place into something exactly opposite to what it was before. The family archives intimate that Sir William was more alarmed than delighted at this information; and it is supposed that the journey to Bath would have been deferred till after Mr. Outline had finished Powerscourt, if my lady had not been taken ill with a violent stomach disorder the next morning, for which the physicians could find no remedy but an immediate use of those waters which King Bladud fortunately discovered, to the unspeakable advantage of all tender husbands and indulgent fathers.

CHAP. IV.

There Affectation with a sickly mien
Shews in her face the roses of eighteen;
Practis'd to lisp, and hang the head aside,
Faints into airs, and languishes with pride;
On the rich quilt sinks with becoming woe,
Wrapp'd in a gown, for sickness and for shew.
RAPE OF THE LOCK.

THE speedy abatement of lady Powerscourt's complaint announced the wisdom of the prescription; but she was a long time extremely languid, out of spirits, and too nervous to bear the fatigue of returning home to the " flaky snow" and " warping wind," that were concomitant to the mountains surrounding Powerscourt. In proof that her case required a warmer situation, the very proposal of leaving
Bath

Bath brought on a relapfe, and the extreme delicacy of her health would not even fuffer her to fpare Sir William juft to take a little peep to fee how Mr. Outline went on with his extenfive projects. Profound politicians are generally believed to have a real as well as an oftenfible reafon for their actions; and though her ladyfhip pleaded that if he did go fhe might probably expire without having his dear hand to clofe *her* eyes, it is fufpected, that, like a good wife, fhe wifhed to keep *his* from witneffing fcenes which might irritate a more profeffed ftoic. Convinced that Mr. Outline's tafte would appear to confummate advantage if no impediments obftructed his defigns, fhe dragged Sir William every night to the rooms or the theatre, places fhe was abfolutely obliged to attend, in order to prevent the low fever which attacked her every evening that fhe was perfuaded to pafs at home.

In a little time the penfive languor of lady Powerfcourt's countenance, unfortunately miftaken for the gloom of difcontent, and the fingular manners of her conftant attendant, excited general obfervation; and the report that fhe was a pretty young creature facrificed by her mercenary parents to a rich, foolifh, jealous, old inamorato, gave an eclat to her character, which neither conftant indifpofition, nor the moft fcrupulous attention to the variations of drefs would otherwife have excited. Ladies of the firft confequence invited her to their whift parties; her box at the play attracted the moft elegant beaux. The former found that fhe loft money with the beft grace imaginable, and the latter difcovered that fhe had an infinitude of wit. That mercilefs complaint

ennui,

ennui, which all Sir William's long histories and still longer arguments had rather increased than diminished, fled at the first touch of the fascinating wand of public admiration. Some say, that the tyrant only yielded one victim to secure another; 'tis certain, that while lady Powerscourt dressed, talked, laughed, and was considered as in the highest ton, Sir William concluded a long letter to his steward with a complaint, "That he felt exactly like a fish out " of water."

Intoxicated by pleasure and adulation, her ladyship anxiously wished to extend her triumphs beyond the narrow bound of a Bath season. The itinerant world, at whose idol shrine she had resolved to sacrifice, had now transferred its scene of empire to London, and she was impatient to shine a peerless star in a new hemisphere; but some difficulties stood in the way. She had seen enough of life to be convinced that Sir William's stiff drapery, formal manners, and obsolete opinions, formed as direct a contrast to the easy accommodating laws of modern etiquette, as the sturdy oak of the forest does to the bending ease of the pliant willow. She had heard observations infinitely to his disadvantage; and though she could collect no more than that he was a bore and a quiz, she was very sure that these cabalistic terms of fashion must import every thing that was horrid and detestable. Since her evil stars had, previous to her *entrée* in the great world, bound her for life to such a partner, she must make the best of her hard fate, and endeavour to balance the misery of his society during one part of the year against the advantage of spending his money during the remainder.

mainder. Lady Morgan had affured her, that of all places in the world a hufband was leaft wanted at London. The late hours and perpetual routine of engagements left no leifure for domeftic converfation; and, fhe added, Sir Ralph was fo entirely of her mind, that he always devoted the time fhe fpent there to the amufements of hunting and fhooting groufe.

Having received information that the improvement of Powerfcourt had advanced fo far as to defy the poffibility of their being completed, or indeed comprehended, by any perfon but the projector, fhe became very anxious that Sir William fhould look a little after his eftate, and at leaft be there in time to attend the approaching audit. But the worthy baronet was by this time become very uneafy about the ftability of poffeffions more fragile than the wide domains of which his anceftors had left him unrivalled lord. His good fenfe taught him the wide diffimilarity between his own manners and thofe of the gay fantaftic train who conftantly hovered round his lady whenever fhe appeared in public. He was certain that the *monkeys* (for he honoured them with that appellation) would be pert enough to laugh at his way when his back was turned; and he had feen fo many ftrange things in this world, that if he returned to Wales inftead of accompanying his lady to town, they might fill her head with ftranger notions than fomehow or other the poor thing had already acquired. Her prefent fituation rendered contradiction very difficult; but if he fhould like her behaviour in town no better than he had done at Bath, he refolved, when once his fon and heir was fafe in the world, to tell her very plainly, that fhe was welcome to make
herfelf

herself as happy as she could at Powerscourt,
but that he never would agree to any more jour-
nies of pleasure. Solacing himself with this
scheme of future resistance, he yielded to the
present torrent; and, assuring her that he had
no wish to return to Wales without her, they set
off for Berkeley-square.

I would not recommend the countenances of
the Powerscourts on their arrival in London, as
models to a painter who wished to embody the
fair idea of connubial happiness. Though the
lady's might derive a few lively traits from the
hope that she was entering upon a scene of con-
quest, yet the apprehension that Sir William was
projecting secret hostilities placed her exactly in
the situation of a general whose movements are
carefully watched by a strong army of observation which it would be imprudent openly to attack. Sir William's dislike of the journey increased every step he took, and he entered London with a firm expectation that the place and
the people would prove equally disagreeable. In
lieu of the taste and elegance with which lady
Powerscourt was every where fascinated, he saw
nothing but impertinence and frippery. The
late hours were insufferable to a man who rose at
six, dined at three, and dismissed his household
with family prayers at ten. He was shocked at
the refinement which banished serious discussion
from polished circles; and he never could fully
comprehend the duties of laborious idleness, the
arcana of modern visiting, the vanity of universal acquaintance, or those restraints upon the
emotions of genuine nature which fashion pre-
scribes and insipidity adopts. Every thing Sir
William heard and saw had to him an air of the
marvellous. He could scarcely believe that the

admirer

admirer of vertù, who piqued himſelf upon his
knowledge of Greek and Roman ruins, might
be ignorant of the architectural magnificence of
the capital of the Britiſh empire. He thought
the pure honour of a peer or a ſenator muſt be
ſullied by condeſcending to admit a profeſſed
ſharper to be the companion of his convivial
hours. He never could reconcile Sunday routs
with his notion of a ſteady well-regulated family; and he abſolutely interdicted lady Powerſcourt from aſſociating with what was then termed the *firſt* circle, when he came to know that
ſome of its fair members occaſionally diſpenſed
with the ſanctions of female decorum.

This way of thinking was certainly very ſingular; but Sir William's prejudices in theſe and
a variety of other inſtances were not to be van-
quiſhed by the light artillery of raillery, which
was frequently played off againſt him in public,
or by the more formidable battery of ſighs, tears,
and faintings, by which his gentle lady ſtrove to
induce him to ſpeak and look like other people.
Even the tender argument, that a man who really
loved his wife muſt adopt all her ſentiments, and
conform to all her wiſhes, was ineffectually op-
poſed to the rigid pertinacity with which Sir
William defended the principles that he had ever
conſidered to be the out-works of religion and
morality. The circumſtances which had induced him to put his " free condition into circum-
ſpection" did not appear to him to favour the
claims of female ſupremacy; and he entertained
the very heterodox notion, that when a lady falls
violently in love, the favoured gentleman has a
right to expect that ſhe will make an obliging attentive wife, rather more ſtudious of his humour, than devoted to the indulgence of her own.

This

This is not the only notion in which the lords of the creation are miſled by that vanity of which nature has given them a preponderant ſhare. The delicacy of the female mind may very poſſibly be attached to the ſpendid titles, large poſſeſſions, or handſome equipages of a gentleman, when the gentleman himſelf, conſidered apart from all theſe appendages, would never *ſtrike* any body ſuperior to his dairy-maid.   Would it not be unjuſt to charge a Counteſs with inconſiſtency, becauſe ſhe neglected her noble Earl, when all the time her heart had been only attracted by the luſtre of his coronet ?   The noble Earl's chagrin entirely proceeds from the deluſions of ſelf-flattery, which whiſpered that his individual ſelf was the all-potent load-ſtone, when in reality the magnetic influence darted from his elegant villa and liberal ſettlement ; or perhaps an enamelled watch and diamond hoop-ring, might form the infatuating taliſman.   I hope this explanatory rule will be applied to all matches which proceed from the ſtrong attachment of a " diſcreet young creature" to a " very good ſort of a man a few years older than herſelf."   It might preſerve many a reſpectable bachelor from the vexation of diſappointment, and prevent the cenſorious from fixing the charge of inconſiſtency upon many a lady's character, who rather deſerves admiration for unſhaken conſtancy.   But to return from my digreſſion—

Faſhion, who in one of her whimſical moments elevated Lady Powerſcourt into a firſt-rate toaſt at Bath, capriciouſly denied her in London the eclat to which ſhe now conceived herſelf entitled.   The gloſs of novelty was paſt, and the attraction of the ridiculous was leſſened by the appearance of freſh eccentricities in newer characters.

racters. She dreſſed with greater taſte, and her
repartees poſſeſſed ſuperior wit and brilliancy;
but the gazer and the liſtener no longer announced her triumph.

My matronly friends aſſure me, that one
prime ingredient of marriage felicity is, that you
always have a helpmate at hand, to whom you
transfer the burden of faults and misfortunes.
Lady Powerſcourt could find no other reaſon for
her going out of faſhion, than that Sir William,
not content with his own ſingularities, had abſolutely prohibited her from daſhing in a grand
ſtyle. No entreaties would prevail upon him to
let Lord Jehu drive her in his phaeton up the
park in a morning, though his ponies were the
ſweeteſt little ſpirited creatures in the world,
and the ride would be of infinite ſervice to her
health and ſpirits. Her head was nine inches
lower than any body's at the opera, and though
moſt ladies wore fruit and vegetables by way of
aigrette, and lady Morgan ſported a beautiful
bunch of amethyſt grapes with a little gold chaf-
finch pecking at them, ſhe herſelf muſt wear nothing but plain riband and blond. She might
not even play for gold; nay, Sir William was ſo
puritanic; and ſuch an enemy to a little harmleſs
mirth, that ſhe was forced to be as cautious in
avoiding a *double entendre* or a witticiſm upon
prieſtcraft, as if ſhe were wife to the Archbiſhop
of Canterbury. What woman of ſpirit could
brook ſuch reſtrictions? If ſhe muſt be moped
up, better return and ruſticate at Powerſcourt,
than ſit like Tantalus within reach of the deſired
enjoyment which ſhe was not permitted to ſhare.
She hinted to her huſband ſomething like a wiſh
to do ſo in a moment of moody diſcontent, oc-
caſioned by his peremptory declaration that ſhe

                                            ſhould

should not go to a masquerade, though the ticket was procured, the dress bespoke, and the party formed for the happy occasion. He for once cordially acquiesced in her wishes, by declaring, that it was the very plan he meant to propose. " I am sure, my dear," said he, " your health " has been greatly injured by living in this " smoky unwholesome place; and the late " hours and constant racketing have worn your " poor nerves all to pieces. You have quite " lost your colour, and are not half so cheerful " as you used to be when galloping over the " Welsh mountains; but a little good country " air will soon set all to rights again; and so " take leave of your friends; for, since you " wish it, I am determined to set off for Pow- " erscourt on Monday morning."

The general tenor of Sir William Powers- court's character was yielding philanthropy, but he could at times assume a quiet firmness which disconcerted opposition. Her Ladyship must either dispute or faint, and she chose the latter as the most gentlewomanlike style of contradiction. Sir William was very sorry, and very assiduous to restore her; but the reviving fair saw no signs of compunction in his countenance, nor did he, by inquiring after the cause of her disorder, give her an opportunity of pointing out the only means of preventing a relapse. Indeed, he was become rather callous to die-away arguments; and though his native candour spurned suspicion, their frequent recurrence led him to doubt the existence of the stomach spasms whence this disagreeable excursion had originated. I mean by these observations to caution my readers, to be very sparing in the use of these *chef-d'œuvres* of female generalship, because the

too

too great frequency of an ambuſcade only puts the enemy more conſtantly upon his guard. Violent hyſterics, floods of tears, and every ſign of gentle deſpondency, confirmed Sir William in the conviction that his Lady's life depended upon her removing immediately from a place where ſhe was ſo dreadfully indiſpoſed ; and ſhe found herſelf on Monday morning on the road to Caernarvonſhire, maugre the opinion of all the fine ladies of her acquaintance, united to her own, that ſhe was much too weak to bear the journey, and would certainly expire before ſhe got twenty miles out of London.

CHAP. V.

With here a fountain, never to be play'd ;
And there a ſummer-houſe, that knows no ſhade ;
Here Amphitrite ſails through myrtle bow'rs ;
There gladiators fight, or die, in flow'rs.

POPE.

THE traveller who purſues a road with which he is unacquainted always finds unexpected pleaſures mingled with unforeſeen misfortunes. A bright ſunbeam often diſſipates the gloom of a dreary country; the inconvenience of a rugged road is frequently counterbalanced by the magnificence of the ſurrounding ſcenery ; an occaſional companion relieves fatigue ; and even the mortification of a bad inn and indifferent accommodations generally tends to heighten the reliſh of future convivial enjoyments.

The

The pilgrim who speeds along the road of life generally encounters a similar mixture of pain and pleasure, not merely in the aggregate, but intimately blended in every event. The rose grows so close to the thorn, that you cannot gather it without encountering a painful sensation; while on the other hand our attention is diverted from the minute wound by the exquisite fragrance of the flower. The pains and pleasures of man, like the world he inhabits, partake of the vicissitude of his own character. I beg pardon for these seemingly irrelevant reflections; but the garrulity of old age can seldom resist an opportunity of moralising.

Nothing could be more melancholy than the situation in which I left lady Powerscourt in my last Chapter, except that of some fair damsel in romance, whom a terrible Saracen is carrying away to his enchanted castle. The twentieth mile-stone was passed, yet Atropos, though oft invoked, forbore to extend her mortal shears, when an unexpected source of consolation suddenly presented itself—not in the shape of a knight armed *cap-a-pie* with spear and buckler, nor in the more modern accoutrement of a fine gentleman with a brace of pistols; and, to say the truth, though a rencontre with lord Jehu just at this crisis might be a very popular incident, I am glad that sir William, for whose character I cannot help feeling a degree of regard, was not drawn into any military adventures. I enjoy the idea of his respectable figure, perfectly satisfied with his victory, riding composedly by the side of his chariot, and wondering if he might venture to get into it at the next stage. Lady Powerscourt's consolations were derived from the philosophic temperament of her own mind.

mind. She recollected that she should have it in her power to display such a wardrobe as had never before blazed on the astonished inhabitants of Caernarvonshire. That Powerscourt was now converted into a perfect paradise, and she should reign the unrivalled Armida of the enchanting region, every part of which would announce her directing taste. Prudence stepped in also to the aid of Patience, and whispered that though she had been defeated in a conflict for superiority, yet, if she carefully kept her own secret, Sir William would never betray her, and she had only to say that she was tired of London, which was in reality nearer the truth than she imagined. Perhaps a degree of remaining pique might suggest the resolution that, as she now perfectly understood her husband's temper, it was only studying the art of tormenting instead of the art of cajoling on any future occasion; and then, though she might not be able to triumph, she would at least make good her retreat.

These placable ideas so happily prevailed, that when they stopt at St. Alban's for refreshment, her ladyship on alighting offered her hand to the baronet with the best grace in the world, and anticipated his inquiries how she had borne her journey, by declaring that he was quite right in supposing the country air would do her good, for that she already found herself much better. Sir William was equally delighted with the change, and puzzled to guess at the means by which it had been effected. Somebody or something was very much to blame; but for his life he could hardly tell where the fault lay, whether in the contagious atmosphere of London, in his Lady's caprice, or his own suspicions. However, he now found himself invested with plenitude

plenitude of power; and, like a prudent monarch, he began to confider in what way he fhould exert it; but his generous heart had been fo foftened by his Lady's conceffions, that he pofitively refolved upon no further exercife of his prerogative, than that Lady Powerfcourt fhould pay her formal vifits by herfelf in future, and that he would never more wear his white and filver.

Peace and unanimity prevailed during the remainder of the journey. It was night when they entered the old manfion, and the examination of its beauties was deferred till the next morning; but the tranquillity of the good baronet was then put to a fevere trial. The faloon was certainly fitted up in the moft elegant manner; but the houfekeeper removed every idea of comfort by her information that the chimney fmoked fo violently, that it was abfolutely impoffible to have a fire; and, confequently, that it muft be ufelefs nine months in the year. The afpect of the dining apartment was equally dreary; the profpect indeed was enchanting, but the fafhes ftarted about an inch from the frames; and the warped doors were unfavourable either to a graceful exit or entrance, as it was only by means of kicking and pufhing that any one could either advance or retreat; and as the chimney, the windows, and the doors, were all conftructed uniformly, any alteration was dangerous, perhaps impracticable. The ready invention of Lady Powerfcourt difcovered, that, as thefe could only be proper for fummer apartments, fome little fnug parlour could be fitted up for general refidence; and they proceeded to the library. This was lofty and extenfive; but Mr. Outline's tafte for decoration feemed to have
annihilated

annihilated its primary intention ; for the mul-
titude of bufts, models, and ftatues, left no fpace
for books. Sir William continued his moralif-
ing tour through the reft of the ftate apartments,
which might be truly faid " to keep the promife
to the eye, and break it to the fenfe," and concluded his journey in the great hall, where, as he
fought in vain for the long oaken tables and
forms which ufed to adminifter to the regale-
ment of his tenants at Chriftmas and other fea-
fons of periodical feftivity, her Ladyfhip reminded him, how charmingly it was now appropriated to the purpofe of a ball-room or a
theatre. She directed his attention to a light
gallery at the upper end defigned for an orchef-
tra, and beautifully decorated ; but this elegant
embellifhment was not in a ftate to bear infpection, it having broken down with old Morgan the
blind harper, who had exhibited in it the preceding evening juft by way of hanfel, he faid, while
the houfemaids and gardeners were footing it a
little below for recreation becaufe his Honor
was coming home again.

Sir William left my Lady to conftruct ways
and means for fupporting the tottering edifice,
and, with a deep figh and a fecret murmur
againft new-fangled trumpery, proceeded to
examine the out-door fcenes. The tafte of Mr.
Outline for objects had induced him to remove
feveral ufeful edifices to inconvenient fituations,
while he occupied their places with erections of
no form nor likelihood, which continually drew
from the impatient baronet the exclamations of
" What is this for ?" and " What does this
mean ?" The ftews were all drained, and their
places occupied by the ruins of a naval amphi-
theatre, while the ftream that fupplied them was
taught

taught to hop from pebble to pebble in diminu-
tive imitation of old Conway's foaming flood,
which roared, in proud magnificence, at a little
diftance. The windmill had given way to a
temple dedicated to Æolus; and the pigeon-
houfe was fucceeded by an aviary of foreign birds,
none of which, in Sir William's opinion, were
fo beautiful as the goldfinch, or fung like the
nightingale. As walls were unpicturefque, they,
and the fruit-trees which they fupported, were
every where metamorphofed into ha-ha's! A
fine grove of oaks, which fcreened the houfe
from the north winds, was cut down to admit
the profpect of a bleak mountain; and the place
of the hardy forefters was occupied by the tender
magnolio and frail accacia, at leaft by their
remains, for the beautiful exotics had been already killed by the frofts, or broken by vernal
ftorms. In fhort, to adopt the owner's defcription of the houfe and gardens, " The former was
" very tafty and very inconvenient; and in the
" latter there was nothing that you wanted, but
" there were ruins and heathen gods in abun-
" dance."

Sir William's difguft did not prevent Lady
Powerfcourt from exhibiting herfelf to infinite
advantage in the office of Ciceroni, and fhe continued to point out the beauties of the new
improvements, till her neighbours had exhaufted
every topic of adulation, and her own tongue
grew weary of the pleafing tale. It is fuggefted,
that the inconveniencies I have enumerated afterwards ftruck her more forcibly than any one
elfe; and that her reafon for hating Powerfcourt
was, that no human creature could be well or
comfortable in fuch a cold dreary wildernefs fort
of a place. Nor did her fplendid attire afford a
                                    more

more permanent fatisfaction : in fome articles
of drefs fhe was anticipated, in others out-
fhone ; and none excited aftonifhment after
their firft exhibition. Alas ! if happinefs be
not feated in the mind, even the gratification of our wifhes will not enfure its poffeffion.

A few months after her Ladyfhip's return to
Powerfcourt, my Heroine firft faw the light ; and
though Sir William had rather it had been a boy,
he received the little ftranger with all the enthufiaftic joy of the fondeft parental tendernefs.
He thought the winning ways of the dear little
cherub muft communicate that happinefs to the
maternal bofom, which fomehow or other (a
favourite expreffion of Sir William's) it had
hitherto failed to experience. But while the
exuberance of his own joy was difplaying itfelf
in the ufual ftyle of overflowing benevolence
and hofpitality, his Lady was ruminating on the
poffibility of being at Chefter races ; and, contrary to the opinion of her matronly friends, fhe
refolved on the hazardous expedient of a too
early appearance in public. A fevere cold was
the immediate confequence ; and the neglect of
the firft maternal duty, joined to inattention to
her own fafety, was foon obferved to have occa-
fioned a total change in her conftitution. Years
of ill health, confinement, and fevere fuffering,
proved the melancholy forerunner of premature
death.

From the account I have already given of
lady Powerfcourt, the reader will not fuppofe
that patience tempered the bitter cup of woe
with its lenient fweets. Her mind was deftitute of natural ftrength, her temper poffeffed no
native gentlenefs, her education taught her rather

ther to conceal than to fubdue the irritability of her difpofition; and, being folely confined to the acquirement of a few external accomplifhments, no mental treafures were laid up in ftore againft the bitter day of adverfity. The lofs of health and beauty at five-and-twenty may certainly be confidered as a fevere deprivation; and when to thofe evils lamenefs and occafionally fevere fuffering were added, it could only be a compofed and elevated mind that could patiently fupport the fevere conflict. Lady Powerfcourt's ideas of pleafure had been adjufted to the limited model which fafhion and fortune prefent to their narrow-minded votaries: what confolations could they provide to mitigate the horrors of a fick chamber, when the foul can only divert the prefent gloom by confolatory retrofpects of its paft conduct, or exhilarating anticipations of its future reward?

The paffive fpirit of interefted dependance could fcarcely fupport the wearifome petulance of the unhappy fufferer; and though Sir William's philanthropy and habitual eafinefs made him exert more forbearance than generally belongs to the character of a hufband, his gentlenefs fometimes proved unequal to the arduous conflict, and he felt a depreffing inquietude which even the fmiles of his little girl could not conftantly divert. Though calamity renders the felfifh mind ftill more callous to the forrows of others, it ftimulates benevolence to encreafed exertions. Lady Powerfcourt was juft relieved from one of her fevereft attacks, when her fervant brought her a letter, which, after a flight perufal, fhe toffed contemptuoufly upon the table.

" You

" You feem difturbed my dear," faid Sir William, who happened to be prefent.

" No wonder," returned her ladyfhip; " furely I have troubles enough of my own " without being peftered with other people's; " but it is like the ufual inconfiltency of that " thoughtlefs creature's character."

" Whom do you mean?" faid the benevolent baronet, whofe attention was roufed at the idea of fomebody being in diftrefs.

" I mean a very imprudent, but a very dif- " tant relation of mine, who flung herfelf away " in marriage with lord Milford's tutor, a little " before I became lady Powerfcourt; and fhe " fhe is now, as fhe might have forefeen, " ftarving."

" Poor foul!" faid Sir William, reaching the letter; when finding by the perufal that it contained an appeal not only to the humanity but alfo to the honour of his lady, he fixed his eyes upon her with fome degree of refentment, and exclaimed, " How came you to forget the " poor woman? Why, you promifed to do " fomething for her hufband!"

" She interprets general expreffions too large- " ly," refumed her ladyfhip; " I have done " her a great many favours, and fhould have " done her many more; but I found out that " fhe was bafe, ungrateful, and not worthy of " my notice."

" I am forry for it with all my heart," re- plied Sir William; " fhe really writes like a " fenfible woman and a good Chriftian."

" Moft people with whom I happen to dif- " agree, are fo in your opinion."

" My dear, I am forry to hear you difturbed; " your fide is in pain again I am afraid."

" It

" It was a great deal better; but this woman's
" impertinence brings on all my old com-
" plaints."

" No, no, it won't; only keep yourself
" quiet; but pray, as I am quite a stranger to
" the story, will you tell me what this Mrs.
" Evans did, to make you so very angry with
" her ?"

" I told you, Sir William, she fell in love
" with a nobleman's tutor, and married him
" contrary to the advice of all her friends.
" My father was so incensed, that he declared
" if she starved, he would never take the least
" notice of her any more. But I was very kind
" to her, and I sent her some of my cast-off
" clothes when I married, which, I suppose, en-
" couraged her to the unheard-of impudence
" which she has been guilty of. Because she
" had been a sort of humble friend when we
" were quite girls, she had the effrontery to
" beg me to introduce her husband to you; a
" fellow whose grandfather was nothing but a
" travelling pedlar. Did you ever know such
" audacity ?"

Doubtless Sir William would have felt very
angry, if one of his own relations had contami-
nated the blood of Powerscourt by mixing it
with the " puddle of a pedlar," and his resentment might have continued, till he discovered
that he had it in his power to do the disgraced
couple an act of service; but he thought it
very ridiculous that a family of yesterday should
in this instance pretend to the same delicacy
with one that could be traced through untold
centuries. Her ladyship, perceiving that the
glow of resentment did not kindle in his countenance so fast as she expected, added by way

of climax, " And she sent the letter the very day when she knew I intended to receive company;—only think of endeavouring to occupy my attention at such a time."

" I think," said Sir William emphatically, " that poor Mrs. Evans has been very unfortunate in applying when you were either too much engaged by pleasure or pain to attend her. But a promise is a promise, let people claim it when they will."

Lady Powerscourt's conscience here gave her a severe pang, and she confusedly answered, that she was sure she never meant to make any engagement; she durst swear that she never said so; at least, if she had, she had quite forgotten it.

" Very likely, very likely," replied the good man; " you never meant what you said, and so forgot all about it. But you see she has remembered it, and perhaps the world may think that it is owing to me that you have not kept your word, at least according to Mrs. Evans's account of the matter; however, I will try to clear up the mistake; and as she is your friend and relation, they shall not be left destitute."

Sir William here rose and hurried out of the room, while lady Powerscourt loudly disclaimed the word *relation*, protesting Mrs. Evans could not be nearer than a second cousin, which she counted nothing at all.

CHAP.

CHAP. VI.

One self-approving hour whole years outweighs
Of ſtupid ſtareis, and of loud huzza's.

POPE.

THE benevolence of Sir William Powerſcourt was not confined within the narrow limits
of relations and friends.   It was not annihilated
by the ſuppoſition of ingratitude, nor did its delicate ſenſibility ſhrink from the contact of human infirmity.   It ſeemed a ray of that beneficence which cauſes the ſun to riſe upon the evil
and the good, and the rain to fall upon the juſt
and the unjuſt.

Nor was his idea of charity limited to the
virtue of beneficence. Combining with his natural placability of temper, it produced the moſt
cordial deſire of being at peace with all mankind,
and made ready forgiveneſs almoſt outſtep of-
fence.   He mounted his horſe, and rode to
Llangollen.   On the road he meditated not on
the faults of lady Powerſcourt, for perhaps his
imagination was afraid of venturing into ſuch
an ample field, but on the ſpeedieſt means of
alleviating the evils which her neglect had cauſed.
Having heard an excellent character of the
Evans's from ſome neighbouring gentlemen, he
haſtened to the cottage which ſheltered modeſt
worth.   He found the wife engaged in the
humble offices of domeſtic buſineſs, while the
huſband was rocking a little baby to ſleep, and
penning his Sunday diſcourſe.   However inele-
gant

gant thefe occupations might be, Sir William Powerfcourt fancied that they both looked like very fenfible people, and very good Chriftians.

The bufinefs of introduction was foon adjufted. Poverty had enfeebled but not extinguifhed the light of lettered fcience and polifhed manners which formerly irradiated the Evans's, and benevolence had entirely banifhed all ceremonious referve from their refpectable gueft. He informed Mrs. Evans that he had a little girl as pretty as that which lay afleep in the cradle, but that her poor coufin lady Powerfcourt had fcarcely enjoyed a day's health fince it was born. At the mention of lady Powerfcourt a deep blufh fuffufed Mrs. Evans's face, which, though in reality it proceeded from her anxiety to know the effect of a letter which fhe had fecretly difpatched without her hufband's confent, and contrary to his known opinion, Sir William miftook for the glow of refentment, and very much difliking to fee any body angry, he attempted a conciliatory explanation of his wife's conduct. His defence indeed amounted to little more than that, when people were much engaged either by pleafure or pain, they were apt only to think of themfelves; yet fo powerful was his rhetoric, that the burning blufhes on Mrs. Evans's cheek were foon quenched by a flood of tears; and though Sir William was not abfolutely unacquainted with tears of anger and difdain, he was convinced that thefe were of a milder quality. Mrs. Evans's grief was accompanied by the livelieft expreffions of regret for lady Powerfcourt's fufferings, and the moft anxious wifhes for her recovery. Sir William's eyes fhone with kindred fenfibility, he drew his chair clofer to the fire, preffed her hand with the freedom of long intimacy, and cheerfully partook of the homely fare

fare with which the hospitality of Mr. Evans
had covered the little deal table.

He then took occasion to ask the particulars
of their situation, and soon found that it was
penurious in the extreme. Every resource had
been tried, every friend applied to ; but resour-
ces are not inexhauftible, and even friends do
not always answer the calls of indigence with
prompt relief. The favour which had been folicited of lady Powerscourt was only her recommendation to a neighbouring clergyman, who
allowed his curates the fplendid flipend of fifty
pounds per annum. This circumstance, unin-
tentionally difcovered, drew from Sir William a
deep figh, and the exclamation of " Well, I
" could not think that poffible !"

The little girl now awoke, and the good
baronet, who was become a great connoiffeur in
nursery tranfactions, feemed much attracted by
its infantine charms. Finding that the difficulty
of procuring fponfors had hitherto caufed the
chriftening ceremony to be delayed, he offered
himfelf to undertake the office, adding a few
words expreffive of his fenfe of its folemn importance ; and having prefented the mother
with what he called his ufual offering on fuch
occafions, a bank-note of fifty pounds, he took
leave of the enraptured pair with many kind
affurances that they fhould foon hear of him
again.

Providence feemed to affift Sir William's generous refolution of making ample provifion for
oppreffed merit. His domeftic chaplain, on receiving the prefentation to a valuable prebend,
with noble moderation vacated the living of
Powerscourt, worth near four hundred pounds
per annum. The character and abilities of Mr.

Evans

Evans femed to point him out as an eligible fuc-
ceffor; but it appeared to be an infuperable difficulty to gain lady Powerfcourt's approbation of
fuch a plan. Luckily, however, the lady was
not quite inexorable. The humane concern
which Mrs. Evans expreffed for her illnefs had
been placed in the ftrongeft point of view, and
if it had not wrought upon her gratitude, it at
leaft, by recalling to her memory the obliging companion and the attentive friend of her younger
years, perfuaded lady Powerfcourt to acknow-
ledge, that in her prefent fituation fuch a neighbour would be a defirable acquifition. Her apprehenfion of being difgraced by the recognition
of her coufin was relieved by the fortunate communications of fome morning vifitors, who, having heard that Sir William had publicly announced his intention of providing for Mr. Evans,
flew to inform my lady that he was the " *charm-
ingeft* and moft *delightfuleft* preacher in the
world; that Mrs. Evans too, though an excellent manager, was an amiable agreeable creature, quite the gentlewoman both in manner
and appearance "

Sir William had purpofed uffering in his intended difpofal of the living of Powerfcourt,
by obfervations on the lofs they fhould fuftain by
Mr. Jones's removal, and how highly defirable
it was to have an agreeable neighbour at the
rectory. He intended next to allude to Mr.
Evans's reputed fkill at back gammon, and to
inquire if his wife was not a very chatty con-
verfable woman; but my lady flopped his exordium in the midft by one of thofe fweet fur-
prifals, in which the reader will perceive fhe
abounded, and begged him as a favour to com-

pliment her coufins with the prefentation,—a requeft which was granted with equal aftonifhment and joy.

Thofe who have been accuftomed to dread the cenfures of their own hearts, and to fuppofe that an unwarrantable indulgence of the irritable paffions muft produce felf-condemnation, will probably wonder that lady Powerfcourt fhould wifh for the foeiety of a perfon whofe prefence muft adminifter perpetual reproach to her confcious mind; but her moral creed was formed upon different principles. She thought it as much impoffible for a perfon of fortune to behave ill to an inferior, as for a beauty to be capricious, or a wit fatirical. Each of thefe characters had a privilege to be rude, tyrannical, and cenforious; and as their faults required no atonement, every body was bound, upon the fmalleft change of behaviour on their parts, to lofe the remembrance of paft ftorms in ravifhing admiration of the prefent gentle breeze. Though endued herfelf with that trembling fenfibility which bleeds at every pore, fhe doubted the exiftence of feeling in the fubordinate orders of mankind; and though fhe had left her friend finking in all the horrors of want, without ftretching forth her hand to fupport her, fhe would have thought that friend the moft ungrateful being in the world, if fhe had refufed to dedicate her time to the tafk of endeavouring to alleviate her real or fancied forrows.

Mrs. Evans certainly could feel, but fhe could alfo forgive. In her behaviour to lady Powerfcourt fhe appeared to remember nothing but that fhe was the friend of her early youth, and the wife of her revered benefactor. " It is my
" duty,

" duty," fhe ufed to fay to her hufband, when he kindly reproved her for devoting fo much time to the painful and unwholefome confinement of a fick chamber: " Confider," fhe continued, " how much we owe to Sir William's bounty, and how much it befits us to " try to alleviate thofe troubles with which " Providence thinks fit to prove the worthieft " of human hearts." In this opinion Mr. Evans acquiefced, and only cautioned her not to injure her invaluable health.

Ten years fucceffively rolled away without producing any remarkable change at Powerfcourt. The Evans's continued to devote their chief attention to the duties which gratitude, fympathy, and pity required. Soothed by their fociety, enraptured by the attractive fweetnefs of his enchanting daughter, and fuftained by the exalting confcioufnefs of a life of ufefulnefs and rectitude, Sir William endured the hourly vexations by which the increafed irritability of lady Powerfcourt's temper contrived to cloud every enjoyment in which fhe could no longer partake. It feemed as if her example was intended as an awful warning to the pride of beauty and the pride of wealth. She lived to be difgufting and dependant, but fhe did not live to feel and acknowlege that her faults required the righteous chaftifement.

Sir William's deportment at her death was marked by that decent propriety which characterifed all his actions. He did not affect to be inconfolable, but he treated her memory with becoming refpect. He fubmitted to the inconvenience of the little parlour and the fummer apartments, becaufe it would look like unkindnefs to his poor wife to reftore things to their

old ſtate again.   From the ſame motive he kept
the temples and ſtatues in good repair, though
he either forgot their names or miſtook their
ſituations ; and though he rather diſliked dogs,
he permitted an old black ſpaniel to be his conſtant companion, becauſe it ſeemed to be the
only thing to which ſhe ſhewed any attachment.
Yet bitter remembrance would ſometimes ex-
tort from him, in the company of very particular friends, the confeſſion, " that the poor
" woman had very odd ways, but people who
" are always ill are apt to be whimſical."

It was the general opinion of the country,
that the good baronet would never more en-
gage in a matrimonial connection, and this
ſeemed to be the more extraordinary, as it was
known he ardently wiſhed to tranſmit his fortune and honours to a lineal deſcendant of his
own name.   Whether influenced by delicacy
ariſing from paſt happineſs, or corroded by the
recollection of paſt ſorrows, it is certain he never appeared perfectly at eaſe when love or
marriage was the topic of converſation ; and
though remarkable for uniform civility, the
words, " fine feeling," and " acute ſenſibility,"
when uſed in their general import, always drew
from him an emphatical " *Nonſenſe !*"

CHAP.

CHAP. VII.

———She was fair beyond your brighteft bloom,
  (This Envy owns, fince now her bloom is fled,)
Fair as the forms that, wove in Fancy's loom,
  Float in light vifion round the poet's head.

Whene'er with foft ferenity fhe fmil'd,
  Or caught the orient blufh of quick furprife,
How fweetly mutable, how brightly wild
  The liquid luftre darted from her eyes!

Each look, each motion, wak'd a new-born grace,
  That o'er her form its tranfient glory caft:
Some lovely wonder foon ufurp'd the place,
  Chas'd by a charm ftill lovelier than the laft.

MASON.

MY readers whom I introduced in the beginning of my fecond Chapter to the marriage of Geraldine Powerfcourt with the earl of Monteith, will perhaps complain of the intervening circumftances which retard my account of the events immediately fubfequent to thofe aufpicious nuptials. They will probably blame me for beginning in the middle, and then going back to the firft part; but I have not even yet quite unravelled the clue which led to that event, and muft entreat their patience a little longer. Nothing is fo impofing upon the generality of the world as an air of fuperior information and felf confidence; I fhall therefore, inftead of acknowledging myfelf to have been in an error, proceed to ftate, that this apparent inconfiftency is the effect of plan, and fanctioned by authority.

I can-

I can plead the example of many ingenious luminaries, who folely owe their reputation to a fkilful generalfhip in the arrangement of their plans. Some have chofen to make a fecond volume take precedence of the firft; others have objected to the formality of a beginning; and a third fet have difdained the pedantry of a conclufion. Several of the wits of the laft age wrote pages on their own pre-exiftent ftate; and many writers of our times have penned volumes, which, if they have any meaning, tend to prove that it would have been better had they not exifted at all. Some fuppofe the road to fame lies through the labyrinth of inexplicable paradoxes; while others, who publifh one book to difprove what they have written in another, feem to think that, in order to advance, it is neceffary to move backward like a crab. In vain does Criticifm attempt to reftrain thefe excurfive flights:—the modern Pegafus is too reftive to endure the rein, and too volatile to attend to the lafh; and moft writers have fucceeded, who have attempted to found their reputation on the broad bafis of fingularity; for what greater proof of originality and fpirit can be given than by doing or faying fomething which furprifes or terrifies every body?

But though thefe huge Leviathans may thus tofs and fport as they pleafe in the great deeps of literature, the leffer fry of authors muft fubmit to fome precautions, or endure the harder alternative of annihilation. Our morofe tafkmafters not only impofe upon us the hard laws of having a beginning, a middle, and an end; but they ftate the neceffity of unity of defign, and an attention to coftume in age, place, and character. As I purpofed, therefore, to treat

of

of the effects arising from the marriage of lady Monteith, it became necessary for me to hurry into the midst of the scene, and to bring forth Powerscourt-house in " high pomp jubilant ;" and like Homer, Virgil, and Milton, to adjust relative circumstances in an episodical manner. In one respect I differ from these high authorities, by making myself the relator; but even here I have an ingenious fiction ready to obviate critical asperity. It is only supposing me the old Nestor of the fable, or the chorus of the scene, and I may tell as many long stories as I please, and moralise whenever I have an inclination, without offending against any of the statutes of Parnassus in that case made and provided, I will now introduce my Heroine upon the stage.

The connection between a lively sensible girl and a sickly petulant parent could be but slender; the concern, therefore, which Geraldine felt for Lady Powerscourt's death was soon overcome. She had long considered Mrs. Evans as more truly fulfilling the maternal character; and she felt for her judicious, firm, but affectionate reproofs, that filial deference which the eternal whine of her mother's complaining censures failed to inspire. Under the care of an experienced governess and celebrated masters, procured at unsparing expence, she rapidly acquired every female grace and suitable accomplishment; but it was to the instructions of Mrs. Evans, and to the tender friendship of her daughter Lucy, that her mind was indebted for its richest treasures.

At the age of seventeen she appeared an enchanting beauty; polite, sensible, accomplished, affable, and generous; the idol of her father,
the

the delight of her friends and dependants, the envy of the neighbourhood, and the object to which every man of fortune in the county secretly aspired :

" —-She was indeed the glass
" Wherein the neighbouring youth did dress them-
" felves."

Miss Powerscourt's example would sanction a small absurdity ; and her enchanting manners excited a herd of awkward imitators. They forgot, however, that it was her wit which supported her opinion, and her graceful beauty that gave elegance to the form of a bonnet, or adjusted the drapery of a robe.

Some fastidious observers, who, cold to the fascination of captivating loveliness, contemplate "the human form divine" with the same cautious discrimination with which they would analyse the merits of a picture, pointed out some shades in this fascinating portrait. They observed, that her vivacity at times approached to levity ; that, under the form of easy *nonchalance,* her eye was on the watch for adulation ; and that the perfections which nature had so liberally bestowed lost their most delicate attractions in the consciousness of possession.

To these observations Candour replied, that even levity was pardonable in youth and beauty, when it appeared to be the artless offspring of a happy innocent heart ; that inexperience would apologise for the faults which proceeded from an exuberant flow of animal spirits, a strong desire to please, and a disposition uncommonly prone to the most generous disinterested confidence ; that it was impossible for her to escape the knowledge

of

of her own perfections, when every tongue was
loud in her praife, and there were none to difpute
her claim to pre-eminence ; and that it was even
amiable in her to wifh to difplay thofe excellencies which feemed ever to communicate delight
to others.   I have ftated the debates which were
caufed by the appearance and manners of Mifs
Powerfcourt, and fhall only obferve, that in point
of numbers the applauders had it.

Many were the detractors and imitators which
the fair Geraldine excited ; but one young lady,
who was neither her rival nor her copyift, loved
her with unaffected tendernefs. The character
of Lucy Evans was perfectly her own ; it was
caft in nature's moft artlefs mould, and finifhed
by the unremitting attention of an intelligent
mother and an exemplary father. Inferior to
her friend in perfonal charms and expenfive
accomplifhments, fhe was yet very pretty, very
fenfible, very amiable, and as well educated as
the daughter of a country clergyman need wifh
to be. Early taught the difference between a
young woman whofe fortune muft arife from
the favings of four hundred pounds per annum,
and the heirefs of twice as many thoufands, fhe
never made the indulgences of Mifs Powerfcourt the model for the regulation of her own
enjoyments and defires. She had read much, fhe
had thought more ; her leifure for ftudy and
reflection was greater than her friend's, and her
mind imperceptibly acquired fuperior energy.
Her knowledge of the world was confined to the
manor-houfe and the rectory ; at the former fhe
fometimes met mixt characters; her fenfibility
made her ftrongly feel their improprieties, and
her fincerity generally betrayed thofe emotions.

The ladies were friends in the ftricteft fenfe

C 3

of

of the word; but when I own that there was
no other young perfon within feveral miles with
whom Mifs Powerfcourt could properly form an
intimacy, my readers will probably condemn me
for afcribing the term friendfhip to an intimacy
which rather proceed from chance and locality
than from tafte and felection, and will probably
predict that it was very likely to be annihilated
in the rude changes of the joftling world. The
following pages will difcover how far they are
right; it fhall fuffice for me at prefent to affirm,
that, at the time I am treating of, the attachment
was mutual and fincere.

While the fair Geraldine bent over the harp
with the grace of a Calliope and the execution
of a Cecilia, Lucy fat quietly at her plain work
in a corner of the room, and enjoyed the applaufe which her friend's mafterly performance
ever excited. But when Mifs Powerfcourt's
fkill in mufic, drawing, embroidery, fillagree,
and every other fafhionable acquirement, had
been difplayed, Mifs Evans could not wholly
efcape obfervation, at leaft if any perfons in
company were fufficiently liberal to turn their
eyes from the dazzling fplendor of fortune to
the mild luftre of modeft independence. Though
her obfervations did not proceed from a mouth
exquifitely formed, nor were enforced by eyes of
peculiar brilliancy, they befpoke a correct intelligent mind, and were accompanied by an arch
naïveté, or an ingenuous earneftnefs, which
feemed at once to develope the fpeaker's artlefs
amiable mind. Exulting at the attention which her
Lucy's remarks obtained, Mifs Powerfcourt ever
delighted to lead the converfation to topics on
which fhe knew her to excel; and when the
party was large, modeft diffidence was often

charmed

charmed out of its intended silence by the affectionate artifices of the mistress of the feast.

Without attributing too much to the allurements of wealth, it may readily be believed, that Miss Powerscourt's hand was an object of general contention. After having, in the space of two years, refused more unexceptionable offers than the most invincible heroine of modern romance can boast, she was introduced to the Earl of Monteith at Chester race-ball, and at her chaperon's request accepted him for a partner. Their similitude in graceful beauty, age, fortune, and connections, pointed them out to the whole company as a most suitable match; and a little policy was admitted, that the peerless pair might not be separated the whole evening. The next morning his Lordship appeared early upon the course, where dismounting without once discussing the merits of the race-horses, or attending to the weighing of the drivers, he took his seat in the stand next to Miss Powerscourt, and during the whole morning seemed to forget that he had several thousands depending upon the issue of the course. In the evening he was again at the ball, again requested the hand of his former partner, and, without once spraining his ancle or complaining of insufferable heat, danced till three o'clock the next morning. Every body was now sure that he was captivated, and the whole county were on the tiptoe of expectation.

On the very day of her return to Powerscourt, Geraldine set out in search of her Lucy, and entreated that she would come and spend a little time with her at the manor. It was impossible for Miss Evans to avoid observing, that her friend's account of the ball, the dresses, and the

manners

manners of the company, was very much embarraffed, and deftitute of its ufual vivacity. On
entering the dreffing-room Geraldine locked the
door, and, throwing her arms around her Lucy's
neck, told her fhe had a fecret to divulge which
was of the greateft importance. On receiving
a promife of inviolable fecrecy, Mifs Powerfcourt attempted to explain ; but after feveral ineffectual attempts to begin the difcovery, fhe faw
fome company coming over the lawn, and, promifing her friend to be more explicit at another
time, fhe unlocked the door and haftened to
receive her guefts.

It was more than a week before Mifs Evans
could find leifure from her domeftic occupations
to vifit Powerfcourt-houfe, in order that fhe
might receive the facred truft. She now found
her friend's lively fpirits ftill more fubdued ; fhe
was abfent, frequently fighed, played with her
mother's picture, which hung fufpended by a
pearl chain on her bofom, fketched figures upon
the table with her netting needle, and, though
unufually affectionate in her expreffions, feemed
lefs inclined to confide the ftory of her troubles
than at their former interview. Neither Mifs
Evans's difpofition nor education were in the
leaft romantic ; fhe could only perceive that her
friend had met with fome great vexation; and
fhe was too delicate to endeavour to pierce the
veil which concealed thofe forrows ; fhe therefore contented herfelf with fecretly wifhing the
painful anxiety fpeedily removed.

But, though Mifs Evans was thus fhort-fighted,
my readers have probably difcovered enough of
the diforder to acquit me of introducing extra-
neous matter, though I fhould inftantly revert to
Lord Monteith. On dancing with Mifs Powerfcourt

court the firſt night,. he publicly declared that
ſhe was the fineſt girl he had ever ſeen : the
converſation in the ſtand convinced him that ſhe
was uncommonly-clever ; and at. the interview
the ſecond evening ſhe appeared with.ſuch captivating grace, that he loudly proteſted ſhe was
the moſt elegant woman in the world ; and that
Geraldine Powerſcourt was almoſt enough to
induce any man to ſubmit to the yoke of marriage. The friends to whom he uttered theſe
rapturous exclamations reported them to their
mothers and ſiſters, who repeated them to their
acquaintance ; but the rough maſculine ſentiment, when filtered through the organs of
female delicacy, ſpoke in a much ſofter and more
inſinuating tone. All the ladies proteſted that
the Earl of Monteith was.deeply enamoured with
Miſs Powerſcourt ; that he thought her the divi-
neſt creature that ever exiſted ; that he was
dying for an opportunity of throwing himſelf at
her feet ; and that his whole earthly happineſs
depended upon her. This high-flown language,
repeated by every viſitor, certainly vibrated on
the ear of the fair Geraldine with a pleaſing
ſound. She conſidered the abſurdity of the
expreſſion to be entirely chargeable on the re-
peater, but that the ſentiment was undoubtedly
his Lordſhip's. She only anſwered by the words
" How ridiculous ! How infinitely abſurd !" but
ſhe bluſhed and ſmiled while ſhe reproved, and
made no effort to change the converſation to a
more *ſenſible* ſubject. Every body obſerved, that
ſhe ſighed frequently, talked leſs, and could remember none but plaintive tunes. The lovely
pair were therefore certainly mutually ſmitten ;
and it was earneſtly hoped that Sir William
would

would not waywardly attempt to interdict their
union.

A month elapfed, yet the enamoured fwain
had neither flung himfelf at the feet of his dul-
cinea, nor taken any other ftep to fecure the prize
upon which his whole earthly happinefs depended. This delay; though it coft the lady a little
chagrin, was yet upon the whole beneficial to
his Lordfhip's caufe. She had time to reflect
upon all he had faid, and all he had looked, at
their former interviews; and though her own
knowledge of his character was limited to the
obfervation of uncommon elegance of figure and
a gentlemanlike addrefs, the whole world (I mean
that part of it with which Mifs Powerfcourt was
acquainted) protefted that he was a moft amiable
and accomplifhed Nobleman. Thefe vague in-
definite terms may be compared to the outline
which travellers frequently prefent of newly-
difcovered countries, leaving fpace for fucceeding adventurers to embellifh the chart by placing
rivers, bays, and mountains where they fuppofe
they may be found. Mifs Powerfcourt exercifed
all her inventive powers to fill up the fketch of
Lord Monteith's character. She marfhalled all
the virtues and agreeable qualities, and placed
them in the propereft ftations. Wit was fupported by tafte and learning, generofity was cir-
cumfcribed by prudence, and heroifm was tempered by the moft melting fenfibility. In fine,
the portrait was enchanting, but the likenefs was
ideal; the fair defigner however, like Pygmalion,
became deeply enamoured with the creature of
her own imagination.

CHAP.

CHAP. VIII.

O, ten times fafter Venus' pigeons fly
To feal love's bonds new made, than they are wont
To keep obliged faith unforfeited.————
O Love, be moderate, allay thy ecftafy:
In meafure rain thy joy, fcant this excefs:
I feel too much thy bleffing, make it lefs,
For fear I furfeit !

SHAKESPEARE.

LORD MONTEITH was quite a Benedict, and had determined not to encumber himfelf with a wife, unlefs he found it impoffible to be happy without one. He haftened from the rural fhade and moping folitude, which, if not the mother, is certainly the nurfe of Love. He plunged into the diffipation of London, vifited the court, the opera, the pantheon mafquerades; but the lovely form of the Cambrian enchantrefs purfued him to ev.ry retreat. Nay, even at the gaming-table, when hundreds were depending upon the odd trick, fhe rofe to his view in all the fplendor of her ball-room ornaments; bending her waving plumes, fhe gently ftruck him with her magic fan, and, begging him to be attentive to the delightful dance which was juft begun, made him lofe the game.

If my limited obfervation of the male character may be trufted, the difference of foul in the two fexes is no where more plainly feen than in their manner of encountering vexation. A lady in Lord Monteith's circumftances, upon finding her heart irrecoverably loft, would have

devoted

devoted her time to woods and groves, and, only
breathing her paſſion to ſome dear confidante,
would have found a luxurious indulgence in
complaining of her ruthleſs ſtars ; but his Lordſhip, when he diſcovered that even cards and
dice could no longer occupy his mind, ordered
poſt-horſes, and in leſs than forty-eight hours
arrived at the ſeat of his friend Lord W. in
Caernarvonſhire, to conſult on the propereſt
method of making propoſals to the lady who had
cauſed ſuch cruel devaſtation.

It was agreed, that a very gallant addreſs to
Miſs Powerſcourt ſhould be incloſed in a reſpectful letter to Sir William ; and, to give the
proceedings more weight, Lord W. offered to
be courier. He found the father and daughter
téte-á-tête ; the latter roſe on his announcing
particular buſineſs ; but on his adding, with a
ſignificant look, that it concerned Lord Monteith,
ſhe ſeemed rather to loiter in her attempt to
leave the room. " Stay, my dear love, if you
like it better," ſaid Sir William, " for I have no
ſecrets from you." The permiſſion was very
agreeable ; ſhe walked to the oppoſite window,
and ſeemed only occupied in playing with her
favourite Italian greyhound, while her father
was circumſpectly examining the ſeal of the
packet, and decyphering the armorial honours of
the Macdonalds.

" Here is a letter too for you, Geraldine," ſaid
Sir William. She turned to receive it ; but
encountering the eyes of Lord W. the livelieſt
confuſion was imprinted on her countenance.
She would have given the world to eſcape the
explanation, which, but a moment before, ſhe
was impatient to hear. Luckily a ſervant announced the arrival of Miſs Evans, and ſhe
haſtened

haſtened to receive her friend, while Lord W. as he attended her to the door, politely whiſpered that her triumph was complete, and entreated her to be as merciful as ſhe was invincible.

Sir William had by this time peruſed his letter, and ſunk into a profound reverie, from which he was rouſed by the eulogium which lord W. pronounced on the rank, talents, fortune, and connexions of his noble friend, the warmth of his attachment, and the uncommon excellencies of Miſs Powerſcourt.

Though Sir William liſtened with the moſt delighted attention to the panegyric on his daughter, he diſcovered great uneaſineſs during the deſcription of lord Monteith's paſſion; and as ſoon as lord W. had ended his harangue, he expreſſed his hopes that the account was not quite true. His noble gueſt took fire at the imputation of exaggeration, and confirmed every thing he had before aſſerted with violent proteſtations.

"Then I beg your lordſhip's pardon," ſaid Sir William.; "and I do aſſure you, that I had "not the ſmalleſt deſign of offending; for, I "dare ſay, you never told me more than what "you thought was truth; and very poſſibly "lord Monteith may think ſo too. Young "men and women are apt to ſuppoſe them- "ſelves in love, and I hope it is no more in the "preſent caſe; for I ſhould be very ſorry to "have my girl make a worthy gentleman mi- "ſerable."

Lord W. pleaded that his noble friend was certainly one of the firſt matches in the kingdom.

"Undoubtedly,"

" Undoubtedly," replied Sir William ; and
" yet, no difparagement to the Macdonalds, the
" Powerfcourts are quite as ancient and re-
" fpectable. But, to tell you the truth, I am
" not very fond of lords, at leaft not for fons-
" in-law. Geraldine will have enough if her
" hufband has not a fhilling, and I would rather
" fhe fhould beftow herfelf upon fome worthy
" man who would keep up my family, than
" fink my name and fortune in that of any_
" peer in the three kingdoms."

Lord W. obferved, that by a fuitable arrangement in the marriage-writings the family name
might be preferved.

Sir William rather fretted at thefe expedients.
" I have told you, my lord," faid he, " that I
" think very well of the Macdonalds; it is an
" ancient na.e, and an honourable family; it
" has given L.rth to a great many true lovers of
" their country ; but I hope lord Monteith will
" not be offended with me, if I fay that I pre-
" fer my own. In fhort, my lord, there is a
" young man whom I think of for Geraldine ;
" and a great bieffing, let me tell you, fhe will
" be to him."

Lord W. recollected a young man of the
name of Powerfcourt, whofe education had
been defrayed at Sir William's expence, and
who occafionally vifited at the manor ; but as he
was known to be entirely dependent upon his
patron's bounty, no one fuppofed him the def-
tined hufband for the heirefs of Powerfcourt.
His lordfhip's aftonifhment was fo great that he
could not help afking, whether the lady affented
to this extraordinary difpofal of charms which
might add honour to a dukedom.

" I have

" I have not yet told her my plans," faid Sir
William; " fhe is very young at prefent, and I
" would not cut fhort her happieft days. She
" is fo attached to me, that I am fure it will be
" almoft death for her to leave me; but as fhe
" is my only child, I muft marry her to keep
" up my family. I affure your lordfhip, fhe is
" a very fenfible girl, and will have no notion
" about dukedoms, unlefs other people put it
" in her head."

Lord W. afked if the happy youth knew his
envied deftination.

Sir William did not like to be thus
catechifed; he, however, anfwered in the
negative. " I don't think it right," faid
he, " to have young men made vain. He is a
" modeft good lad now, and will enjoy his
" fortune better, and know how to do more
" good with it, for having been without one
" when he was young. I affure you, my lord,
" you are the firft perfon to whom I ever men-
" tioned my plan, though I formed it as foon
" as my wife died, never intending to marry
" again. It is out of refpect to lord Monteith
" that I mention it, becaufe I would not have
" him think that I refufe his addreffes in an
" uncivil manner. But had I not better write
" a few lines to his lordfhip, as he was fo po-
" lite as to write to me?"

Lord W. promifed to be a faithful reporter
of what had paffed, and they feparated mutually diffatisfied, lord W. conceiving Sir William to be the moft extraordinary old quiz he
ever converfed with; and Sir William wifhing
the flafhy young men would let his daughter
alone, being certain that fhe was perfectly happy
if they would not torment her.

While

While this scene passed in the breakfast-parlour, Geraldine was perusing her letter in the dressing-room, commenting on its passionate but respectful contents, and owning to her dear Lucy that it was impossible to deny lord Monteith's merits. She could now repeat all the adventures of Chester races; her account was lively and interesting, yet sufficiently sentimental to explain to Miss Evans the reason of her absence and her sighs. She waited her father's summons with impatience, and flew to dinner with so light a foot as would scarcely have pressed down

> " The gossamer
> " That idles in the summer's noon-tide air :"

but it was observable, that she returned with

> " Even step, and musing gait,
> " Sober, stedfast, and demure."

I need not account in diffuse terms for the change. Sir William had informed her of his absolute rejection of lord Monteith, in a manner which evidently proved that he expected she would be as well satisfied with his conduct in this particular, as she had been in every preceding instance, it never occurring to Sir William that she could be at all interested in the addresses of a stranger.

Though Miss Powerscourt had certainly acted with girlish precipitancy in attaching herself to the idol of her own imagination; and though, with the common philosophy of nineteen, she supposed nothing so irretrievable as a wandering heart, she really was what Sir William esteemed her to be, a very amiable and

very

very fenfible girl. She not only loved her father's perfon, but fhe alfo venerated his character. The emphafis that he laid on the word *ftranger* induced her to reflect on the hazard of beftowing her hand upon a perfon with whom fhe was fo flightly acquainted; and though fhe continued to believe that lord Monteith poffeffed all the real virtues of which fhe had conjured up the refemblance, yet fhe thought there would be no impropriety in letting the latent excellencies expand. In fine, fhe was too refpectful as a daughter to eftablifh an open oppofition to her father's intentions, and too delicate as a female to think of encouraging an addrefs which wanted the folemn fanction of paternal approbation. If lord Monteith's paffion were fincere, it would not be repreffed by difficulties; and if it ftood the trial, fhe knew the warmth of Sir William's affection to her too well to fear his final rejection, when he fhould know that her happinefs depended upon his affent.

If my readers think thefe refolutions too magnanimous to correfpond with the character of a young lady accuftomed even to that folicitous indulgence which prevents our wifhes, who never viewed the world but on its brighteft fide, and who never faw

"Hard unkindnefs' alter'd eye
"Mock the tear it forc'd to flow;"

let it be remembered, that fhe had in Mrs. Evans a friend of a fuperior caft to what moft heireffes can ever hope to poffefs; a friend who, having no finifter views, had no occafion for fervility or flattery;—a friend, who to an exalted

alted turn of mind united the courage to en-
force unpleasant truths, and generosity to overlook casual errors.

We have seen that gratitude to Sir William
reconciled Mrs. Evans to the painful task of attending lady Powerscourt during her long illness. When death terminated what she conceived to be her duty in that particular, she considered the situation of his daughter. Young,
amiable, idolised, possessed of superior beauty
and uncommon vivacity, by what more noble
method could she evince her gratitude to the
father, than by shewing the unwary girl the
shoals and quick-sands which abound in the
voyage of life?

Mrs. Evans's early knowlege of what is called
the great world convinced her, that though refinement may interpose its flimsy veil, the un-
amiable passions prevail in the higher circles as
much as in the cottage; and that the pilgrim
who wishes to pursue a safe course must unite
the serpent with the dove. While, therefore,
she strongly recommended to Miss Powerscourt
the extirpation, not the concealment, of every
ungenerous, violent, and selfish principle, as
the happiest means of ensuring internal peace,
she taught her to apprehend external danger
from the violence and selfishness of others, however concealed by the fair appearance of polished manners, or even by professions of attachment. But, above all, she strongly imprinted on her pupil's mind a veneration for her
father's character. She not only pointed out
his active benevolence, patient gentleness, and
firm integrity, but led her to consider the general propriety of his opinions upon any subject with which he was thoroughly acquainted;
and

and though his recluse habits had caft an air of
fingularity over his natural good fenfe, yet his
plain firm ftile of thinking was not only better but
wifer than that flexible judgment which bends,
contracts, or expands, as the world, that is, as
caprice determines. Nothing could be more
judicious than thefe inftructions. Mifs Powerfcourt's parts were lively and brilliant, quick in
difcovering the ridiculous, and powerful in ex-
pofing it. Though virtue, benevolence, and
fond indulgence, muft have obtained the warm
affection of her grateful heart, her refpect for
fuch a father could only be founded on the perfuafion which fhe had imbibed in her early
youth of the natural fuperiority of his uncultivated underftanding.

The confcioufnefs of yielding to a weaknefs
which Mrs. Evans would difapprove had kept
her from informing Lucy of the ftate of her
heart prior to lord Monteith's declaration, and
the fame fentiment forbade her difcovering any
ftrong uneafinefs at her father's rejection of his
addreffes. In relating the affair fhe only obferved with a fuppreffed figh, that fhe thought
his lordfhip infinitely the moft amiable and deferving of any of her fuitors; but fince her father
difapproved the connexion, fhe fhould acquiefce
in his decifion, and heartily wifh the earl happy
with fome other lady; in which wifh, however,
it may be queftioned whether fhe did not make
a little ufe of the long bow.

The enamoured earl was not at this time in fo
quiefcent a ftate. He was quite in a humour
for

    " Moving accidents by flood and field ;"
Or,
    " For hair-breadth 'fcapes in th' imminent deadly
      " breach."

                                One

One time he refolved to ftorm the caftle and free the lady from durance; at another time decided to ftretch his rival in the bloody duft. The probability of the fair one's being offended by the firft project foon made him abandon that; and there feemed fo much cruelty in killing a man who did not even know that he was an impediment to his happinefs, that his lordfhip's cooler judgment pronounced that the latter would be too fanguinary. After confidering all the plans which ancient and modern romance fupplies, the old fcheme of Jupiter and the fhower of gold was preferred. But it was not to Danaë that the Caledonian Jupiter defcended in that form; it was to Danaë's waiting maid.

The very evening after this phenomenon had taken place, Mifs Powerfcourt faw a letter upon her dreffing-table, fuperfcribed in characters which fhe perfectly recollected. The Cambrian Abigail was not an adept in her profeffion; for on being queftioned how it came there, fhe neither affirmed that fhe faw a Cupid fly in with it at the window, nor even hinted that it might be conveyed there by fairies, or rife out of the table by the power of enchantment. She neither invoked goblin nor witch, but fimply owned that lord Monteith begged her to deliver it, and fhe thought there could be no harm in complying with the requeft of fuch an agreeable gentleman.

" If you do not know your duty to my father, " Bridget, I know mine: return it immediately " to his lordfhip; but ftay; I think I will add " a few words."

Mrs. Bridget bleffed her goodnefs, and began an harangue on his lordfhip's virtues, which her miftrefs filenced with a look, and fhe retired.

The .

The opener of Pandora's box was a gentleman. Let the gentlemen therefore behold one of the sex whom they brand with the stigma of curiosity, sitting with a Pandora's box sealed before her, yet forbearing to lift the interdicted lid. She wrote a few lines which expressed her abhorrence of a clandestine correspondence, without intimating perpetual enmity against the correspondent, and, inclosing his lordship's letter, rung her bell, and ordered it to be delivered by the very first opportunity. She refused Mrs. Bridget's attendance that evening, and betook herself to the repose which conscious rectitude and self-possession can alone enjoy.

CHAP. IX.

—— A prudent father,
By nature charg'd to guide and rule her choice,
Resigns his daughter to a husband's power,
Who, with superior dignity, with reason,
And manly tenderness, will ever love her ;
Not first a kneeling slave, and then a tyrant.
                                        THOMSON.

LORD Monteith and his friend were forced to project fresh measures ; for Mrs. Bridget was so unwilling to offend her dear generous young lady, that she refused to appear any more upon the stage, and yet her gratitude to the dear generous young gentleman induced her to consent still to take a part behind the scenes. She suggested that her lady would soon pay a visit to a neighbouring family; that she would go on horseback, only accompanied by Mr. John the groom; that the road lay through a neighbouring coppice, but that lord W. as well as Sir William had keys of the ridings; and she concluded with observing significantly, that Mr. John was a very well-behaved man, no listener, and too *discreet* to say any thing.

The excursion was undertaken at the appointed time; but the instant Miss Powerscourt entered the wood, she saw a gentleman on horseback approaching, whom in another instant she knew to be lord Monteith. Her first intention was to turn back, but she was prevented by John's having dropped the key in the long grass, just as he had locked the gate. Anger was useless, indeed unreasonable; for the poor man was endeavouring to repair his carelessness by looking for it very anxiously. Though she could not but suspect that the rencontre was concerted, she had sufficient confidence in her own dignity to overcome her first agitation. Retreat was impossible, and she advanced slowly to the dreaded interview.

On the gentleman's side there was expressed an infinitude of love, admiration and despair, blended with some degree of resentful sensibility at the idea of being compelled privately to solicit a blessing to which he had thought himself entitled publicly to aspire. On the lady's there appeared a just sense of female decorum, and a steady resolution to repress any acrimonious observations on her father's conduct. But the most interesting part of the conversation took place after lord Monteith had explained Sir William's reasons for rejecting his addresses, and asked

aſked her if ſhe would accept the lover he de-
ſigned to propoſe.

" Aſſuredly I will not," was her anſwer.
" Should my father ever expreſs ſuch intentions
" to me, I muſt be as firm in refuſing my hand
" where I cannot beſtow my heart, as I now am
" in rejecting your addreſſes while he diſap-
" proves of them."

" Moſt admirable of all human creatures !"
exclaimed Monteith, " I will patiently commit
" my deſtiny to the care of a lady whoſe exalted
" ideas increaſe my eſteem for her at every
" interview ; yet permit me to add one more
" inquiry. Might I venture, madam, to hope,
" or ſhould I have been too preſumptuous in
" hoping, that if I had been honoured by Sir
" William's approbation, I ſhould not have en-
" countered the terrors of your refuſal ?"

Miſs Powerſcourt's reply was confuſed, and
inarticulate ; yet the deep crimſon which fluſhed
her, half-averted face, and the ſoftneſs of her
accent, did not reduce him to deſpair. She
perceived it did not ; and ſoon as ſhe had recollected herſelf, ſhe added, " I know the goodneſs
" of my father's heart ; I know his unbounded
" affection for me ; and I am confident that he
" will perſiſt in no plan that would make me
" miſerable. But let me entreat you, my lord,
" not to purſue a method of addreſſing me
" which muſt either make me mean in my own
" own eyes, or diminiſh my reſpect for your
" character." His lordſhip bowed, and proteſt-
ing inviolable obedience and unaltered love, rode
off juſt at the inſtant that John found the key
which enabled Miſs Powerſcourt to purſue her
expedition. Her conduct in this interview did
not leſſen her in her lover's affections, for he

vowed

vowed to lord W. that she was an angel in a human form, and that he was determined either to die or obtain her.

Nor did the Evans's, to whom Miss Powerscourt impartially related this incident and that of the letter, feel any diminution of the love and esteem which the many amiable qualities of their charming young friend had long excited. On the contrary, Mrs. Evans bestowed warm encomiums on the marked propriety of her conduct, and Lucy's eyes shone with that humid lustre which the praises of her dear Geraldine always called forth. Sir William's scheme for the intended disposal of his daughter's hand excited general surprise, mingled with some share of disapprobation; and though uniform respect for his character prevented Mrs. Evans from expressing any doubt of the propriety or practicability of the scheme, the artless open-hearted Lucy was so strongly persuaded of its impropriety, that the moment Miss Powerscourt retired, she could not avoid reprobating the absurdity of allowing her friend so little influence in an affair so infinitely momentous to her own happiness.

" It is certainly wrong," replied Mrs. Evans, " and may be added to the instances I have fre- " quently repeated to convince you of the ne- " cessity of conforming a little to the notions " of other people; for I have often observed, " my dear girl, that you have more tenacity of " opinion than one generally meets with in a " young woman of nineteen. Do not suffer " singularity to creep upon you; for though " it now only appears in wearing your hair " smooth, while all your acquaintance have " theirs curled, or in expressing your dislike to

music

" mufic when all the world is mufical, it may
" twenty or thirty years hence induce you to
" lay more abfurd fchemes for the marriage of
" my grandchildren than even Sir William's fo
" much reprobated plan."

Lucy replied laughing, " I will put my hair
" in rollers this very evening, which will, I
" truft, remove your apprehenfions refpecting
" the prepofterous matches of your grandchil-
" dren."

" If you, my dear," continued Mrs. Evans,
" recollect the circumftances of Sir William's
" life, and analyze his character, his prefent
" defign will appear the natural refult of both.
" The virtues which fpread profperity and joy
" all around him are not the refult of thofe
" refined feelings, thofe elegant fufceptibilities,
" which ufurp the place of folid virtues in the
" eftimation of too many. They are the effect
" of reflection, of principle, of chriftian prin-
" ciple, my dear, that firmeft foundation for all
" that is truly excellent in man. But though
" his idea, that the gifts of fortune are only
" an accountable ftewardfhip, makes him uni-
" formly and perfeveringly upright and gene-
" rous, it does not fupply thofe nicer touches
" of the heart which nature never originally
" beftowed. Exclufive of what he feels for
" Geraldine, I queftion whether his heart was
" ever touched by any fentiment livelier than
" univerfal benevolence."

" How came he to marry then ?" inquired
Lucy. The air of *naïveté* with which fhe fpoke
would have diverted Mrs. Evans at another time;
but when applied to the prefent fubject it re-
called painful fenfations. " It was not a love-
" match," faid fhe after a long paufe; " and
" I fear

" I fear lady Powerſcourt did not ſtudy to ex-
" cite thoſe ſentiments of eſteem and attach-
" ment in Sir William's mind, which her en-
" gaging attentions would have inſpired.
" Though I believe he never felt a ſtronger tie
" than what aroſe from habit and compaſſion,
" his natural goodneſs made him behave to her,
" during the trial of a long ſickneſs, with ſo
" much tenderneſs, that he was univerſally ac-
" counted a moſt excellent huſband. You
" know, Lucy, he is not apt to make obſerva-
" tions on people or incidents which do not
" immediately affect himſelf. The world ſlides
" by unnoticed, if it do not elbow him; and
" though this may conduce to the tranquillity
" of his mind, it prevents him from enlarging
" his ſtock of information. Can you, however,
" wonder from what he has felt, and from what
" he has obſerved, that he ſhould ſuppoſe mu-
" tual attachment unneceſſary in a union be-
" tween two worthy people? and you will al-
" low Miſs Powerſcourt and her couſin anſwer
" that deſcription."
" Moſt certainly they have the beſt hearts
" in the world; but is not lord Monteith too
" a moſt worthy character, and in point of
" rank and fortune a more deſirable match?"
" Fortune, my dear, though in moſt marri-
" ages a very neceſſary ingredient, is of little
" conſequence in the diſpoſal of Miſs Powerſ-
" court; for her hereditary affluence is ſo great,
" that ſhe may poſſeſs every indulgence ſhe can
" wiſh for, without the neceſſity of her huſ-
" band's adding any thing to the paternal ſtock.
" I am not one of thoſe who ſlight the advan-
" tages of rank; I allow it to be deſirable; but
" if you balance againſt it the apparent juſtice
" of

" of beſtowing a rich heireſs on her father's
" neareſt male relation, who is educated in the
" ſame principles, and will reſide upon the
" ſame ſpot where his anceſtors have flouriſhed,
" who will moſt probably continue to diffuſe
" the ſame noble benevolence and patriarchal
" hoſpitality; I proteſt, when I think of theſe
" advantages, I can condemn nothing but Sir
" William's characteriſtical indifference to the
" ſtate of his daughter's affections. But I ob-
" ſerve, Lucy, that of late you always ſeem
" uneaſy and ſilent when we talk of Henry
" Powerſcourt; are not you and your old
" friend and playfellow upon as good terms as
" uſual?"

" Yes; quite ſo."

" Then ſhould you not rejoice at the proſpect
" of his good fortune?"

" So I do; but poor lord Monteith—I cannot
" help juſt now thinking of him. I am ſorry
" at my very heart that he ſhould be left un-
" happy, he is ſo uncommonly amiable."

" Pray," ſaid Mrs. Evans, " how came you
" to know that he is ſo uncommonly amiable
" and excellent?" Miſs Evans confeſſed that her
informant was Geraldine.

" Ah, poor Geraldine!" ſaid Mrs. Evans,
" the eye I ſee has outſtepped the judgment;
" I hope it has not miſled it. What very amia-
" ble qualities could ſhe diſcover in a ball-room?
" Does the indirect mode of his purſuing your
" friend, ſince her father's rejection, argue any
" very exalted excellence?"

" No," ſaid Lucy, " indeed it does not; but
" do, my dear mother, make allowances for his
" very ſtrong attachment. I am afraid too my
" ſweet friend's heart is irrevocably his, and
" ought

" ought she to marry Henry Powerscourt, all
" worthy and good as he is, while her affections
" are another's ?"

" Your mother's conduct," replied Mrs.
Evans, " has shewn her decided opinion upon
" such a question, nor has she ever found rea-
" son to regret the preference which has made
" her the wife of the worthiest of men.   Yet,
" if in the present conflict of Miss Powerscourt's
" passions I could hope that my warning voice
" might be heard, I would entreat her to con-
" sider, whether, since her attachment is not
" the result of long acquaintance and impartial
" observation, but the transient start of sudden
" preference, it be not at least possible that her
" father's plan for her happiness may be the
" most eligible ?   She can never now have an
" opportunity of knowing lord Monteith's real
" disposition previous to the marriage ceremony.
" The cautious lover will disclose nothing
" which is disagreeable, where he studies to re-
" commend himself to favour ; and what can
" she learn from the vague or perhaps interested
" communications of others ?   Charge her
" then, my dear Lucy, in your moments of
" endearment and privacy ; if your Geraldine's
" happiness be dear to you, charge her to reflect
" on Henry's known virtues, his modest diffi-
" dence, ingenuous gratitude, and gentle, yet
" generous disposition.   Ask her, if these are
" not the qualities which must insure happiness,
" and warn her not to mistake a transient liking
" for an insurmountable attachment."

Miss Evans burst into tears at her mother's
pathetic injunction, and promised obedience.

CHAP.

CHAP. X.

True dignity is his, whofe tranquil mind
   Virtue has rais'd above the things below ;
Who, every hope and fear to heaven refign'd,
   Shrinks not, though Fortune aim her deadlieft
    blow.   -   BEATTIE.

WHILE Youth with democratic violence
pulls down Reafon from her fovereign feat, and
commits the helm to a rebel rout of paffions ;
Age, finding thefe riotous principles quiet and
manageable in his own particular territories,
fuppofes it eafy for others to keep them in equal
fubjection, and affirms that the abfolute unlimited
monarchy of the ci-devant princefs is not only
the beft mode of government, but actually the
moft feafible. It is not wonderful that Youth
fhould deny the power of thofe reftrictive principles which time and experience gradually introduce ; but certainly Age might remember the
fentiments that it once felt.

The above obfervation, though profoundly
true in general, is, I confefs, irrelevant to the
cafe before us ; for Sir William Powerfcourt had
exactly the fame opinion of love at the time I
am treating of, as he had forty years before ;
and Mrs. Evans was of fo fingular a tafte, and
had fo thorough a contempt for a " fet of features and complexion," that, like Defdemona,
fhe faw her hufband's " features in his mind ;"
for when fhe felected Mr. Evans, who had no
perfonal graces to boaft of, fhe not only encoun-
tered embarraffed circumftances, but difpleafed

D 3   her

her relations by rejecting a rich and handfome, but abandoned admirer.

A few days after the events related in my preceding Chapter had taken place, Sir William's bailiff begged his Honor's leave to tell him fomething that made him unhappy. It was, that he had twice feen a very fine gentleman whifpering with Mrs. Bridget in *Ellis*'s temple in the dark hour. The groom, he added, feemed to know fomething about it, for he laughed, and faid Bridget had got a London fweetheart ; but Roger fomehow thought, though he knew that fecond-handed gentlemen in London dreffed as fine as their mafters, that this looked to be another guife kind of body. Sir William thanked Roger for his fidelity, fhook his head, and obferved that the world grew worfe and worfe every hour; to which obfervation Roger, who was of the fame age with his mafter, cordially agreed.

Previous to thefe communications of faithful Roger, Sir William had felt a confiderable fhare of uneafinefs. He recollected that Lady Powerfcourt was very fond of relating long narratives of refiftlefs beauties, who, by their unrelenting cruelty, had compelled their defperate lovers to carry them off in chariots and fix, furrounded by armed footmen, maugre all their tears and cries; and though Sir William had always confidered thefe tales to be entitled to an equal degree of credibility with thofe of Mother Goofe, his anxiety for Geraldine reminded him, that if Lord Monteith had ever happened to hear any of thefe ftories, they might have put fomething in his head which he would not otherwife have thought of. He determined therefore to inform Henry Powerfcourt of his

defigns

defigns in his favour, and to confign his daughter to a hufband's protection fome years fooner than he had intended.

That young gentleman paffed the college vacations at Powerfcourt, and excited the efteem of every intelligent obferver by his ingenuous diffidence, unaffected gentlenefs, and a thoufand unequivocal proofs of a generous, grateful heart. His countenance was open, and his features agreeable, though they had no pretenfions to beauty; his figure was naturally good, but he feemed quite at a lofs how to manage it to the beft advantage. He was faid to poffefs very refpectable literary talents, but the perpetual raillery of the lively Geraldine againft pedants made him profoundly filent upon topics which he was beft qualified to difcufs. Of the world he was totally ignorant; and he feemed, like his refpectable kinfman, to be not very anxious to be initiated into its myfteries. Afraid of being abfurd, he never ventured to trifle; ignorant of the fmall talk of the day, too ftudious and retired during his college refidence to enrich his mind with alma mater anecdote, or to learn the art of practical joking; confcious of his dependant fituation; folicitous to avoid intrufion; and ever fearful of offending; he certainly appeared with a referve and gravity unufual at his age; and he might in a mixed company juftify Geraldine's obfervations, that he looked like perpetual prefident of the club of the humdrums.

Mifs Powerfcourt's vivacity found continual employment during her coufin's vifits in what fhe called teaching him the graces, and rubbing off college ruft. But though an exuberant flow of youthful fpirits made her fometimes purfue

thefe

thefe topics further than her good nature would have permitted, had fhe known that it gave pain to the object of her raillery, fhe felt for him the tendernefs of a fifter, and treated him with the confidence of a friend. Her heart was truly generous: I do not fpeak of that light, tranfient, and fometimes affected difregard for money which young people, who have never experienced its utility, often carelefsly difplay; but of that real liberality which could circumfcribe its own defires to increafe the comforts of thofe around it. Far therefore from regetting the fums which Sir William expended in Henry's education and fupport, or viewing the progrefs which he made in the good Baronet's affections with envy or jealoufy, fhe continually urged him immediately to beftow upon the valuable oddity, as fhe ftiled him, that independence which his noble mind richly deferved. " I even tell him," fhe would fay to her Lucy, " that in fo doing he will make " me happier; for I cannot help feel- " ing that I was thrown in the way moft unfea- " fonably to mar that dear fellow's expectations. " But for me, you know, Lucy, he would have " been heir to all my father's princely for- " tune."

Such folicitude for Henry's intereft had convinced Sir William that his fcheme was in the moft profperous way; and when, deeming the golden harveft of hope to be fully ripe, he informed his daughter with a fignificant fmile that he had fent for her coufin to Powerfcourt upon bufinefs which fhe was materially concerned, he certainly thought that he was communicating welcome intelligence. Far different were the agonized feelings of Geraldine, feelings which her anxiety to fave her elated father from the

pangs

pangs of sudden disappointment could scarcely restrain. She flew to Lucy, and, throwing herself into her arms, conjured her by all their infantine tenderness, if she ever loved, ever pitied her, to do something to save her from the dreadful alternative of a detested marriage, or offending an almost adored father.

Lucy mingled her tears with Geraldine's with more than the common sensibility of friendship. She could recollect nothing but her mother's solemn adjuration, and she repeated her arguments with fidelity; but the moment of strong passion was unfavourable to cool consideration. " O cease, my dearest girl!" interrupted Miss Powerscourt, " cease to urge the only proposal " to which I cannot accede. Even your mother, " all prudent, all self-possessed as she is, would " strongly reprobate solemn perjury. Had this " union not been proposed, my regard for Lord " Monteith should never have induced me to " have taken any step contrary to my father's " will, nor should he have discovered that the " sacrifice I made to filial duty was at the expence of my happiness. But to bind myself " for ever to another, when my heart is irrevocably his; to shut out every hope that time " might remove my father's reluctance; honour, " delicacy, affection, nay, even my esteem for " Henry Powerscourt, all strongly forbid such " an unhallowed bond!"

Lucy was quite a convert to these arguments; but when Geraldine again called upon her to suggest some plan of conduct that might obviate these threatened evils, the artless weeping girl could form no other scheme than that she should throw herself at Sir William's feet and own a pre-engagement. Miss Powerscourt seemed not

to have fufficient courage for a difcovery which
fhe apprehended muft produce difagreeable
events; but while depreffed and unrefolved, fhe
feemed firm in nothing but that fhe would
ultimately reject her coufin's hand. The important eclairciffement came from another
quarter.

I fhall pafs over many unimportant converfa-
tions to give a fuller account of the interview in
which Sir William unequivocally, and in fure
expectation of a joyful acceptance, informed his
kinfman of his defign to make him the heir of
his fortunes, and the depofitory of his daughter's
happinefs. But when he expected to fee the
highly favoured youth break out in a ftrain of
grateful rapture, (for even his phlegmatic
temper expected rapturous acceptance when
Geraldine was the gift,) how cruelly was he difappointed to fee his countenance betray diftrefs
almoft bordering upon defpair, and to hear him
in grateful, refpectful, but decifive terms, reject
the radiant, the alluring prize. Sir William ftood
motionlefs with aftonifhment to fee the " cloud-
capt tower" he had been fo many years erecting
prove in one moment to be only " the bafelefs
fabric of a vifion;" and as I conceive my readers
muft be equally planet-ftruck, I cannot help
afking them, in a tone of exultation, whether I
have not attained the grand climax of improba-
bility? whether the legends of modern romance,
modern poetry, or the modern drama, can produce a fituation fo novel and ftriking?

That a prudent, diffident young man, who,
without having abfolutely laid a plan to make his
fortune, was anxioufly folicitous to be relieved
from a dependance which he feverely felt; that
fuch a one, I fay, without any preconcerted
defign

design upon Lady Bridget Autumn's estate, or the jointure of the duchess dowager of Witherington, should refuse the young, lovely, fascinating Geraldine, when offered to him by her father, with the immediate possession of three thousand a year; and a certain assurance of an additional five thousand per annum on his death; I think I have been too diffident in only challenging my contemporaries in the circle of the Belles Lettres to rival me in the non-natural: I might also call upon the *philosophers* of the new school, and ask the illustrious sophists if they can form a paradox more perfectly incomprehensible.

But, notwithstanding my passionate love of fame compels me to adopt the most fashionable, that is, the certain method of obtaining it, I cannot quite conquer the common foible of old people, that of looking back to the times I have seen, and thinking them somewhat better than the present days. Indeed now and then I am rude enough to conjecture that the modern Parnassus is seated very near that " windy sea of land," which Milton names the Limbo of Vanity, the residence of.

" All th' unaccomplished works of Nature's hand
" Abortive, monstrous, or unkindly mix'd."

Regretting that simple elegance and rational amusement should be sacrificed to high-sounding phrases and inconceivable wonders, signifying nothing, I sometimes invoke the shades of Addison, Goldsmith, and Fielding ; and, after having contemplated the forms of nature or morality which their antiquated pages present, I in vain endeavour to be amused with ghosts and dungeons, incident without character, or character without effect. These last sentences recal my
wandering

wandering pen, by suggesting to me that criticism may be as jejune and irrelative as the novel or poem which it condemns; and that the satirist of the taste and morals of others must from prudence avoid exhibiting any thing reprehensible in her own.

Taught by that "warning voice" to shun the rock of digression, I must inform my readers, that the absurdity of my plan may be rather apparent than real. Henry Powerscourt might have some private reasons for his extraordinary conduct. He might have a pre-engagement; and no lover under twenty would hesitate to offer a few annual thousands on the shrine of Cupid. He might be enamoured of academic shades, and think, like Shakespeare's Henry VI.

"Marriage! alas, my years are yet too young,
"And fitter is my study and my books:"

Or the vivacity of Geraldine might intimidate him as much as Beatrice's did Benedict, and induce him to offer "to go on an embassy to "Prester John or the Antipodes, rather than "encounter that lady's tongue." What his real reasons were must not now be developed; but, knowing the pain of curiosity, I cannot help owning, notwithstanding my usual reserve, that I know them, and that they shall be explained in their proper place.

The reader must remember that I have left fir William in rather an awkward situation. Some little hope that there might be a mutual misunderstanding induced him to repeat the offer; and, in a tone that indicated not only surprize but displeasure, he asked Henry if this was what

he

he meant to refuſe? The embarraſſed youth gave a heſitating " Yes," and turned aſide to conceal the ſtrong emotion of his agitated heart. " You are not ignorant, Henry," ſaid ſir William, " that my fortune is entirely at my own " diſpoſal, and that all your inheritance is an " eſtate of your father's, ſomewhat under a " hundred a year."

" I know it, ſir," anſwered Henry in a voice ſcarcely audible ; " I know too how infinitely " I am beholden to your bounty, and that I " could ſacrifice my life to prove my grati- " tude."

" Pho! pho!" ſaid ſir William, " a fiddle- " ſtick about gratitude and ſuch nonſenſe ; " talking about theſe things is not to the pur- " poſe ; I meant to have been a greater friend " to you than I have been ; but I ſuppoſe you " have ſome reaſons for your behaviour, and " ſo I ſhall only add that I wiſh you a better " offer."

He then left the room, while the afflicted Henry, wretched at the idea that he had offend- ed the perſon whom of all others he moſt revered and eſteemed, ſunk upon a ſofa, and fell into a painful reverie on his paſt conduct. His mo- tives appeared ſo laudable, that he could not upon retroſpection wiſh the deed undone ; he only feared that his voice, his looks, his words, or his manner, had not ſufficiently indicated the deep veneration which he felt in his heart.

In a converſation which took place the ſame morning between ſir William and his daughter, the former animadverted on Henry's unaccount- able conduct in terms more acrimonious than he had ever before uſed. As a proof of the un- common ſweetneſs of Miſs Powerſcourt's diſpoſition,

poſition, ſhe appeared not only to forgive the affront, but ſhe even pleaded for the bold re-fuſer with all that enchanting eloquence by which ſhe had ever been accuſtomed to influence her father's mind:

" I cannot, my dear ſir," ſaid ſhe, " condemn " Henry's behaviour ; on the contrary, I think " it proceeded from that inviolable regard for " honour and ſincerity which you tell me has " been from time immemorial the charaĉteriſtic " of our family. A mean intereſted perſon " would have thought that your predilection in " his favour gave him an abſolute right to treat " me as he pleaſed ; he would never have con- " ſidered whether I was the wife he would " voluntarily have preferred. Looking only " at the greatneſs of my dowry, he would at " all times have ſilenced the compunĉtions of " his conſcience, by remembering that I was " obtruded upon his choice, when perhaps his " heart felt a ſecret preference for another."

While Miſs Powerſcourt ſpoke; her look, voice, and manner, were uncommonly beautiful and impreſſive. Sir William gazed upon her with inexpreſſible delight ; and when ſhe ſtopped, he only obſerved, that he thought there were few young men in the kingdom who would not have been overjoyed at ſuch a pro-poſal.

" Parental partiality," reſumed Geraldine, " muſt not decide on ſuch an important " point ; but let not my deareſt father, through " his fondneſs for me, ſwerve from that noble " integrity which has ever been the rule of his " aĉtions. From motives of delicacy to my- " ſelf I muſt entreat that the events of this " morning may make no difference in your " opinion

" opinion of Henry. Indeed I fhould think
" that as the highly-liberal plan you had formed
" in his favour is now fruftrated, this is the
" propereft time to give him the independence
" you defign for him. Suppofe you immedi-
" ately refign the Merionethfhire eftate. It is
" but five hundred a year you know ; and if
" fuch a defalcation in your revenue fhould any
" way derange your cuftomary charities, per-
" mit me, my dear father, to furrender part of
" that very ample allowance which you give
" me. It really is much more than I know how
" to fpend ; it only makes me thoughtlefs and
" extravagant ; and I am fure that abridging it
" would be a good moral leffon."

" Speak no more, child, upon this fubject,"
replied fir William ; " nobody fhall fay that I
" brought a young fellow up, and then let him
" ftarve becaufe he was not willing to marry
" my daughter ; but there is no neceffity for
" choofing the very time of his difobliging me
" to make him independent, as you call it. I
" have been put out of humour this morning,
" and I will take a ride round my farm to get
" myfelf comfortable again. I don't fee that
" Henry's ftaying here longer is of any ufe, and
" I fhall tell him that he may as well fet off for
" Oxford when I come home."

Henry was roufed from his ftupor by a letter
from Geraldine, which I fhall tranfcribe :

" To HENRY POWERSCOURT, Efq.

" Your conduct, my noble coufin, during
" the trying incidents of this morning, fuper-
" adds to the efteem and confidence which I
" have ever felt for you, the indelible tie of
" fervent

" fervent gratitude. If I ever appear to forget
" your generous behaviour, add to the lift of
" thofe infamous women of antiquity whom
" you have often reprobated, the more in-
" famous name of Geraldine Powerfcourt, who
" bafely neglected the difintereſted friend who
" rifked all his faireſt hopes to alleviate her for-
" rows.

" Be not grieved, my ever-refpected Henry,
" at the apprehenfion of my father's anger.—
" It muſt not, it fhall not continue. His own
" excellent heart will not permit the difappoint-
" ment of a favourite plan to infpire laſting
" refentment againſt the worthy youth who is
" an honour to his name. Perhaps, under the
" prefent circumſtances, it will be better for
" you not to meet, at leaſt till he can fee you
" without too keenly regretting that you cannot
" be his fon. I have heard you exprefs a wiſh
" to vifit Italy ; does that wiſh continue, or has
" it been fupplanted by fome other defire ? Say,
" in what way can I prove that mine is not a
" mere wordy gratitude ; write to me as foon
" as you get to Oxford, for I can taſte no
" true fatisfaction unlefs I hear that you are
" happy.

" GERALDINE POWERSCOURT."

I hope it will not be deemed an imputation on
Mr. Powerfcourt's fortitude, if I ſhould affirm,
that on reading this letter his eyes were obferved
to be fuffufed with tears. With a faltering voice
he ordered his horfes. He attempted to write a
few lines, but his hand was too tremulous, and
his thoughts too confufed to perform the taſk.
The deſtined heir of Sir William Powerfcourt,
renouncing all thofe fplendid profpects which
had

had opened upon him, returned to the academic
shades which, warm with the most sanguine
hopes, he had left the week before. He returned poor in every worldly possession, dejected,
and dismayed; but rich in integrity, rich in the
noble consciousness of approving virtue.

CHAP. XI.

——Here, before Heaven,
I ratify this my rich gift. O Ferdinand!
Do not smile at me that I boast her off;
For thou wilt find she will outstrip all praise,
And makes it halt behind her.

SHAKESPEARE.

THE Earl of Monteith was too ardent a
votary of Cupid, to hear with indifference of
his rival's proceedings. On the first intelligence
that Henry was arrived at Powerscourt, his lordship's valet received orders to examine and clean
the locks of his silver-mounted pistols, and to
have a sufficient quantity of powder and ball
ready at the shortest notice. Alarmed for his
lord's life, Beaufoy instantly informed lord W.
of this bloody preparation, who again prevailed
upon his young friend to wait patiently for the
effect of Miss Powerscourt's evident predilection
in his favour.

Meantime the " tall long-sided dame" whom
Hudibras characterises as a " tattling gossip,"
having received some hint of what was really
intended at Powerscourt-house, blazoned it with
all her powers; and, knowing that the intelligence

gence muſt be particularly intereſting at W. park, ſhe put her ſwifteſt winged emiſſaries into motion. Theſe, gentle reader, were not aërial ſylphs, or " Iris gliding down her painted bow:" modern proſe is ſeverely reſtricted from the uſe of ſuch ornamental machinery. I can only introduce a lame dowager of conſummate prudence and known candour, who had her old horſes driven ten miles through the dirt to wonder with Lady W. that any young Lady could reject Lord Monteith, and accept Henry Powerſcourt, and to reprobate the extravagant demand of eight hundred a-year for pin money, on which the intended bride had poſitively inſiſted:— Another of Fame's buſy meſſengers was a gentleman fox-hunter, a man of extreme caution and undoubted veracity, who affirmed at Lord W.'s public dinner, that he had met two barriſters and a ſerjeant at law riding poſt to Sir William's that very day. On one of the company obſerving, that three lawyers conſulting upon a ſettlement was rather unuſual, Squire Weſtern affirmed with an oath, that one of his neighbours told him Sir William would have it ſo :— " Theſe lawyers," ſaid he, " are ſad quarrel- " ſome fellows, and if two of them ſhould diſ- " agree, I will have the third ready to be um- " pire; for the wedding ſhall take place next " week." Nobody now could doubt his teſtimony, the words were ſo very like what Sir William would ſay.

When the gentlemen adjourned to the drawing-room, the buſy ſprite I have before alluded to had taken poſſeſſion of that goodly field, and inſtigated a lady, at the hazard of engroſſing too much of the converſation, to enumerate all the bride's paraphernalia. One part of the com

pany

pany indeed affirmed, that they were told Mifs Powerfcourt fecretly difapproved of the match; but three young ladies, influenced by the fame fupernatural agency, protefted that they knew better. They were, they faid, her very intimate friends, and were entrufted by her with the fecret of her attachment to her coufin, which had fubfifted from their earlieft years.— During thefe narratives, the countenance of Monteith varied from the crimfon glow of rage to the livid hue of jealoufy; and, as he was not fufficiently verfed in the fcience of felf-command to conceal his ftrong emotions, the ladies were all highly entertained with the idea that he really was very much in love ftill; forgetting, or perhaps having never read in the fable, that what is fport to one may be death to another.

It was only by repeated obfervations, that all thofe reports could not be true, and that the lady's word deferved confidence, that lord W. could prevail upon his noble gueft to fufpend the execution of his fanguinary defigns. At this crifis the unexpected, the tranfporting intelligence arrived, that Henry was certainly gone in difgrace from Powerfcourt; but neither the lame dowager, the cautious fox-hunter, the criticifing lady, nor even the *intimate friends* of Geraldine, could tell why.

The ftate of affairs, both at the park and at Sir William's, foon underwent a furprifing revolution. The lovely Geraldine, with fteps once more light as the wood nymph's, flew to communicate to her dear Lucy the intelligence which her fparkling eyes, and the fmiles that played around her fafcinating face, had already anticipated. Lord Monteith had renewed his
addreffes

addreſſes in the moſt paſſionate but reſpectful terms ; and Sir William, contraſting ſuch ſtrong attachment with Henry's cold refuſal, had declared, that as his own plans were fruſtrated, he ſhould have no longer any objection to his lordſhip, provided ſome peculiar conditions were granted, with which Monteith joyfully complied. " Felicitate me, Lucy," added Miſs Powerſcourt, " upon the happy change in my " ſituation. I ſcorn the mean affectation of " keeping a generous heart in ſuſpenſe. I have " owned to my father, that I regretted his re- " jection of Lord Monteith. Nay," added ſhe, leaning her bluſhing face on Miſs Evans's ſhoulder, " I have confeſſed that my affections " are irrevocably fixed upon the moſt conſtant, " the moſt generous of men."

I will truſt that the active imaginations of my readers will delineate all the ſcenes of joyous congratulation, courtſhip, and preparation, which intervened between Sir William's acceptance of Lord Monteith's offers, and the nuptial ſolemnity; and will only premiſe, that, as the principal figures on the canvaſs were people of elevated rank and deeply in love, the execution muſt be maſterly. An enamoured Earl muſt certainly expreſs his ſentiments in more dignified periods than an enamoured Viſcount ; and if this obſervation be extended through all the " privileged orders," my prudence in ſhrinking from the hazardous attempt of recording the loftier flights of heroic love is worthy of ſome credit ; particularly in theſe times, when every noveliſt permits his plain Williams and Richards to addreſs their miſtreſſes in terms that would formerly have been allowed only to an Archduke or a Count Palatine, except indeed the hero were a

profeſſed

profeſſed Knight-errant, to whom the uſe of extravagant hyperbole has belonged from time immemorial.

Let it then be ſuppoſed, that after the noble lover had many times repeated his injunctions to Phœbus to " gallop apace his fiery-footed ſteeds," and had chided creeping Time for not " ſpeeding on the lagging hours," the auſpicious morning at laſt arrived, and the lovely pair, attended by many of the neighbouring gentry, and a numerous cavalcade, compoſed of Sir William's tenants, proceeded to the pariſh church, where Mr. Evans joined their hands, amid the acclamations of hundreds, whom the unrefined but liberal hoſpitality of the worthy baronet had aſſembled on this joyful occaſion.

Though female delicacy would gladly have eſcaped the oppreſſive ſtate of public celebration, yet Geraldine was determined not to oppoſe her father's known predilection for all thoſe antiquated cuſtoms which were derived from the feudal barons, whom he gloried in imitating.— Gratified in the object of her choice, Lady Monteith preſided with unaffected ſweetneſs and poliſhed grace at thoſe feſtal entertainments by which Sir William ſtrove to diffuſe on all around him the overflowing ſatisfaction of his own heart.

I ſhall here perhaps be aſked, how his general diſlike to lords and love-matches, his plans in favour of Henry, and his wiſhes to perpetuate his own name and family, could be ſo ſoon forgotten. This laſt objection is anſwered by obſerving, that a clauſe in the marriage-ſettlement ſecured the inheritance of Sir William's fortune to the ſecond ſon of this marriage, who was expreſsly enjoined to receive the name of his maternal grandfather; or, in cafe of no fecond fon, the eldeft daughter was to convey the Powerfcourt honours to her hufband. A difpofition like Sir William's, though prone to purfue a favourite fpeculation with eagernefs, will not renounce every future good, becaufe its primary wifh has proved impracticable, but will fpeedily return to that harmonized tranquillity which beft accords with its natural feelings.—— When the doating father faw that Lord Monteith beheld his Geraldine with nearly the fame idolizing preference as he did himfelf, he forgot that he was a Peer, and he almoft became a convert to the opinion, that a love match was well enough now and then.

Befide the claufe already mentioned, the deed of fettlement contained another of a very extraordinary nature. It was, that on Lady Monteith's fucceeding to her inheritance, two thoufand pounds a year fhould be folely appropriated to her, that is to fay, not merely the income, but the abfolute power of giving or bequeathing it to whomfoever fhe chofe. Lord Monteith's lawyer ftated this demand to be extremely adverfe to the interefts of his noble client, whofe whole fortune was entailed upon the iffue of this marriage; and even Sir William thought that his dear girl was a little unaccountable, in afking for a power injurious to the interefts of her own children. The lady, however, perfifted in the requeft, which was indeed the only one fhe urged; and the matter being referred to Lord Monteith, he, with lover-like complacency, infifted that all oppofition on the part of his counfel fhould be immediately withdrawn.

It

It was alfo ftipulated, that Sir William fhould be gratified with the company of his daughter and fon-in-law for three months every year at Powerfcourt. The good baronet, on propofing this condition, explained the motives to lord Monteith: " I do not doubt, my lord, but that " as you will foon have a pretty large concern " in thefe parts, you will be anxious to get ac- " quainted with the neighbourhood, and to " know the characters of your dependants. I " am now, my lord, very old, and every thing " muft foon be your's and Geraldine's. It gives " me pleafure to think that I fhall leave you a " fet of upright worthy tenants; and I truft " you will act a father's part by them, as I " and my anceftors always have done. I will " introduce them all to you before you leave " us. Poor fouls! they have been ufed to " have their landlords live among them on free " and fociable terms, and it will grieve them " not to fee the chimnies of Powerfcourt fmoke " as they ufed to do. However, I fhall not " expect that your lordfhip can live here more " than four months in the year when it comes " to be your own; I know you have a feat in " Parliament, and when very particular bufi- " nefs is going on, you muft certainly be in " London; for the affairs of the nation are of " more confequence than the interefts of fifty or " fixty country yeomen. You have a very " fine caftle too of your own near Loch Lo- " mond, falling quite to decay, I hear, your " anceftors having neglected it for feveral years. " That is a fad pity, I think: doubtlefs, my " lord, you will wifh to go down there and fit " it up again. Geraldine will be very happy to

E 2   " affift

" affist you in beautifying it, and making it a
" comfortable refidence."

It will not be very furprifing that fome local
reflections fhould induce Sir William to lay a
particular ftrefs on the word *comfortable*.   Lord
Monteith, ftarting from a reverie, exclaimed,
" O, undoubtedly !" Sir William, who difcovered that he had been totally abfent during his
whole harangue, perceiving the object which
had fixed his attention, fmiled, and forgave
him.   Nor will my readers be inexorable,
when I tell them that the object was the
beautiful Geraldine, who, with her " loofe
hair floating in the wind," unconfcious that fhe
attracted any obfervation, fwept the foft ftrings
of her harp in a neighbouring alcove, and
chaunted, with her melodious voice, the following air :

Come, Cupid, with ambrofial flowers,
Rear'd in thy own Idalian bowers,
　　My nuptial wreath adorn ;
Here let the purple am'ranth bloom,
Mix'd with the lily's chafte perfume,
　　And rofe without a thorn.

O ! hafte, each claffic fymbol choofe,
The laurel facred to the Mufe
　　Of elegance and tafte ;
With thefe thy Mother's myrtle bind,
Beft emblem of a placid mind,
　　With gifts perennial grac'd !

I do not afk thy frolic hand
To weave the perifhable band
　　That fades on fafhion's brow ;
My conftant foul a tie requires,
Firm as the virtue which infpires
　　And dignifies my vow.

Give

Give me the mild perfuafive art,
Which holds the captivated heart
    In unregretted toils ;
Shed thy own luftre o'er my face, .
When beauty mourns each ravifh'd grace,
    And youth no longer fmiles.

Perplexing doubts my bofom tear ;
Oh ! let me fan with veftal care
    The Hymeneal fire ;
Guard it from paffion's wild extreme,
And bid his falutary beam
    With life alone expire * !

Having now gradually led my readers to that
point where I at firft rather abruptly introduced
them, I fhall endeavour to proceed ftraight forward during the remainder of my narrative.

---

* Mrs. Prudentia is very forry that fhe has not
abfolutely conformed to the opinion of the Re-
viewers, who beftowed fuch liberal praife upon her
profe, by entirely banifhing the vagrant Mufe.   She
has a moft unlucky knack of " hitching into rhyme;"
and when the bantlings are produced, fhe had rather
that they ftuck on the top fhelf of a book-cafe,
than that they fhould be immediately committed to
the flames.   With regard to their advice of publifhing her poetical productions feparately, fhe can
only anfwer, that fhe has repeatedly made the unfortunate experiment.   Her bookfellers all agree in
one fentiment, " Poetry will not go off."

CHAP. XII.

As humorous as Winter, and as fudden
As flaws congealed in the fpring of day.
His temper, therefore, muft be well obferv'd.
Chide him for faults, but do it reverently.

SHAKERPEARE.

LORD MONTEITH was one of thofe common characters which the world every day pro-
duces, and which a very little penetration will
eafily unravel. His abilities were not confpicuous, and his application to the improvement
of them had been as great as a rich heir, early
become his own mafter, ufually beftows. He
poffeffed a great deal of good temper, and that
open-hearted eafy generofity which always fuc-
ceeds in fecuring general good opinion. His
paffions were naturally very ftrong; and, never
having been taught the neceffity of reftraining
them, they were encreafed by continual gratification, till they fomewhat refembled the impetuous torrent. Nature intended him to be
humane and beneficent; but a neglect of difcipline and conftant indulgence had introduced
an indolent felfifhnefs. Yet ftill, if a good
deed required no great exertion, or if an object in diftrefs luckily prefented itfelf at a moment when he was difengaged from any favourite purfuit, he would not only fhew a noble
liberality, but alfo enjoyed a noble pleafure from
the benevolent deed.

A character

A character like lord Monteith's rather fitted its poffeffor to follow others, than to be a leader. Unhappily for him, his birth and fortune obtruded him into notice, and placed him in fituations to which his natural talents were unequal. The fplendour of his rank and his reputed munificence furrounded him with parafites ; and the impetuofity of his temper prevented him from having any directing friend. Lord W. at whofe houfe he lately refided, was a man of the world, very folicitous that his noble gueft fhould form a proper matrimonial connection ; but extending the idea of propriety no farther than to the fortune, the family, or perhaps the perfonal graces of the lady ; and though the young earl, during his paroxyfms of love, added to thefe allurements every angelic quality, he did not accurately define what thofe angelic qualities really were. Such was the man whom the purblind god, in one of his capricious moments, felected to be the hufband of the beautiful, animated, intelligent Geraldine Powerfcourt ; whofe feelings, exquifitely fufceptible, had been accuftomed to the regular tenor of gentle manners, uniform confiftent goodnefs, and every fond indulgence and mild endearment that parental tendernefs could beftow.

The fentiments with which the young couple approached the altar of Hymen were as diffimilar as their characters. The bridegroom thought no further of the awful ceremony, than as it was the means of putting him in poffeffion of an elegant and beautiful woman, upon whofe account he had felt a great deal of uneafinefs. He fuppofed that this event would of courfe greatly increafe his ftock of happinefs ; but as to any abridgment of his former plea-

fures,

fures, or any ferious duties impofed by the character of a hufband, he had not the leaft idea
of fuch difagreeable reftrictions. He was, indeed, firmly of opinion, that inclination would
in future ftrongly attach him to home, and that
he fhould find the fociety of his beloved " a
perpetual fountain of domeftic fweets;" but
fhould that expectation be difappointed, (and
fome of his married friends had complained
that they had been taken-in on a fimilar occafion,) would any body pretend to fay that he had
no right to make himfelf as comfortable as was
in his power? He had already a fine houfe,
elegant carriages, and a numerous retinue; he
was very feldom at home, to be fure, but he
believed that the houfe-keeper and the fteward
went on very well; and fhould he (which was
fcarcely poffible) find no more attractions in
his own fire fide when graced by the prefence
of a charming wife, he faw nothing in the
marriage ceremony which forbade his making
himfelf happy elfewhere.

The more correct principles and refined imagination of Lady Monteith taught her to confider the man whom fhe vowed to love, honour,
and obey, as the partner of all her joys and forrows, the lord of her deftiny, the guardian of
her character, and the guide of her conduct.
Confcious that death alone could diffolve the
folemn bond into which fhe had juft entered, her
moft anxious wifhes were pointed to one end,
that of being for ever amiable in her hufband's
eyes. She determined to ftudy his difpofition
with the moft affiduous care, to comply with his
peculiarities, and by imperceptible, becaufe
gentle, means, gradually to infpire that delicacy
of tafte and fentiment which even her partial
                                judgment

judgment difcovered to be wanting in his character. Had her obfervations been more profound, fhade after fhade muft have appeared;
yet, perhaps, had fhe even feen the whole portrait in its true colours, her ftrong predilection,
and the fanguine hopes which inexperienced
youth (and I muft add youthful vanity too) had
tempted her to form of being able to make a
complete revolution in his character, would
have encouraged her to attempt the hazardous
experiment. She never reflected, that the tender
indulgence to which fhe had been accuftomed
muft render the perpetual renunciation of her
own defires a painful tafk; nor was her experience fufficient to teach her, that the refinements
which fhe meant to introduce, like delicate
exotics, could only flourifh in a congenial
foil.

The firft inftance that the bridegroom gave of
that habitual felf-indulgence, and difregard to
the wifhes of others, which might be faid to be
the predominant feature in his mind, was an
impatience to leave Powerfcourt long before Sir
William had finifhed have his plans of feftal
glee. His lordfhip had, with vifible *ennui*,
endured the tedioufnefs of a public day, and
given fuch half-civil anfwers to the exclamation
of " I heartily wifh you joy, my Lord!" which
burft upon him from every quarter, as to excite a
doubt in the congratulators, whether he really
was or was not glad that he was married. At
dinner, he was only amufed by obferving the
indifcriminating appetites of country gentlemen;
and when the cloth was removed, as he found
himfelf the object of general attention, he determined to give no vexatious preference; and
therefore confining all confideration to his own

E 3   reveries,

reveries, he continued drawing lines upon the
table with the madeira or claret, and proceeded
no further in the way of difcourfe than by a hum'
or a fmile. While his right-hand neighbour
was defcribing the beft method of improving
land, his left explained the advantages of inland
navigation, and the gentleman oppofite addreffed
to him a long narrative explanatory of the difficulties attending a law-fuit which had been
awarded to him at the laft Caernarvon affizes.
Their manner was verbofe, and they talked all
together: his lordfhip, therefore, concluded
that they faid nothing worthy of attention, and
that the chagrin he felt arofe from the want of
fuperior fociety.

He feized the firft opportunity of withdraw-
ing from the company to the countefs's dreffing-
room, and on entering flung himfelf upon a fofa,
with fo loud a yawn as to alarm her ladyfhip and
Mifs Evans with ferious apprehenfions that he
was taken ill. " Are not you well?" exclaimed
the former with tender anxiety. " It is impof-
" fible to be well among fuch boors," returned
his lordfhip. " I have been talk'd at all the
" afternoon, and cannot for my foul remember
" one fingle fentence that has been uttered. I
" am determined to go to London the firft op-
" portunity : living here three months would
" be the death of me. I proteft, my chaming
" Geraldine, that you put me in mind of a rofe
" growing in the middle of a wildernefs."

Lady Monteith could fcarcely enjoy a compliment which conveyed fuch ftrong contempt for
what fhe had ever been accuftomed to view with
affectionate regard. She fmothered a figh, and
affumed a faint fmile. But the fmile and the figh
were alike difregarded. Her lord's attention was

now

now engroffed by a favourite fpaniel; with that he amufed himfelf for a few moments, and then dropped afleep upon the fofa.

Another incident a few days after this difplayed his humour in a ftill ftronger light. Sir Ralph and Lady Morgan fent an invitation in form, requefting the honour of the bride and bridegroom's company at their feat to a dinner and a ball given in honour of their nuptials. The invitation was written on an elegant card, decorated by her ladyfhip's own pencil with Lilliputian Cupids lighting their tiny torches. Twenty years ago the Morgans were people in high life, and even the gallant Monteith would not then have blufhed to have appeared at her ladyfhip's parties; but twenty years are fufficient to annihilate mighty empires, and muft unqueftionably caufe great revolutions in a private family. Juft before his affairs were irretrievable, Sir Ralph difcovered, that to be one of the very firft people is a preliminary ftep to becoming nobody; and his lady reflected on the danger of coquetry and diffipation before the laft falfe ftep had irretrievably ruined her character. They had fufficient good fenfe to refolve on mutual amendment; plans of retirement and œconomy were immediately adopted, and regular perfeverance in thefe falutary meafures had enabled them to refume their old family fplendor a little before Lady Monteith's marriage. Certainly at this period nobody knew the Morgans; and her ladyfhip's knowledge of the fafhionable world was fo antedated, that the very card fhe intended fhould announce her indifputable claim to fuperior elegance, convinced Lord Monteith that fhe muft be a mere *fal lal,* and that the vifit would

prove

prove a *bore* . as a natural confequence, he determined not to go.

On the day appointed, the countefs, attired in
all her bridal fplendor, in compliment to her
father's old friend, waited for her lord's approach
to lead her to her chariot.   Her lord appeared in
his morning difhabille, and in a half-whifper
announced his refolution not to go.   "I hate
" flate vifits,". faid he, "and I never could
" endure country balls in all my life."—" But
" this," returned the countefs, raifing her plead-
ing eyes, "is abfolutely given in compliment to
" us."—" Never mind, never mind," continued
his lordfhip, hurrying her to the carriage, and
at the fame time holding a handkerchief to his
mouth : " You can make an apology.   You fee
" I have got a terrible tooth-ach ; upon my foul,
" I would not go for a thoufand pounds.
" Come, your father waits ; you will be too
" late."   At thefe words he lifted her into the
chaife, and then, with the voice of one in extreme
pain, exclaimed, " Beft compliments—forry I
" can't do myfelf the honour—make hafte, my
" love ; if you are too late, I fhall be mifera-
" ble."

Lady Monteith had now, for the firft time in
her life, the painful tafk of apologizing for what
fhe conceived to be a moral impropriety in the
conduct of a perfon whom fhe tenderly loved.
Unufed to difguife, fhe faltered in her excufes,
which, indeed, feemed rather to make the affair
worfe than to improve it.   She found every
thing at the Morgans in flate array ; the entertainment was conducted with great decorum ;
and nothing but the lamented abfence of Lord
Monteith feemed to render deficient the èclat of
the fcene.   To compenfate for the bridegroom's
rudenefs

rudenefs, the bride thought it her duty to exert
herfelf with greater affiduity; but her attentions were ungraceful, her wit forced, and her
laughter artificial. After having endured a moft
irkfome evening, fhe returned home, and found
that the noble invalid had completely banifhed
his tooth ach and his chagrin, by witneffing the
amufements of an afs-race.

Lady Monteith liftened with feeming intereft
to the ludicrous accidents to which ruftic competition had given rife, and then ventured upon
a gentle expoftulation on his abfenting himfelf
from a fcene which muft have afforded him
fuperior pleafure. Her defcription of the entertainment and the company made his lordfhip a
convert to her opinion, and, unfolicited, he fet
off the next morning to the Morgans, to make a
perfonal apology for his abfence. He found
them fo unexpectedly agreeable, that on a flight
invitation he fpent the day with them, and returned home, not afhamed of his own caprice,
but vexed that he had miffed the pleafanteft party
that had occurred fince his refidence in Caernarvonfhire. Not that he was any way to blame;
his earlieft recollection did not furnifh him with
one inftance of his having acted wrong; the
fault lay entirely in the unlucky Cupids and the
painted card.

The feafon of the year of which I am now
treating was May, a period when the country
holds out its pleafures only to the ftudious, the
induftrious, and the contented. It is of all
times the moft infipid to the fportfman, who,
being deprived of all chance of breaking his
neck or blowing out his brains, is obliged to
hurry up to town to avoid the puerility of gather-
ing primrofes, and liftening to the cawing of
rooks.

rooks. Lord Monteith had already found his nuptial felicity lefs perfect than his expectations had conceived; but this, for the reafons I have above ftated, could not be from any error in his own behaviour, or any impropriety in his own judgment: nor did it proceed from the imperfections of his adorable Geraldine, who proved to be the angelic creature he had before fuppofed her: it was all owing to the odious country, to Sir William's odd ways, and the *twaddling* people whom he fuffered to vifit him. In London he fhould undoubtedly enjoy the expected paradife; there his lovely girl muft attract univerfal admiration; he fhould breathe another air, enjoy a different fociety, receive the congratulations of all his own friends; in fhort, he muft fet off for town immediately.

When, with many polite expreffions of regret for being obliged to fhorten his vifit at Powerfcourt, lord Monteith firft acquainted Sir William with the neceffity of his going up to town, the latter difcovered great furprife that he fhould choofe to go to that difagreeable place juft when parliament was fo near breaking up, and that there was no more national bufinefs of importance to fettle. "This," faid he, "feems to " be the very time that you fhould take a trip " to Scotland, to examine the plans of your ar- " chitects, to fet them to work, and to get the " foil fmooth and ready to plant next autumn. " I am afraid, my lord, you are not naturally " fond of a country life; but it is only becaufe " you have never been ufed to it. Get ac- " quainted with your neighbours; confider the " intereft which you have in the fcenes around " you; remember how much good you may " do in a fpot where you reign like a little king,

" compared

" compared to what you can do in London, and
" you will foon be as fond of Monteith as I am
" of Powerfcourt."

The manner in which Sir William uttered
thefe expreffions was too much marked by dignified benevolence to admit of ridicule; and the
unfortunate lord would have been compelled to
give up his London journey from the mere want
of arguments to defend its expediency, had not
accident favoured him with a convenient reafon for putting his defigns in execution, which
even Sir William allowed to be indifputable.

CHAP. XIII.

So mourn'd the dame of Ephefus her love.
SHAKESPEARE.

ON the mariage of lord Monteith, an exprefs
was difpatched to Kinloch caftle, to inform lady
Arabella Macdonald and lady Madelina Frazer
of the joyful event. The meffenger on his arrival found the caftle attired in the moft fombrous
weeds of woe, owing to the death of its *oftenfible*
mafter, Sir Simon Frazer, who, after having
exifted for feveral years in a ftate of complete
inanity, expired at the patriarchal age of ninety-
two, to the great grief of his inconfolable confort.

As lady Madelina was too much abforbed in
woe publicly to take an active part in the concerns of the family, the difpatches were opened
by

by lady Arabella, who acted as miſtreſs during the ſecluſion of her aunt. She read her brother's account of his marriage to the moſt excellent and beautiful of women, and, after caſting a ſide glance at the chimney-glaſs which reflected her own figure, ſhe proceeded to open a letter from her new ſiſter, which expreſſed a hope that the endearing tie of friendſhip would ſoon be added to that of kindred ; but what appeared to the reader to be the moſt ſignificant part of the epiſtle was that where lady Monteith added a preſſing invitation to their houſe in London, and an aſſurance that ſhe ſhould rejoice in the opportunity of exerting all her abilities to promote the happineſs of any of her lord's friends.

The general etiquette of Kinloch caſtle had eſtabliſhed a rule of decorum which extended to the moſt trivial occurrences. Every motion was to be grave and conſequential ; and a run could only be juſtified by one wing of the houſe being on fire, or by the appearance of an enemy on the coaſt. So ſtrict were theſe injunctions, that lady Madelina herſelf could not diſpenſe with them even upon the affecting incident of Sir Simon's death ; for, on being informed that if ſhe wiſhed to ſee him alive ſhe muſt come immediately, ſhe roſe with her uſual majeſty, and throwing her train into its proper graceful folds, moved with ſlow and ſtately ſteps to the door of the apartment, where ſhe found, to her deep regret, that ſhe was come too late ; a circumſtance the more to be lamented, as he went off in a fit, and had nobody with him but his old valet, who was lame with the rheumatiſm. Theſe obſervations will more clearly point out the groſs impropriety of lady Arabella's conduct, who with a joyful exclamation

tion of " O ! my brother is married, and I will
" go to London," fet off full fpeed to her aunt's
apartment.

The forrows of that lady, though of too deep
a caft to admit more than one narrow ftripe of
daylight, were not fo wholly fublime, as not
to require now and then a few adventitious fup-
ports. The room in which Sir Simon lay in
ftate was contiguous to her own. She vifited it
every day, and was moft feduloufly exact in
having the emblazonment completed in the
higheft ftyle of heraldry. In a remote country,
where few events occur to excite the attention
of the curious, a feudal laird lying in ftate in
his own caftle was an agreeable novelty; and
as the relict was not averfe to the exhibition, Sir
Simon became a much more interefting object
after he was dead, than ever he had been when
alive. All who faw, by repeating what they
had feen, excited the attention of others. Mutes
were ftanding all the way up the ftairs; all the
ftate apartments were hung with black tapers as
big as men; plumes of feathers as large as thofe
of Otranto, and efcutcheons and achievements
were placed at every corner. Several of the lady-
vifitants, after having feen all thefe aftonifhing
things, pleaded the rights of friendfhip, and entreated that their ftrong defire of combating lady
Madelina's extreme grief might wave the rules of
etiquette, and after a little reluctance, they were
admitted into her apartment. She *generally*
fainted upon receiving company, though *fometimes*, if fhe found herfelf exhaufted, fhe only
exhibited a flood of tears, and called upon the
dear fhade of her lamented lord. They *generally*
reafoned her into a ftate of calmnefs and refig-
nation; and *fometimes*, if the vifitants were Frazers.

zers and only the wives or daughters of younger
brothers, they fat down to a confolatory pool at
quadrille. But even here her ladyfhip's fentimental tendernefs was vifible ; for fhe could only
be brought to play at that game from a recollection " that poor dear Sir Simon, when he
" was quite himfelf, was remarkably partial to
" holding a lone-hand."

It was at fuch a time, and when lady Madelina
was engaged with fuch a party, that lady Arabella, forgetting her uncle's death and her aunt's
melancholy, rufhed into the room, health on her
cheek, joy in her eye, and the Monteith packet
in her hand, calling out rather too loudly,
" My brother is married to a Mifs Powerfcourt,
" and has afked me to come to London." The
affecting word *marriage* flung poor lady Madelina
into hyfterics, to which indeed the fudden entrance and loud exclamation had previoufly contributed. On her recovery another fource of
anxiety was ftarted. Who were the Powerfcourts ? What alliances had they formed ?
Had any body ever heard of the family before ?
Luckily, a very fkilful genealogift was prefent,
whofe information entirely obviated all anxiety
upon the fcore of degradation ; and her ladyfhip
became tolerably compofed. It was now declared
to be the univerfal opinion that fhe had indulged
her melancholy quite long enough ; that nothing
was fo good for bad fpirits as a journey ; and
that it would be quite kind and condefcending
in her to pay a vifit to the young couple. Her
ladyfhip for fome time ftrongly refifted the pro-
pofal ; protefted that her intentions were foon to
follow Sir Simon, whofe ghoft fhe was fure ftill
waited for her, and to die upon the very fpot
which contained his facred remains. It feemed

to be doubtful to the lady-comforters, whether Sir Simon had not had enough of his lady's company, for they denied the fact about the ghoft; and at laft convinced her, that it was exceedingly wicked in a perfon of her age to talk of dying. After much diffufe argument, it was agreed that the interment fhould take place a fortnight fooner than was intended; and that when the efcutcheons and achievements had been properly arranged, lady Madelina and her niece fhould prepare for their London journey. The latter clofed the converfation by obferving, that thefe were the only agreeable founds fhe had heard fince her arrival in Scotland.

While lady Arabella fpeeded the joyous preparation, and indulged all the hopes of future pleafures and triumphs which youthful confidence, aided by her early recollection, could fupply, lady Monteith took leave of Powerfcourt with far different fentiments. The one, averting her eyes from the detefted walls of Kinloch with an ardent wifh never more to behold what fhe called a burying place for the living, could only be interefted by fubjects remotely connected with dear, dear London: the latter vifited every fpot which the amufements of her youth had endeared, and took leave of every acquaintance, domeftic, and friend, with the foft regret of remembered kindnefs. Next to thofe fentiments which her ever-revered and beloved father excited, her feparation from the Evans's called forth the moft lively emotions. It was at firft her intention to have requefted that Lucy might accompany her to town; but, had not the propofed vifit of her lord's relations induced her to poftpone that defire till fhe could have been fully at liberty to enjoy the unreftrained plea-

fure of her fociety, the indifpofition of Mrs.
Evans would have fruftrated the fcheme.   That
excellent woman was now confined to her chamber by the increafe of a diforder under which
fhe had laboured for many years; and though
her fituation by no means excluded hope, her
tender domeflic daughter could feldom fteal an
hour from the pleafingly painful tafk of attending her, to breathe her fond wifhes and fonder
adieus to that deareft friend from whom fhe was
now for the firft time in her life going to be feparated.

CHAP. XIV.

Lighter than air, Hope's fummer-vifions die,
If but a fleeting cloud obfcure the fky;
If but a beam of fober Reafon play,
Lo Fancy's fairy froft-work melts away!
But can the wiles of art, the grafp of power,
Snatch the rich relics of a well-fpent hour?
PLEASURES OF MEMORY.

THE young countefs, waving every form of
ftate which might have proved inconvenient in
a fick family, walked down to the parfonage, to
bid farewell to her maternal friend, as fhe conftantly ftyled the refpectable fufferer.   She
came juft at the time when Mrs. Evans was
going to rife, and claiming admittance with the
privilege of long-eftablifhed intimacy, employed
herfelf in airing the good lady's fhawl; while
Lucy was bufily engaged in affifting her mother

to

to drefs, and in fixing her eafy chair in a proper fituation. Mrs. Evans looked at her noble gueft with a tender fmile. "I perceive, my deareft "lady Monteith," faid fhe, "that there is no "alteration in your character. Your goodnefs "and amiable vivacity has fuffered no diminu- "tion from the referve of rank or the etiquette "of dignity; and fee the effect it has upon us. "We can confider you in no other light than "that of our old friend. I admit you to a "fick chamber, and treat you with a little groan- "ing, while Lucy finds you fome employment, "as if you were ftill the playful Geraldine "whom I had ufed alternately to correct and "idolize. Do you remember dreffing my cat "in a blue jacket and trowfers, teaching it to "walk upright, and protefting that it was the "very image of your coufin Henry; and after- "wards, when you faw him crying at the com- "parifon, giving him the new gold watch your "father had juft bought you, by way of confo- "lation?"

"I have many unatoned fins to anfwer for to "Henry Powerfcourt," faid lady Monteith gravely, "worfe than tearing his beft Virgil to "paper my baby-houfe, or caufing the deftruc- "tion of his plaifter-of-Paris bufts by dreffing "them in high-crowned hats and hooped petti- "coats to frighten the houfe-maids. I have "blafted his faireft profpects; but I have not "forgot that I owe him an indelible debt of "gratitude. I have juft received from him an "affecting congratulation. He writes in a "difpirited ftyle, and complains of a low fe- "ver; but his wifhes for my happinefs are "breathed in fuch a ftrong and affectionate "manner, that while I read his letter I felt—
"I know

" I know not what I felt, unlefs it were a wifh
" that I had the power of making him as happy
" as he deferves "

During lady Monteith's fpeech Mifs Evans
was employed in mixing her mother's medicine.
Her hands appeared to tremble, fhe dropped
the cup, and, while apologizing for her awkwardnefs, burft into tears. " Your clofe con-
" finement makes you nervous, my love," faid
Mrs. Evans. " Go into the garden, and water
" your little nurflings; your friend will chat
" with me while you are gone; and I felt fo
" eafy this morning, that I intended to omit
" the draught."

Lucy inftantly obeyed. Her mother's eyes
followed her to the door; they were then lifted
to Heaven, as if enforcing a filent ejaculation,
and finally fettled upon Lady Monteith with a
look of fupplicating earneftnefs.

Silence enfued for a few moments, which
Mrs. Evans hefitatingly interrupted : " Till you
" are a mother, my dear madam, (faid fhe,)
" you cannot know the full force of a mother's
" fears. Mine, perhaps, are exaggerated by
" my prefent weaknefs. It ftrikes me, that
" my dear girl's dejection is even greater than
" my indifpofition, or your leaving us, could
" juftify. While I have any hopes of recovery,
" I conceive myfelf obliged to avoid awaken-
" ing her ftrong apprehenfions upon my ac-
" count; and I believe fhe is not aware that my
" prefent illnefs is attended with fymptoms of a
" more ferious nature than appeared in any
" former attack. If my conftitution fhould
" prove weaker than my difeafe," continued
fhe with a ftill more faltering voice, " I fhall
" leave her to the protection of one of the
" beft

" beſt of fathers ; but men cannot ſo well pene-
" trate into the female heart, they cannot treat
" our little peculiarities ſo delicately as one of
" our own ſex. It would lighten my mind of
" many cares could I diſcover whether my child
" has any ſecret unhappineſs ; even if it ſhould
" prove ſuch as I could not remove, I could
" at leaſt," wiping the tear that would no
longer be ſuppreſſed, " give her a mother's laſt
" legacy of advice and conſolation."

Lady Monteith underſtood this appeal, and
prevented further inquiry by immediately re-
plying, " You think, perhaps, that my deareſt
" Lucy may have entruſted me with ſome ſe-
" crets which ſhe has not revealed to you ; but
" I do aſſure you, if her innocent heart ever
" formed any wiſh or attachment with which
" you are unacquainted, her delicacy would
" ever prevent her from giving me the confi-
" dence which ſhe denied to her juſtly vene-
" rated mother. It is only from ſuch incidents
" as have juſt occurred, that I have gained a
" tranſitory inſight reſpecting what paſſes in
" her mind ; and perhaps my late experience
" may have made me an accurate obſerver."

" Do you mean her behaviour on dropping
" my medicine ?" inquired Mrs. Evans : " I
" ſaw nothing in that, except that ſhe was dif-
" pirited and agitated."

" You forget then," obſerved the counteſs,
" that Henry Powerſcourt was the ſubject of
" our converſation."

A thouſand circumſtances crowded at this
inſtant into Mrs. Evans's mind, which confirmed the ſagacity of her ladyſhip's infer-
ence ; but though the acknowleged merit of
the object leſſened the pain of the diſcovery,
the

the tender mother could not, without apprehenfive terror, be convinced, that love had " paled
the rofes on her daughter's cheek."

" I know of no one," faid fhe, "to whom
" I could with greater confidence entruft my
" darling's happinefs; yet fo many crofs acci-
" dents occur to blaft our faireft fchemes, that
" I own I wifh her heart had proved lefs fuf-
" ceptible. I do, however, hope that fhe is
" not a volunteer in her affections. You can,
" my dear Lady Monteith, pardon my folici-
" tude; but can you tell me whether Henry
" entertains reciprocal fentiments?"

Her ladyfhip appeared embarraffed by this
inquiry. " I think," faid fhe, " at prefent—
" I mean—I can hardly explain myfelf—Henry
" is too much attached to his ftudies and retire-
" ment; but I hope his chagrin—I mean his
" habits of feclufion, will wear off. His fitua-
" tion has been very peculiar. It has hardly
" given fair play to his affections. I truft he
" will very foon be made independant; I know
" he poffeffes great fenfibility, and I am per-
" fuaded that when his circumftances are per-
" fectly eafy, when he feels that he is his own
" mafter, if opportunities for frequent inter-
" views fhould occur, our Lucy's mild excel-
" lencies muft ftrike him in the moft forcible
" manner. I know her general character has
" attracted his warm approbation."

Another tear ftole from Mrs. Evans's eyes.
" I fee," faid fhe, " my poor girl has woven
" a net which will fatally entangle her peace of
" mind during the happieft hours of youth."

" No," faid Lady Monteith, with energy;
" if my friendfhip can break this fatal web,
" my Lucy fhall never be unhappy. Nothing
" in

" in my power fhall be omitted to forward the
" union of two hearts that feem formed in the
" fame mould. But if Henry, contrary to my
" expectations, fhould never fhew that par-
" tiality for my fweet friend which her excel-
" lence deferves, even Henry is not worthy
" of her, and I will affift her naturally-ftrong
" fenfe and refined delicacy in conquering an
" ill-placed attachment. I will keep her fe-
" cret with religious care: I will feife the firft
" opportunity to have the dear girl with me;
" I will endeavour to fathom Henry's heart,
" and without oftentatious eagernefs, will fet
" her merits as ftrongly in his view as propriety
" and decorum will admit. If all fhould fail
" of the defired effect, fhe never fhall be left
" to mufe over her griefs in folitude. I will
" amufe and confole her, nor fhall fhe ever feel
" a forrow which it is in my power to re-
" move."

Mrs. Evans thanked the countefs for thefe generous intentions, yet fighed at the fear of their being
impracticable. The return of her daughter neceffarily gave a check to the converfation, which
now turned to the fubject of Lady Monteith's
expected vifitants. Her lord had pointed out
to her the fingularities of Lady Madelina's character; but his only obfervation on his fifter
was, that fhe was the prettieft creature he had
even feen, and that fhe fluttered up and down
the caftle like a bird in a cage. " I expect,"
faid Geraldine, " that I fhall be much capti-
" vated by the fair reclufe, whofe behaviour at
" returning into the world after a long eftrange-
" ment muft be exceedingly interefting and na-
" tural. My lord has her picture. It exhibits
" lovelinefs perfonned; but it was drawn pre-

" vious to her leaving England; the character
" of the girl therefore is moſt predominant.
" I ſhould name it untaught nature."

" And what·traits," inquired Mrs. Evans,
" do you ſuppoſe have been added by her re-
" ſidence in the wilds of Scotland ?"

" O, an infinitude !" replied the animated
Geraldine, anxious to divert Lucy's dejection,
which the morning exerciſe had not quite removed. " As Lady Madelina was uncommonly
" ſevere, her pupil muſt be the eſſence of com-
" plying ſweetneſs. As ſhe was illiberal,
" proud, and reſerved,—gentle Candour, yield-
" ing humility, and frank generoſity, muſt
" mark the mind of a young woman who has
" had ſo many opportunities of obſerving the
" oppoſite odious faults."

" Do young women always obſerve faults,
" and ſhun thoſe they diſcover ?" demanded
Mrs. Evans.

" No—only a gifted few, and principally
" my Lucy and myſelf. I ſee, my dear Mrs.
" Evans, you are going, as uſual, to cenſure my
" propenſity for determining characters from a
" mere outline, and condemning or admiring
" in the groſs. I have often laboured hard to
" convince you, that this faculty is one of the
" peculiar gifts of nature, and that though *you*
" muſt judge from experience and conſidera-
" tion, *I* may draw as clear inferences from
" an intuitive art of gueſſing Ah! I ſee you
" ſtill ſhake your head incredulouſly; but Lucy
" ſhall be my evidence. Do not I find out
" people wonderfully ſoon, Lucy ? Am not I
" completely miſtreſs of their characters and
" propenſities before you can have adjuſted the
" propriety of their head-dreſs ?"

Lucy

Lucy with a smile acknowledged her friend's superior quickness; but added " You forget " one little circumstance. It has frequently " cost you the trouble of a walk to the par- " sonage to say, O Lucy! I was quite wrong " in my opinion of Mr. or Mrs. Such-a-one. " I hope you have not mentioned what I " thought of them."

" You are the severest satirist that I know," said her ladyship; " but upon this occasion I " am sure I shall never plead guilty. You and " Arabella shall meet; and if you once pronounce " me right, your dear mother will be easily led " to think me in future infallible. But," con- tinued she, glancing her eye upon her watch, with a painful consciousness that the moment of separation was near, " I have a favour to ask. " I know that you and Mr. Evans object to " the introducing this dear girl to scenes above " her fortune; I know that you are tenacious " of her valuable society; yet remember our " early endearments, and spare her to me as " soon as the engagements into which I am " now thrown will permit me to claim her." Mrs. Evans, with a dejected look, answered that her father should decide.

Lady Monteith felt the significance of this answer, and expressed her sense of it by dropping a tear upon Mrs. Evans's hand, which she at that moment pressed to her lips. " Dear, " amiable, second daughter," said the good woman, " my anxious wishes, my fondest af- " fections, follow you into that thorny and in- " tricate path which you are now going to " tread. I understand enough of the great " world to know that a character like yours " must attract observation, illiberality, and

F 2 " envy.

" envy. Your defire to pleafe will be called
" vanity; your fprightlinefs, levity; your fine
" accomplifhments, an invidious affectation of
" fuperiority. Through this dangerous trial,
" remember, innocence alone will not fupport
" you, and fenfibility will betray you. Keep
" in mind my oft-repeated maxims, that no
" human character can be perfect, and that it
" is dangerous to our peace to contemplate
" with too fteady an eye the failings of thofe
" with whom we are intimately connected."

" I will remember all you fay to me, and all
" I have faid to you," refumed the amiable
bride. " I will frankly own, that my inexpe-
" rienced heart flutters at the idea of the plea-
" fures and the diftinctions which await me.—
" I fhall have many trials, perhaps many
" enemies ; but where fhall I find friends to
" whom I may fo fafely difclofe all my heart, as
" I do to my dear Mrs. Evans and to my
" Lucy ?"

" Make your hufband your friend ; endea-
" vour to gain his confidence, and beware of
" forming dangerous intimacies, unfanctioned
" by experience, which may tend to leffen your
" attachment to him. Strive to exalt the pre-
" ference your charms have excited into firm
" efteem ; and if you fhould not at firft fuc-
" ceed, or not fo completely as you wifh, do
" not fink into dejection. Remember, time
" will overcome every difficulty, and patience
" will foften every forrow."

Mifs Evans, who had left the room during
the preceding fpeech, now haftily re-entered.—
" I have brought you," faid fhe, " my ever
" dear Geraldine, one other little keep-fake."—
Lady Monteith, opening the paper, found a
purfe,

purse, which she remembered her friend had been anxious to finish with the most perfect neatness.

"I cannot take it," replied the countess; "I know that when you netted it, you said "you meant it for Henry Powerscourt."

"He wants none of my purses; you shall "have it, for you will value it most."

"But if you have promised it my love," observed Mrs. Evans.

"No—he never knew my intention, and "never shall."

"He is infinitely more careful of his valua- "bles than I am," resumed the Countess, ming- ling a smile with her tears; "You have given "me so many nice things already, and I am "such a random creature—if I should lose it"

"Though you are going to be very happy, I am "certain *you* would not lose my present without "sincere pain.——You will never forget me, "Geraldine; you will often write to me; and "if I should not be punctual in my replies, you "will never call it neglect." The friends wept a moment in each other's arms; Lady Mon- teith's eyes asked her Lucy to accompany her part of the way to the manor; but as the latter made no offer of that kind, she forbore to name her request. Once more she repeated her assurances of inviolable regard, and they parted.

I have gratified my own taste by entering into a diffuse description of this interview. Perhaps it was in no way more extraordinary than com- mon life often affords. They who, disdaining the softer touches of the mental pencil, only enjoy the bold design which sketches the wildest storm of the passions, where the sun of reason

never

never beams, and where difcretion never controls the raging elements, will pafs over the uninterefting page that defcribes attachment without caprice, dejection ftruggling with a fenfe of propriety, and fimplicity affecting a difguife which it cannot fupport. Such readers will not join in the reflections of Lady Monteith, who, reviewing, during her folitary walk home, her friend's behaviour, and rightly afcribing her unwillingnefs to accompany her to a fear of being led to difcufs a fubject to which fhe was unequal, exclaimed, " Dear, artlefs, amiable " girl! Where fhall I find another Lucy?"

Early the next morning the Monteiths fet off for London. At parting with his daughter, Sir William difcovered the deep yet firm regret of difinterefted affection. " I fhall mifs you very " much, my dear love," faid he ; but it is for " your good, fo I fhall not complain. I muft " look for amufement to your letters now, in- " ftead of your pretty prattle. Don't be caft . " down, child ; for I fhall not be dull if you " are happy." The tender Geraldine could " only anfwer with her tears.

At this inftant Mr. Evans, who had been from home the preceding morning, interrupted the . family party by his characteriftic adieus. " I " truft, my dear lady, you are going to make " many hearts happy; you will leave many " aching ones behind you here." Then turning to Lord Monteith, whofe bofom glowed with fentiments which Nature meant he fhould have been better acquainted with, " Providence," faid the good man with patriarchal fimplicity, " has intrufted you, my Lord, with a rich " jewel. Wear it at your heart."

" That

"That I will," replied the young Earl, shaking him cordially by the hand; "and for the "share you had in giving it to me, remember, "when I am Prime Minister, you shall be "Archbishop of Canterbury." A sudden glow of pleasure brightened the general dejection.—— Sir William, enjoying the tribute to his daughter's worth, thus hastily extorted from her Lord, more than he would have done a studied compliment, tenderly pressed his son-in-law's hand, and led his drooping daughter to the chariot.—— The carriages drove off. London, and its round of pleasures, soon regained possession of his Lordship's mind, unaccustomed to the finer emotions; while his lady's eyes oft turned to take another view of Powerscourt. "Farewell," said she to herself, "ye dear scenes of "my youthful pleasures. Farewell to the home "and the protection of the best of fathers! I "enter upon an untried, and, if I may trust "to the experience of others, a perplexing "world. Will the husband of my choice, the "future master of my destiny, treat me with "such uniform tenderness as my indulgent pa-"rent did? Will he guide my inexperienced "steps, like my dear Mrs. Evans? or, may I "unbosom to him my inmost soul, as I did to "my sympathising Lucy? Ah! could I but be "sure that I shall return in a few months sa-"tisfied with my own lot, find my dear father "unchanged in health and spirits, Mrs. Evans "well, and my Lucy happy!" A tear obscured her radiant eyes, when my Lord roused her from her reverie, by telling her the number of miles they were from London.

CHAP.

CHAP. XV.

Come then, the colours and the ground prepare!
Dip in the rainbow, trick her off in air,
Choose a firm cloud before it fall, and in it
Catch, ere she glance, the Cynthia of the minute.

POPE.

ON the close of the first day's journey, Lady Monteith accidentally inquired how far they were from Oxford. "Admirably recollected!" cried his Lordship; "I have always intended to "go there, and never could find time. We "will take it in our way to London."

"Don't you recollect," said the Countess, "that by the last accounts from Scotland our "friends intend to be in town before the end "of this week?"

"O! we shall run all over Oxford in a day "or two. Beside, suppose they do get to Port-"land-place before us, my housekeeper is the "civilest, best-bred creature you ever saw, in-"finitely superior to the myrmidons near Kin-"loch-castle. She will make them very fine "courtesies, and they will glide about and get "over their first wonder before we reach "town."

"But will that be perfectly respectful and "accommodating?"

"My dear Geraldine, if you take so much "pains to accommodate other people, they will "soon give you a surfeit of courtesy. My good
aunt

" aunt in particular ; fhe has had her own way
" years enough ; and for fear fhe fhould take
" up any idea of managing me, I fhall fhew
" her at firft that I mean to pleafe myfelf, and
" never care what fhe or the world think about
" it."

The excurfion to Oxford being now as irrevocably fixed as the ancient laws of the Medes
and Perfians, Lady Monteith privately difpatched her own fervant to town with the beft apology her invention could frame to her expected
guefts.

On entering the feat of the Mufes,

——Mother of arts
" And eloquence, native to famous wits,
" Or hofpitable, in her fweet recefs,
" City or fuburban, ftudious walks and fhades ;"

the Countefs felt a refined pleafure, uninter-
rupted by any painful recollections, till her
Lord, as he hurried her from the Theatre to the
Ratcliffe Library, fuddenly exclaimed, " Have
" you not fome curiofity of your own to ex-
" hibit at Oxford,—a quondam lover ? How
" you blufh, you little tyrant ! I muft fee him.
" I once intended to cut the fellow's throat ;
" but I am quite in charity with him now.——
" Where is he ? we will have him with us at
" the hotel this evening "

" Indeed, my Lord," ftammered Lady Monteith, " I am afraid he cannot come. He is
very ill."

" Ill !—O ! then we will go and fee him.—
" What college does he belong to ?—Come, we
" can go to his rooms firft."

" Not without fome previous notice," faid
the Countefs. " His complaint is on his fpirits,

F 3   " and

" and we fhall only agitate him. It is a low
" fever."

" A low fever!" replied his Lordfhip with a
loud laugh. " A ftrong love-fit you mean.——
" You fpirited him off very cleverly, Geraldine;
" and juft in time to fave his life ; for I had
" written a challenge for him. I wonder, by
" the bye, why you came to refufe him ; for
" he muft be one of your own accommodating
" fort of people, to give up a charming girl to
" a ftranger, and afterwards fall fick about her
" himfelf. We will have him ; the fight of
" you, and a bottle or two of claret, will cure
" his low fever."

" You are all in the wrong," replied Lady
Monteith, who could fcarcely fummon fufficient
fpirits to parry this attack ; " but all your
" manœuvres fhall not make me gratify your
" curiofity by explaining this enigma. I will
" write to Henry, and afk him to give us the
" meeting ; but pray, remember, that he really
" is unwell, and alfo naturally timid and re-
" ferved. Spare your raillery therefore ; for,
" though you will be wide of the mark, his fen-
" fibility is fo acute, that it may give him pain."

Lord Monteith, with truth, declared that he
never defigned to give any one uneafinefs. On
returning to the inn her ladyfhip difpatched the
following letter :

" To HENRY POWERSCOURT, Efq.

" It is impoffible to pafs through Oxford
" without feeling a folicitude for the health of
" my valuable friend ; and if it be fufficiently
" reftored to bear the exertion, your company
" this evening would afford me peculiar plea-
" fure

" fure. Lord Monteith joins anxiously in this
" wifh. His impatience to be introduced to
" one, on whofe merits he has often heard my
" father expatiate, would have carried him to
" your apartments; but I doubted how far you
" might be able to bear his vifit. Come to us,
" my dear Henry, if you poffibly can; perhaps
" my lord's playful vivacity may enliven you.
" To fee you well and happy is the only addition
" now wanting to the felicity of

Your ever-faithful
" and grateful friend,

"GERALDINE MONTEITH."

The fervant who carried this epiftle returned
with the intelligence that the gentleman had
been very ill, and was gone for change of air to
fome friend's houfe a few miles in the country;
but that his fervant happened to come to his
lodgings to enquire for meffages juft as he was
there; and that he had given him the letter to
carry to his mafter. " How far was his friend's
" houfe from Oxford?" The fervant could not
" tell. Did he know the name of the gentle-
" man at whofe houfe he was?" No. " Nor
" the name of the place?" Still a negative—
" Blockhead!"—but I fhall omit the epithets by
which my lord expreffed his fenfe of difappointment; for though they conveyed to his
terrified lady the idea of his being in a towering
paffion, habit made them pafs trippingly from his
tongue without any confcioufnefs of having
uttered them. While Lady Monteith therefore,
pale and trembling, reflected upon the uniform
fuavity of her father's manners, a turn or two
acrofs the room fet the earl perfectly to rights
again,

again, who, advancing to her with a smile which
perfectly became him, begged the favour of her,
as he had lost the diversion of quizzing a chum,
to amuse him with a game at picquet.

No other incident worth recording occurred
during the remainder of their journey to London. On their arrival at their town residence, a
number of servants ranged themselves on each
side the entrance to welcome their approach.
Though Monteith had not bestowed much
trouble in sacrificing to the Graces, he possessed
all the natural elegance of a Belvidere Apollo.
He presented their new mistress with a look of
benevolent freedom, which his features were
particularly calculated to express; and he told
them, that she was come to make them all as
happy and as good as herself. The countess's
heart felt agreeably elated. She cast a benignant
glance around, and advancing to the housekeeper,
who stood at the head of the female party, after
an assurance of general good-will to all, she
pressed her hand with that graceful affability
which was concomitant to all her actions; when
the words "Lady Madelina" instantly changed
the scene.

Her ladyship was indeed advancing *in propria
persona*, bridling with stiff dignity, rendered yet
more stubborn by a smothered sense of affront.
She congratulated her nephew in terms solemnly
sententious, and then bent her knees to the bride
with the overstrained lowliness of proud humility. Monteith, though he knew his aunt's character, felt thunderstruck; and the timidity
which her ladyship's dress, figure, and manner
excited, annihilated all the polished elegance of
Geraldine. The parties, therefore, stood like
what the sportsmen call hounds at a fault, till
Lady

Lady Madelina waved her hand for her niece to go up ſtairs firſt; which the latter declining, the former wheeled round, and, in the ſame conſequential manner, reaſcended to the drawing-room. Lord Monteith, as he followed in the proceſſion, muttered to himſelf, " No! this will never do."

The ceremony of being properly fixed in their chairs took up ſome minutes; and after three introductory hems, Geraldine ven·ured to try the ſound of her own voice by expreſſing her regret that they were not in town at the time of Lady Madelina's arrival; the only anſwer to which apology was a majeſtic bend. Again the young counteſs made an effort at converſation, by hoping that her ladyſhip's health had not ſuffered from the fatigue of her long journey; another bend, and a negative, was the anſwer. "Silence again reigned unrivalled queen," till her empire was terminated by the entrance of her ſworn enemy Lady Arabella, who, having given the finiſhing arrangement to her dreſs, ſwam into the room to eclipſe her new ſiſter in thoſe qualities of wit and beauty for which ſhe had heard ſhe was diſtinguiſhed; and certainly, if feature alone could denominate the latter, and volubility the former, the fair Geraldine muſt have hid her diminiſhed ſplendour.

Nature, who had beſtowed upon the Earl of Monteith the ſtriking advantages of a fine figure and an agreeable countenance, had been ſtill more bountiful to his ſiſter, whoſe face and perſon had all the regular lovelineſs which the vaineſt mother could ever deſire for a darling daughter. Theſe ſuperior attractions appeared in her earlieſt years; and as the ſyſtem of policy purſued by the houſe of Macdonald did not add

any

any lucrative temptations to the charms of their females, this rare bounty of nature was treasured with the most unremitting care, as a sure means of securing an honorable establishment. The plan of her education consisted in avoiding whatever was bad for the eyes, bad for the shape; and bad for the complexion ; and in acquiring whatever was perfectly elegant and suitable for a young lady of the first fashion.

I have already mentioned the mournful incidents which in her seventeenth year banished the lovely Arabella from London, and confined her within the secluded walls of Kinloch. The same event put a stop to her improvements and her pleasures. The confined education of her present protectress, Lady Madelina, had not even paced the narrow circle of female accomplishments ; and her observations had been wholly limited to the neighbourhood where her local pre-eminence allowed her to reign undisputed sovereign. No wonder, therefore, that she conceived her niece to be a miracle of erudition, because she could speak French with tolerable volubility ; or that her jejune performances in music and painting should meet with unbounded celebrity among the visitants at the castle, where few understood, and none dared to censure. But, exclusive of the pleasure which even gross adulation bestowed, the three years which she spent in Scotland formed one continued period of mortification and regret.

Lady Madelina's recollection of those early difficulties which had at last influenced her to reward Sir Simon's long and generous attachment, determined her to rescue her niece from similar trials by adopting her for her heiress to those ample possessions which her uxorious hus-

band

band had alienated from his own family. But upon becoming perfonally acquainted with her; and finding that all the beauty and all the virtues of the race from old Donald to the prefent times were centered in the peerlefs Arabella, fhe grew paffionately fond of her, or rather blindly partial to what fhe fancied the fummit of all human excellence. To banifh her chagrin, and to awaken reciprocal attachment, fhe treated her with unbounded indulgence; but as indulgence always defeats its aim, it neither made the young lady grateful nor happy. On the contrary, fhe grew every day more capricious, vain, and wretched. She could not love or refpect a perfon who neither checked her faults nor ftrengthened her virtues. She foon learned the art of turning her aunt's weaknefs to her own advantage, and confidered the favours fhe received as a tribute rather than an obligation. Without one fenfible friend to enlighten her judgment, without one correct model by which to form her character, fhe miftook affectation, elegance, and faftidioufnefs, for delicacy.

Nor did her diflike of retirement proceed from a relifh for polifhed fociety and refined pleafures. She only thought that the power of her charms was limited to too narrow a fphere; and fhe wifhed, like the fair Phaëton of the laft age, to "obtain the chariot for a day," that "fhe might fet the world on fire."

Though an invitation to London had at firft infpired a heartfelt complacency for her new fifter, her reported graces had foon obliterated that idea, and ingrafted in its ftead the baneful germ of envy. Had the lovely Geraldine entertained fimilar ideas, their firft interview might rather have been called the battle of the beauties,

than

than an attempt to conciliate fifterly affection
and reciprocal regard.

Proteus, the poets tell us, could affume a
thoufand refemblances; but, whether he feemed
a lion or a fawn, he was Proteus ftill. Like
him, lady Arabella could tack an infinitude of
modes on her natural habit; but, whether it was
the manner of the dove or the magpie, fhe was
ftill at heart the vain, cold, felfifh Arabella.
After a long confultation fhe had determined,
that the brilliant would be beft fuited to her
intention of intimidating her rival; and having
arranged her drefs in a manner better adapted to
the magnificence of a court-ball than to the eafe
of a private party, fhe burft upon her aftonifhed
fifter-in-law, who in vain attempted to trace a
remote refemblance of that artlefs wild fimplicity
which her creative imagination had affigned to
the unknown "Highland laffie."

The introductory compliments were now
difpatched in a manner diametrically the reverfe
of the dry referve of the former converfation.
Lady Arabella was in ecftafy. The carelefs
fimplicity of the bride's travelling habit could
not pretend to any competition with her own
profufion of ornament; and both the beauty
and the vivacity of Geraldine fuffered from the
chagrin which the manners of her vifitors infpired. Confcious fuperiority always fpeaks in
hyperbole. Arabella had been immenfely tired
with her journey, was rapturoufly delighted with
her new relation, and infinitely folicitous that
they might foon become the ftricteft of friends.

While fhe fpoke, her eye reverted to every
object, except the fubject of her enthufiaftic
admiration. Her aunt viewed her with a complacency which the countefs thought her features
could

could not poffibly have affumed, but which was
fometimes interrupted by obferving what effect
this fparkling converfation had upon the
Monteiths; for, though it could not poffibly
anfwer any end, lady Madelina would have felt
mortified if even her nephew did not acknow-
ledge how infinitely his fifter excelled his wife.
Her obfervations that evening were limited to a
fhort period: his lordfhip had bufinefs to tranf-
act with his banker, which could not poffibly be
delayed; and he foon left them, whifpering his
lady, " Go to bed if you are tired of them."

Geraldine did not conceive herfelf warranted
to follow her lord's advice. She made fome at-
temps to gain a fhare in the converfation; but
the playful wit and eafy fweetnefs which at
Powerfcourt " engroffed all hearts and charmed
all eyes," had now loft all its power, and fhe
funk quietly into the lefs brilliant but ufeful character of a hearer; while her guefts enumerated
the old titles which might be revived in the
houfe of Macdonald, and fettled the exact place
in which the reprefentative of their honours
ought to walk at the next coronation.

They feparated at an early hour. The young
countefs did not find herfelf difpofed to fleep,
unaccuftomed as fhe had been to contempt and
to unkindnefs. Powerfcourt and the friends of
her youth rufhed full upon her mind. " What,"
" faid fhe to herfelf, " am I to expect from
" ftrangers, when thofe with whom I have juft
" contracted the tie of kindred are even ftudi-
" ous to fhew their diflike of me?" To this,
reflection followed a fear, that her lord would
leave her, unprotected, to their pride and folly;
and the bitter tears which fhe had hitherto
reftrained courfed each other down her cheek.

At

At that inſtant lord Monteith entered. He had met with a party of his old friends, who would felicitate him upon his nuptials, and he was returned home in a very joyous humour. "I was very ſorry to leave you, my deareſt Ge- "raldine," ſaid he; "I know it was rude and "aukward to go out the firſt evening after you "came home; but it was not in the power of "man to endure my conſequential aunt, or the "ridiculous automaton that Arabella has be- "come. Did they get a little more tolerable "after I left them? Ha! you are in tears—I "ſwear by heaven, that if they have given you "the leaſt cauſe for uneaſineſs, they ſhall both "leave my houſe to-morrow morning."

Lady Monteith knew enough of the earl's temper to be convinced that this threat would be fulfilled. Her prudence not only determined her inſtantly to avert from herſelf the dreadful imputation of violating the harmony of the family into which ſhe was adopted, but it made her alſo reſolve to aſſume the amiable character of a mediatrix if any contentions ſhould in future ariſe. Happy in the hope that ſhe ſhould ever preſerve her avowed pre-eminence in her lord's affections, her ſorrows ſeemed to diſſipate like a morning miſt, and ſhe anſwered with a ſmile, that ſhe had been wicked enough to be entertained with the eccentricities of the ſtrangers, which doubtleſs proceeded from too recluſe a mode of life, and would certainly be worn off by a little commerce with the world. "I have," continued ſhe, "enough to con- "demn myſelf for;—I have been a petted "child, and, feeling your abſence this evening "more than I ought, Powerſcourt returned to "my memory. But do not reprove me. My "heart,

139

" heart, Monteith, is formed for ftrong at-
" tachments. I have preferred you to my fa-
" ther's houfe and my early friends; yet muft
" I ever 'remember that fuch things were,'
" and ' that they were moft precious.' The
young earl gazed at her with the tendereft
regard, vowed eternal affection, and for a moment wondered how he came to find out fuch
an angel.

But while the amiable Geraldine thus purfued
her early defign of fecuring, meliorating, and
correcting the heart of her lord, his noble relations were employed in adding a little adventitious fuel to their own native fire. The ftranger was arraigned (but not at the bar of juftice
or candour); and found guilty of the following offences, which, as they were fupported by
pofitive evidence, could not afterwards be dif-
proved: Firft, fhe muft be nobody, notwithftanding Mrs. Archibald Frazer, of Annale,
had affirmed that the Powerfcourts were a good
family; for lady Madelina had detected her in
the very act of fhaking hands with a fervant;
befide, lady Monteith's terrified manner at firft
feeing her; proved that fhe had never been in
company with a lady of quality before. Se-
condly, fhe was no beauty; for fhe was not
above the middle fize, and her complexion no
better than a brunette; her features too had
nothing of the Rubens' caft, and were totally
diffimilar to all the firft-rate toafts in the picture-
gallery at Kinloch. Thirdly, fhe was no wit;
for fhe never tried at a repartee all the evening,
and her expreffions were as common as thofe of
a houfe-maid. This degraded creature being no
longer an object of terror to lady Arabella, fhe
refolved to try if fhe could not live upon good
terms

terms with her; and lady Madelina obferved, that as the girl feemed good-tempered, and had a large fortune, perhaps her nephew, who was but a thoughtlefs kind of a young man, could not have done much better.

C H A P. XVI.

Good humour, only, teaches charms to laft,
Still makes new conquefts, and maintains the paft;
Love rais'd on beauty will like that decay,
Our hearts may bear its flender chain a day;
As flow'ry bands in wantonnefs are worn,
A morning's pleafure, and at evening torn;
This binds in ties more eafy, yet more ftrong,
The willing heart, and only holds it long.

POPE.

THE ceremony of congratulatory cards now commenced. It was followed by vifits from thofe ladies who wifhed to form a clofer intimacy, and by the introduction of the bride and lady Arabella at court. The death of Sir Simon, though now nearly banifhed by fubfequent events from the memory of his amiable relic, was ftill too recent to allow of her joining in thefe ceremonies. She could, therefore, only hear from lady Arabella, what fhe would rather have feen, that the bride was completely outdone upon every occafion. The fair narrator's laudable defign of making her aunt happy tempted her to fome fmall exaggerations. The Grecian model of beauty, which the form and face of
Geraldine,

Geraldine refembled, was more confonant to
the public tafte than the round vifage, uniform
regularity of features, and auburn locks of the
northern beauty. The figure of the latter was
indeed more confpicuous; but being lefs cor-
rectly moulded by fafhion, it feemed to yield
in elegance to the polifhed fymmetry of the ever-
graceful countefs. The lily and the rofe were
rivalled by Arabella's complexion; yet lilies and
rofes may be bought at Warren's, which by
candle-light look almoft as well as nature; but
what cofmetic can beftow that " pure and eloquent blood" which fpcke in Geraldine's face,
and might almoft juftify the opinion of the
poet, " that her body thought?"

If from their perfons the obferver reverted
to the drefs and manners of the fifter beauties,
the palm indifputably belonged to the countefs.
In her felection of ornament the correctnefs of
her tafte led her to reject what was exuberant
and fuperfluous; and by ftudying fuitablenefs
rather than fplendor, fhe ever appeared with
the graceful proprity of a woman of fafhion;
while lady Arabella was loft in the maze of taf-
fels and flounces. The terms upon which Sir
William Powerfcourt lived with his neighbours
were not calculated to infpire his daughter's
mind with any ideas of inherent fuperiority,
further than what her own merit juftified. His
family pride was not of a hoftile character. It
rather taught him to refpect himfelf, than to def-
pife others. Educated in the fpirit of benevolence and univerfal good-will, if any indications
of latent vanity fometimes appeared to check
the nobler growth of Geraldine's foul, Mrs.
Evans was ever at hand to eradicate the perni-
cious weed. The internal principle thus fecured,

her

her native good fenfe and obfervation taught her to copy the exterior of politenefs from the beft models which her fituation afforded ; and on her entrance into the firft circles, fhe only appeared to want a little familiarity with peculiar cuftoms, to realize in its fulleft perfection the character of a well-bred woman.

On the contrary, lady Arabella's attempts to fhine, announced the effort, and miffed the effect. Hauteur could not command refpect from thofe who, equal or fuperior in rank, allowed nothing to the claims of a longer pedigree. Confeffedly inferior to moft young ladies of her own ftation in acquired graces, the mere attraction of beauty, though foon felt, was as foon forgotten. The flippant obfervation and fevere farcafm, which at Kinloch-caftle paffed for eloquence and wit, could not endure the teft of more competent judges, who cannot relifh a fneer unlefs recommended by fome other quality than mere malignity. When to thefe confiderations is added the reflection, that the world is generally more inclined to approve thofe who folicit their favour than thofe who command their attention, it will not be wondered at, that general opinion loudly proclaimed lady Monteith a very charming woman ; and that if ever the filence of polite referve was interrupted by repeated inquiries of " What do you think of " Lady Arabella Macdonald ?" the moft candid anfwer generally received was, " Nothing very " ftriking."

The Philofopher who attempts to defcribe the fecret powers of nature will not expect to trace the footfteps of the fovereign Queen, " in crowded cities" or " the bufy haunts of men," but in the fequeftered glen or uncultivated mountain.

tain. The Moralist who, by a defcription of the human character, wifhes to correct the failings of the human heart, will not place his fphere of obfervation in thofe fcenes where fafhion prefcribes a genteel uniformity of manners. The crowded rout, where every body is well-bred; the drawing-room, where every body is well-dreffed; the public breakfaft, where every body is lively; and the opera, where every body is in ecftacies, may prove an author's intimacy with the great world; but however the reader may be dazzled by the glare of finery, the mind commonly complains of meagre entertainment. A few general obfervations will fuffice to defcribe the firft month of lady Monteith's acquaintance with fafhionable life. She trod the giddy maze of diffipation with firm but graceful ftep. The voice of flattery, though foothing to her ear, excited no dangerous emotion. Her character retained its primitive virtues, her heart remained faithful to the impreffion which was now confecrated by indelible ties, and her judgment continued to prefer the mild luftre of connubial happinefs to all the glare of fafhion, and all the fafcination of pleafure.

The earl of Monteith ftill continued to think his Geraldine the moft perfect of all human beings, and himfelf the moft fortunate man in the world. It was impoffible for him to think otherwife; for all his young friends declared him a happy fellow, and his courtly acquaintance pronounced his lady to be the moft divine creature ever feen. It was aftonifhing, they faid, how fhe could acquire fuch an air of high ton in her fecluded fituation; and ftill more wonderful, that the refplendent fame of the fair reclufe had not pervaded the rural fhades by
which

which she was surrounded. " Your taste in " beauty, my lord," they added, " is perfectly " accurate, and the world is infinitely obliged " to you for introducing this paragon to its ado- " ration."

His lordship always went home in raptures from such conversation; but his lady was either gone out with a party, or the presence of his noble relations qualified his transports, and convinced him that one angel cannot protect the joys of the domestic paradise, if spirits malign over-leap the sacred inclosure. The hours intended to be devoted to the endearing charities of private life were most commonly usurped by high dispute and sour contradiction, to which the softening observations of the countess could not always give the air of sportive raillery. Lady Arabella's positive refusal to attend a public breakfast given by one of her brother's greatest intimates, and to which he had thoughtlessly engaged his female inmates without previously consulting lady Madelina, disconcerted the earl so much, that he determined even to give up the pleasures of London, and to betake himself to the wild shores of Loch Lomond, rather than continue where he could not be master of his own actions. To his loud complaints against feminine perverseness, his lady vainly attempted to oppose her observation, that though lady Arabella's refusal to go had rather an air of pertinacity, it merely restricted her own conduct, and could by no means be construed into an attempt to controul his perfect liberty. The truth was, lord Monteith was as desirous of governing as his sister was unwilling to obey; and his querulous hatred of restriction led him to scrutinize every word, look and action, which
                                        seemed

'feemed to militate againft the wifdom of his de-
cifions and the freedom of his conduct. Lady
Arabella's refufal to go to the breakfaft had been
aggravated by fome reflections on the inviter's
rudenefs in not returning her curtefy at Rane-
lagh; to which lady Madelina added, that a neglect of politenefs was the true criterion by which
a plebeian family might always be difcovered.
His lordfhip fo bitterly refented this farcafm,
that, regardlefs of the fair fame of the titled
Macdonalds now committed to his charge, he
refolved to convince the world that peers of the
realm may be as unpolite as commoners; and
though lady Madelina and her niece talked of
removing to a villa near Richmond in about a
month, he determined not to endure the temporary thraldom, but immediately to emancipate
himfelf from their fetters, by fetting out for
Monteith; and, with the inconfiftency which frequently marked his character, he appointed the
very morning fixed for his friend's public breakfaft for his own departure.

Lady Monteith's heart, as I have already hinted,
was not wedded to the amufements of London.
Her natural tafte and early habits did not teach
her to ftart affrighted at the name of folitude,
nor did the recollection of mild colloquial pleafures induce her to regret the fociety fhe was
going to leave. On the contrary, had the manner been better fuited to the project, the propo-
fal of vifiting her lord's hereditary poffeffions
would have met her entire approbation. She
would have rejoiced in the profpect of renewing
thofe ties of gratitude and generofity, which had
been long diffolved; and the hope of reanimat-
ing a forlorn defert region would have afforded
equal gratification to her native benevolence and

inherent love of diſtinction. But while ſhe
recollected her lord's often-repeated preference
of London and abhorrence of Scotland, ſhe
regretted that pique and diſpleaſure, not duty
and conviction, had wrought the deſired change.
Ruminating with deep regret on thoſe traits of
her huſband's character, of which this incident
gave her a full view, ſhe ſhuddered at the idea
of her own miſery if the fatal period ſhould
ever arrive when ſhe ſhould loſe her preſent influence over his affections. What was ſhe to
expect from paſſions ſo irritable, ſo impatient
of control, and from a diſpoſition ſo little influenced by the reſtraints of decorum, or the
opinion of the world!

Mrs. Evans's remembered admonition diverted
her mind from purſuing this melancholy theme;
but, as ſhe traced the chain of her parting precepts, ſhe felt that there was one obſervation
with which ſhe never could coincide. Should
the event which her fears anticipated ever take
place, ſhe knew it would be a misfortune which
time could never overcome, a ſorrow which patience never could ſoften.

While the ſweetly-tempered mind of the
young counteſs framed extenuating apologies,
and concerted a thouſand little acts of attentive
kindneſs, to mitigate the painful effects of her
lord's ſelf-willed negligence upon the minds of
his friends, ſhe was agreeably ſurpriſed to find
affairs in the beſt train poſſible; and a greater
degree of cordiality and good-humour aroſe from
what ſhe ſuſpected muſt have proved the death-
blow to family amity. No ſooner had the earl
announced his intention of ſetting out for Scotland, and trying to make his old caſtle ſomething
habitable, than the active imagination of lady
Madelina

Madelina flew back to the times of her grandfather, when Monteith was in its greateſt ſplendor. She again anticipated the found of the
bugle-horn, reverberating round its projecting
towers, to ſummon the clan to attend their feudal chieftain to a hunting party or a curling
match. Her mind now recurred to the grandeur of a public day, the court glittering with
ſplendid viſitors, the deſolated halls reſounding
with the cheerful notes of the bagpipe, and
numerous ſervants in gaudy liveries conducting
the aſtoniſhed gueſts through the long galleries
to a magnificent entertainment. Fired at the
idea, her countenance loſt its uſual aſperity, and
with an air of melting kindneſs ſhe applauded
the wiſdom of her nephew's project. "By all
" means," ſaid ſhe, " endeavour to reſtore the
" caſtle and its vicinity exactly to the ſame
" ſtate in which it was at the time of your great-
" grandfather. Never be ſeen beyond its walls
" without a train of archers and broad-ſword-
" men. Your anceſtors would not even appear at
" Stirling without fifty atendants, moſt of whom
" were Macdonalds in the right line. It ſtruck
" an awe into the neighbourhood; for not one
" of theſe gentlemen ever condeſcended to en-
" gage in any mercantile purſuits, but dined
" every day at the laird of Monteith's table.
" The country was not then over-run with up-
" ſtart traders, who by introducing manufac-
" tories, as they call them, corrupt all the com-
" mon people, and render them inſolent to their
" ſuperiors. I remember, even when I was a
" child, that if a coach with the Macdonald
" arms quartered upon it did but paſs through
" Glaſgow, all the inhabitants ran to the door,
" and teſtified their reſpect by ſuitable geſtures;

G 2　　　　　" but

" but now you may traverſe the whole town,
" and not one loom ſhall be ſtopped to pay you
" you a proper compliment."

Let not the reader ſuppoſe that Lady Madelina's harangue was intended to have terminated
ſo abruptly. It might have extended to the
length of the expoſtulation of the ghoſts in
Gray's " Long Story," had not Arabella taken
advantage of a cough to rejoice that her dear
ſiſter was going to recruit a little in the whole-
ſome air of the Highlands, after the fatigues
of diſſipated London. The pleaſure which
glowed in her countenance did not, however, in
truth, reſult from her hope that the faded cheek
of Geraldine might ſoon reſume its priſtine
roſes. In ſpite of the contempt which ſhe affected, the abſence of a rival who abridged her
conqueſts and humbled her vanity was the real
ſource of Arabella's joy.

Lord Monteith was ſo delighted to find his
plans thus cordially approved, that his reſent-
ment immediately ſoftened, and he politely offered his aunt the uſe of his houſe in London
till ſhe could fix herſelf in an agreeable reſidence,
Her ladyſhip repaid the favour, by promiſing to
reſtore all the valuable embelliſhments which ſhe
had ſurreptitiouſly conveyed to Kinloch caſtle,
as ſoon as Monteith was reinſtated in its priſtine
ſplendor.

CHAP.

CHAP. XVII.

I rue the riches of my former fate :
Sweet comfort's blafted clufters I lament :
I tremble at the bleffings once fo dear.

YOUNG.

THE day preceding that fixed for her departure from London, Lady Monteith was painfully
furprized by the prefence of an unexpected
vifitor. This was no other than Henry Powerfcourt, who, having at laft determined to vifit
Italy, impofed upon himfelf the fevere tafk of
bidding farewell to that treafure, the lofs of
which had rendered his native country a defart
fcene, barren of every joy and every hope.———
Having thus divulged a fecret, at which before
I only hinted, it ftill remains neceffary to develope the motives that induced this extraordinary
lover to refufe the bleffing which the amiable
fingularities of Sir William Powerfcourt had
placed within his reach.

From his earlieft youth his fufceptible mind
had felt the full power of his coufin's charms ;
but while his admiration rendered her raillery
more exquifitely painful, it prompted the ardent
yet unacknowledged wifh to acquire every laudable quality which could recommend him to
the favour of the lovelieft of her fex. His inexperienced heart knew not the nature of that
paffion to which it was a victim ; if it had, the
native rectitude of his mind would have ftarted

with

with inbred horror at a difcovery that feemed to ftamp every ungenerous, mean, and ungrateful vice upon the unprincipled villain, who dared to lift his felfifh eyes to the angelic daughter of his honoured benefactor. So far, therefore, from taking any indirect means to obtain the object of his wifhes, thofe wifhes were unperceived even by himfelf, and he fancied that he cherifhed no other fentiments than fuch as could be juftified by the ties of friendfhip and affinity. The general admiration which Geraldine attracted feemed to confirm this idea ; and though the inquietude which he ever felt at hearing of her having made any particular conqueft might have removed the delufion, he ftill foothed himfelf with the perfuafion that his anxiety arofe only from a friendly folicitude for her welfare, and he forbore to probe the wound till it became too deep to admit of cure.

The terms of the letter in which Sir William had fummoned him to Powerfcourt excited a wild tumult of hopes and fears, and firft convinced him that the intereft he took in his fair coufin's happinefs was not fo entirely abftracted from felfifh confiderations as he had fuppofed.— A faithful old domeftic, who was the bearer of this epiftle, could not forbear telling the enraptured youth, that the general report of the family pointed him out as the heir and fon-in-law of their refpected mafter. A thoufand expreffions of Sir William's were now recollected in an inftant, and Henry's ardent mind explained their equivocal nature as decidedly fignificant of the generous plan which had been long formed in his favour. His reception elevated thefe hopes into certainties ; for, though Sir William forebore any particular explanation, the uncommon

mon kindness of his manner, and some injunctions to Henry to do such and such things after he was gone, banished every remaining doubt of his intentions.

Nor did Miss Powerscourt's unusual dejection alarm her lover with the apprehension that her sentiments were not in unison with her father's. He thought that a reflecting mind must feel a temporary depression during the period of a decision so momentous to its future welfare. Yet while he regretted the absence of that charming vivacity which he alike dreaded and admired, and anxiously wished that Sir William's expected declaration would release him from that silence which his delicacy prescribed, and leave him at liberty to reassure his mistress's virgin heart by protestations of fervent gratitude and unalterable love, he thought even Geraldine herself never appeared so lovely with all her enchanting graces sporting around her, as she did in her present interesting melancholy.

This golden dream soon terminated. On the fourth morning after his arrival at Powerscourt, Henry surprised Geraldine in an agony of grief too violent to be referred to any other cause than extreme and hopeless sorrow. The solicitude of generous love was instantly awakened, and he entreated her confidence in terms strongly indicative of affectionate sympathy. " If," said the lovely mourner, fixing her radiant eyes upon him with a firm but despairing look; " if " you are indeed the noble disinterested Henry " I have ever supposed you, I may yet be happy; " if not, I am a wretch for life. This is not a " time for disguise and affectation. " My fa-" ther intends that you should be my husband; " but though I esteem your virtues, my heart

" avows

" avows a preference for another, which I never
" can furmount. Nothing but mifery can re-
" fult from our union. Be generous, Henry ;
" and, by refufing me, prevent a difclofure
" which would be deftructive to my father's
" peace, and to which nothing but defpair fhall
" ever drive me."

As all language would be inadequate to defcribe the feelings of Mr. Powerfcourt, I. fhall
only fay, that he filently dropped the fair hand
which he had ardently grafped at his entrance,.
and, after a minute's paufe, ftammered out a
few words expreffive of his refolution to comply
with her requeft. He then haftened to the door.
" Stay," faid Geraldine, whofe heart, relieved
from the burden of her own. forrows, inftantly
felt for him to whom fhe appeared to have transferred the infupportable load ; " Stay, and hear
" the effufions of gratitude, efteem, friend-
" fhip"——" No," faid the tortured youth,.
breaking from her, " if I ftay another moment,.
" I never can refign you."

His fubfequent conduct has been already defcribed, and the myftery of Lady Monteith's
requiring two thoufand pounds a-year to be left
at her fole difpofal will be explained, by obferving that fhe thought even that fplendid donative
would be inadequate as a proof of her efteem
for a man who had evidently facrificed his own
happinefs to her's. Her affectionate wifhes
pointed to Lucy Evans as his beft and moft fuitable reward.

Sir William's refentment at Mr. Powerfcourt's
fuppofed indifference to his daughter's merits
had foon fubfided, and a little after the departure
of the Monteiths he fent him a friendly invitation to come and fee him, with an affurance
that

that he was ready to ferve him in whatever way
he thought proper to point out. Henry determined upon this vifit, with the expectation that
his melancholy would be relieved by frequenting the fcenes in which he had nurfed his infant
paffion, and that the converfation of his refpected benefactor would footh his faddened fpirits.
The air of dejection and indifpofition which
was fpread over his countenance excited the kind
attention of his benevolent kinfman. He took
him all the walks and rides he ufed to take with
Geraldine, and, by way of diverting him, conftantly dwelt upon a theme which he thought
muft be pleafing, the affection of Lord Monteith, and his daughter's happinefs. " It is very
ftrange," Sir William fometimes faid to himfelf, " that Henry refufed Geraldine, and yet
" he don't like to hear of her being happy with
" her hufband ; and after all, they never ufed
" to fall out; and Henry is a very good young
" man, with nothing of envy or malice in his
" difpofition."

He faw but little of the family at the rectory.
Mrs. Evans declined rapidly ; her hufband
feemed to need all the confolations of ftrong
fenfe and chriftian fortitude to fupport the
fhock, and the gentle Lucy funk, like a broken
lily under the beating of " the pitilefs ftorm."
She feemed ftudioufly to fhun converfing with
Mr. Powerfcourt ; and when an interview was
unavoidable, fhe was not only dejected but referved. As he once attempted to recall to her
remembrance the joyous fcenes of juvenile
amufement, when the manor-houfe and the parfonage feemed alternately the temple of innocent
cheerfulnefs, fhe turned fuddenly, and, gazing
at him with a penetrating fmile, obferved,

G 3   " that

" that the temples remained, but they had loft
" the goddefs who irradiated the fcene."

Difappointed in his expectations of finding
confolation in thofe objects which ufed to adminifter delight, Henry at laft anfwered Sir William's inquiries of what he could do to ferve
him, by remarking, that he thought the falu-
brious climate of Italy might be of fervice to
his health, and that the numerous objects which
it prefented to the curious eye might diffipate
the langour which indifpofition excited.———
Though Sir William was convinced that England, particularly Caernarvonfhire, was the moft
healthful climate in the world, and contained a
fufficient number of wonders to entertain any
rational man, yet he thought that the whimfies
of fick people fhould be treated with the fame
indulgence as their palled appetites. His affent was accompanied by a liberal allowance ;
but he charged him to ftep in London, and, if
Lord Monteith and Geraldine had not left it,
to make their houfe his home for a few weeks.
" The company of your coufin," faid he,
" will do you good ; and my Lord is ftill live-
" lier than fhe is. Befide, you may have an
" opportunity of getting the beft medical ad-
" vice the kingdom affords ; and, I charge
" you, don't be guided by outlandifh phyficians
" while you are abroad, for they never can un-
" derftand what is proper for an Englifh con-
" ftitution. I have no doubt, Henry, that
" your good fenfe will keep you from running
" wild, as many of our young fly-about tra-
" vellers do ; and I dare fay you will not dif-
" grace my regard for you, by pretending,
" when you come back again, to like other
" countries better than your own."

No

No phyfician at that time refiding in London who " could minifter to a mind difeafed," or who could " pluck from the memory a rooted forrow," Mr. Powerfcourt did not apply for medical affiftance ; and he regretted that the eftablifhed laws of fociety compelled him either to vifit the fair troubler of his peace before he left England, or, by attempting excufes to which his ingenuous nature was unequal, excite fufpicions of a fecret which he flattered himfelf was confined to his own bofom. He called at Portland-place at an unfeafonable hour, and without previoufly announcing his intentions.—— He was, however, admitted, contrary to his hopes, and found himfelf in the Countefs's dreffing-room before he had acquired fufficient fortitude to fupport the trying interview. He advanced with timid fteps, refigned her offered hand with refpectful coldnefs, and, glancing his eyes over the happy envied Monteith, took a chair, and attempted a perplexed converfation.

His Lordfhip immediately found that his intended raillery had loft all its enticing piquancy. The dejection, embarraffment, and evident indifpofition of his rival affected his good nature, and he ftrove by repeated attentions to diffipate his confufion. But as it rather increafed than diminifhed, his Lordfhip recollected that his behaviour might have an air of infult ; and, after two or three attempts to occupy his own mind by reading the charades written on a fire-fcreen, he at laft confidered, that the moft conciliating conduct he could adopt would be to take himfelf out of the room, which, after defiring Henry to fpend the day with them, he

immediately

immediately did, with too much precipitation to
hear his reply.

Lady Monteith was by this time sufficiently
recovered from the perturbation which native
delicacy and innate benevolence had excited,
to inquire after her father's looks and spirits.
She heard with delight that he seemed perfectly
well. " And," added Henry, " I have the un-
" speakable pleasure to say, that, thanks to
" your generous mediation ! I seem completely
" restored to his favour."

" Do not talk of my generosity, Henry, for
" fear I should enter upon a never-ending
" theme—But our friends at the rectory—Can
" you tell me any good news of them ?"

" Mrs. Evans declines rapidly—she cannot
" continue long."

" O, my dearest Lucy," said the countess,
bursting into tears, " excellent, forlorn girl !
" who will comfort you !"

" Can those be forlorn whom you love ?"
replied Henry. " Your friendship, Geraldine,
" is a blessing which must compensate for every
" other loss."

" You forget that my present situation im-
" poses duties upon me which no longer leave me
" at liberty to fly to that dear girl to comfort her
" filial sorrow. Does she seem sensible of her
" approaching calamity ?"

" I do not know ; I saw very little of her.
" Can you tell me, Lady Monteith, why I
" have been so unfortunate as to lose Miss
" Evans's confidence ?"

" You cannot have lost it ; I know her sen-
" timents too well ; she regards you with all
" the esteem your merit deserves."

" I thought

" I thought myfelf a blank in the creation,
" banifhed from the good opinion of every one
" except your excellent father."

" Indeed, Henry, you muft caft afide this
" mifanthropic humour. It robs you of all the
" amiable candour natural to your character."

" I truft, Lady Monteith, I fhall find it the
" difeafe of the climate. In eight-and-forty
" hours I hope to bid a long farewell to Eng-
" land, to all my forrows, and——" he juft recollected himfelf in time to forbear adding,
" and to you."

" Let me not," faid the countefs in evident
emotion, " engrofs any more of your time,
" which muft be fully occupied with prepara-
" tions for your journey. We fhall, I truft,
" meet on your return, with the reciprocal
" pleafure our early interviews afforded. Per-
" mit to addrefs to you thofe fentiments in
" writing which I find it impoffible to utter in
" converfation."

He replied, " Your letters, madam, will be
" invaluable." Finding his refolution unequal
to the tafk of further converfation, he prefented
his addrefs, bowed, and withdrew.

As Henry Powerfcourt will not for fome
time appear again upon the fcene, I fhall fub-
join Lady Monteith's firft epiftle to him, with
his anfwer. They occafionally correfponded during his refidence abroad; but the remainder of
his letters were irrelevant to the fubject of this
hiftory.

" To HENRY POWERSCOURT, Efq.

' Do not accufe me of departing from the
' delicacy of my fex, if the warm intereft
' which

' which your welfare and happiness excite in-
' duces me to adopt a freedom in my expref-
' fions which our near affinity and long friend-
' ship alone can juftify. Far from feeling the
' cruel pride of conqueft, my heart participates
' in your dejection fo ftrongly, that while I
' fancy myfelf the caufe of your unhappinefs,
' I think it is felfifh in me to enjoy that cup
' of blefling which would otherwife be my
' portion.

' I have reconfidered my conduct from my
' girlifh days. Youthful levity may have led
' me into indifcretions; but my confcience ac-
' quits me of the bafe coquetry of endeavouring
' to excite hopes which I never meant to con-
' firm. Let the friend whom I fhall ever
' efteem, after a retrofpect of his own conduct,
' declare what part of his behaviour expreffed
' fentiments too lively to be applicable to the
' affection of a relation, and the intimacy of a
' companion. If I rightly appreciate the pu-
' rity of his principles, he would have re-
' jected with abhorrence every defign of form-
' ing a connection unfanctioned by my father's
' approbation, and the knowlege of that appro-
' bation was not communicated till my heart
' had loft the power of being juft to the merits
' of the man he propofed.

' When I appealed to your generofity, I knew
' not how painful a facrifice I required. The
' more I feel it, the more I venerate your cha-
' racter; while my knowlege of your firm
' felf-denying fortitude encourages the hope
' that it will be finally exerted for the reftora-
' tion of your own peace of mind; that time
' and abfence will prevent your exalted fpirit
' from bending under an unavoidable difappoint-
                                        ' ment;

'ment; and that your affections will at last be
'just to the merits of some amiable woman,
'who, with virtues superior to what I could
'ever boast, will bless you with the undisputed
'preference. which, much as I esteem your
'merit, I never could bestow. England, my
'dear Henry, contains many fair patterns of
'feminine worth; but I will not point that
'excellence which your judgment will best dif-
'cover. Let it suffice for me to say, that, as
'my happiness must be incomplete while cor-
'roded by the sorrows of those whom I tender-
'ly love, prudential considerations need not
'circumscribe your choice. I owe you a debt
'of gratitude, which a pecuniary recompense,
'however liberal, can never repay. Let me
'hear frequently from you, and let me hope
'that the reasons will soon cease which banish
'you from the sight of

> 'GERALDINE MONTEITH.'

'To the Countess of MONTEITH.

 'I confide in your honour for the conceal-
'ment of a passion which I trust your discern-
'ment has alone discovered. No blame at-
'taches to the conduct of the most amiable of
'women. The audacious but inexperienced
'youth, who presumed to admire the most at-
'tractive pattern of female loveliness he ever
'beheld, deserves to suffer for the presump-
'tuous hopes which a father's preference first
'tempted him to encourage.

 'Anxious to avoid giving pain to that heart
'which I earnestly pray may long continue the
'peaceful seat of connubial happiness, I will
'endeavour to exert the firmness you recom-
> 'mend.

‘ mend. I will pay a ftrict regard to my
‘ health, and court amufement in every jufti-
‘ fiable form. Should I fail in my efforts to
‘ regain my peace of mind, let not the recti-
‘ tude of your principles ftart at the idea of in-
‘ fpiring an unwarrantable fentiment in my
‘ breaft. An innocent attachment fhall never
‘ degenerate into a guilty paffion. I remember
‘ that you are now the wife of the Earl of
‘ Monteith : I remember that I withdrew my
‘ pretenfions in deference to his jufter claim.
‘ Eternal infamy light upon the wretch who
‘ feeks to diffolve a bond fanctioned by every
‘ law human and divine ! Eternal infamy light
‘ upon him who, under the pretence of pure
‘ fentimental attachment, feeks to excite an
‘ undue intereft in a matron’s heart ! I will
‘ never return to England till I can fee you
‘ without emotion in that character ; and this
‘ is the laft letter which fhall exprefs a thought
‘ inconfiftent with the equanimity of an affec-
‘ tionate relation and a fincere friend.

‘ HENRY POWERSCOURT.’

CHAP.

CHAP. XVIII.

O how canſt thou renounce the boundleſs ſtore
  Of charms which Nature to her vot'ry yields!
The warbling woodland, the reſounding ſhore,
  The pomp of groves, and garniture of fields;
  All that the genial ray of morning gilds,
And all that echoes to the ſong of even,
  All that the mountain's ſheltering boſom ſhields,
And all the dread magnificence of heaven,
O how canſt thou renounce, and hope to be forgiven!
                          BEATTIE.

THE intereſt which the appearance and behaviour of Mr. Powerſcourt had excited in lord
Monteith's mind had more permanence than the
ſudden emotions to which his diſpoſition was
ſubject commonly poſſeſſed. His evaneſcent
impulſes might generally be compared to the
impreſſion which a ſtone makes upon the clear
ſurface of a glaſſy lake, which, after having
formed a few tremulous circles, ſoon reſumes
its natural tranquillity. But on the preſent occaſion he thought of his good-tempered rival, as
he termed him, during moſt part of his
journey to Scotland; and, as neither a whiſtle
nor a ſong would always excite new ideas, he
frequently expreſſed himſelf anxious to know
whether the poor fellow had ſhot himſelf: "Yet
"I proteſt, my dear Geraldine," he added, "I
"do not laugh at him; for, upon my ſoul, if I
"were as miſerable as he ſeems to be, I ſhould
"think of nothing but driving out Cupid's
"arrows with a brace of bullets."

As

As lady Monteith's endeavours to divert her lord from suspecting Mr. Powerscourt's attachment had proved ineffectual, she determined, by that full confidence which Mrs. Evans had recommended, to remove every subject of self-condemnation from her own heart. After having bound his honour by a promise of secresy, she delivered to him the letters with which I concluded the last Chapter; and she entreated him, as the affair was too serious for levity, to avoid the distressing subject in their future conversations.

Lord Monteith was a stranger to that " green-eyed monster which mocks the meat it feeds on." The preference his lady had recently given him was too avowed, and her conduct, as well as her principles, too correct to raise suspicion even in the heart of a Leontes. On the contrary, Mr. Powerscourt's behaviour excited his warm esteem; and his frank open disposition compelled him to exclaim, " I cannot think, Geraldine,
" why you preferred me to that noble fellow;
" I hope he will live to come back to England,
" that I may thank him for giving me happiness
" at the expence of his own repose. Let me tell
" you, very few young fellows of my acquain-
" tance would have acted as he has done."

" I hope," said the countess, while heart-felt pleasure lighted up all the charms of her intelligent face, " that I shall have the satisfaction of
" presenting two friends to each other, highly
" deserving of mutual confidence. You see I
" have requested Henry's correspondence; you,
" my lord, must permit me to communicate it
" to you; your superior knowledge of the cha-
" racter of your own sex will enable me to
" discover whether his travels are conducive to
" his

" his repofe; and you will affift my replies by
" pointing out fuch topics as will prove moft
" effectual in promoting this end, ever remem-
" bering that the efteem and gratitude I now
" feel for him muft be fubfervient to the
" ftronger attachment whence they origi-
" nated."

Such were the fentiments of lady Monteith;
and fuch is the conduct upon which the mufe of
hiftory and the mufe of fiction alike delight to
dwell. The uncorrupted mind avows its divine
original, by recurring with fecret complacency
to the portrait of what is perfect, fair, and good.
Though the depravity of modern manners may
obtain tranfient amufement from thofe highly-
coloured fcenes of guilt which the judgment
condemns, the foul only finds conftant gratification in contemplating the lovely pictures of innocence and virtue.

When I recollect that the fubfequent events
of this hiftory will lead my narrative through
many a painful fcene, I feem to fhrink with reluctance from the difgufting tafk of defcribing
fyftematic villany mining the outworks which
decorum and religion have placed around female
virtue, while the unfufpecting heart becomes
entangled by fatanic guile and inbred vanity.
I feel that the part moft analogous to my tafte,
as well as to my powers, would be to depicture
the amiable features of the human character
fhaded only by thofe lighter traits of frailty from
which the moft perfect ftandard of human goodnefs is not exempt. But, knowing that the
unchriftian morals of the prefent age ftrain their
affected charity till they embrace vice, while the
moft glaring enormities are gloffed over by delicate fubterfuges; and refined liberality expatiates
on

on the goodnefs of the heart, while its poffeffor
breaks every precept in the decalogue; I feel
ftimulated by an ardent, though perhaps injudi-
cious zeal, to lend my feeble aid to ftop the torrent of enthufiaftic fentiment which daringly
menaces that heaven-erected edifice that is
predicted to furvive the wreck of worlds.

Impreffed with this idea, I conceive it poffible
to ferve the caufe of principle, by fhowing
through what devious unfufpected paths the
human heart may be led to error; how eafily it
may, by youthful indifcretion, be hurried down
the fteep defcent, till, Hazael-like, it finks into
the infamy which it once fhuddered to name.
Yet, retaining too much native purity to be reconciled to its degraded ftate, and too much fenfibility to ftifle reflection, it fhrinks from life as
from an infupportable burden; and the morning
which rofe in fplendor is clouded by infuperable
gloom before it attains its meridian brightnefs.

If in the execution of this defign the pencil
fhould fail, let Candour remember the intention,
and excufe the unfkilful painter. Perhaps the
imperfect outline may induce fome fuperior
genius, more converfant with life and manners,
to execute the inftructive fubject with all the
glowing energy that its importance requires.

I fhall gratify my own tafte by dwelling a
little longer on that part of lady Monteith's
hiftory, when, unaffailed and happy, fhe fpread
delight and comfort all around her, and her own
heart derived an allowable gratification from the
confcioufnefs of deferved applaufe. The firft
four years of her married life were unembittered
by reftlefs anxiety, corroding difappointment, or
the ftill keener pangs of felf-accufation. But,
left my readers fhould fuppofe that I am now
falfifying

falfifying my own maxims, I in:l: :xhihit a
curfory view of that period wh'ch . .. . .:'d
not include any great forrows . . . . viati-
ons from rectitude, (lill bore .... .arks
of the penalty of Adam.

When the young countefs arr.ved ..Monteith,
fhe was aftonifhed at the cruel ravages which
time and negligence had made in that venerable
pile. Its native magnificence, the fubli ne features of the adjacent fcenery, every ipot of
which feemed by fome traditionary anecdote
connected with her lord's family, and the attachment which the peafantry, notwithftanding
their extreme wretchednefs, expreffed for the
defcendants of their old mafters, kindled in her
mind an agreeable enthufiafm, and fhe rejoiced
in a diftinction which feemed capable of uniting
her own individual happinefs with the general
good. Though fhe continued to think that lady
Madelina carried her ideas of hereditary confequence to a ridiculous extent, a generous heart
would find a fair field to gratify its nobleft paffions in the fupremacy of a wide, domain. She
feemed never weary of wandering through the
romantic fcenery. ' Here,' faid fhe, as fhe one
day refted on the flope of a green hill, over-
hung by a pine-clad precipice, ' I will build a
' neat little village. The houfes fhall all be
' white; there fhall be a garden to each, and a
' refidence in this agreeable fpot fhall be the
' reward conferred upon fuch of my lord's te-
' nants as feem to fulfil their duties with marked
' propriety. I will frequently vifit them; I will
' be their legiflator, their inftructor, their phyfi-
' cian, and their friend. They fhall look up to
' me with gratitude, and my own heart fhall
' enjoy

' enjoy the pure recompence of confcious bene-
' ficence.'

In the improvements which fhe planned at
the caftle, the fame focial and benevolent fpirit
prevailed, though here perhaps it received a more
worldly teint from the dangerous approximation
of vanity. ' Thefe rooms,' faid fhe, ' if em-
' bellifhed in the Gothic ftyle, will fhame the
' feeble glitter of modern frippery. Every
' article of furniture fhall be maffy and fubftan-
' tial, and convey an idea of general ufefulnefs
' rather than a felfifh defire of exhibiting the
' cold enjoyments of unimparted wealth. My
' lord's fortune is ample; I have made to it a
' confiderable addition: how infinitely fhall I
' prefer fpending it upon this fpot, which has a
' local claim to our preference, to fquandering it
' in the unvarying round of a London life!
' Here, without feeling the pain of competition,
' expence may be juftified by the motive of em-
' ploying induftry and diffufing pleafure. I will
' cultivate the efteem of all my neighbours by
' the moft winning attentions. The peculiari-
' ties which entitle me to pre-eminence fhall not
' give them uneafinefs, becaufe they fhall be
' uniformly exerted for their pleafure or amufe-
' ment. Here, without obfervation or inter-
' ruption, I may purfue my plan of influencing
' lord Monteith's tafte, till it gradually affimilates
' to my own. Lady Arabella's predilection for
' a London life, and her acknowledged influence
' over her aunt, prevent me from fearing that
' my fchemes will be fruftrated by the prefence
' of thofe whom I cannot propitiate and wifh
' not to offend. Diftance may, perhaps, dif-
' arm their prejudices; and when perfonal com-
' petition is removed, the reprefentative of their
' family

'family may receive thofe commendations to
' which kindred or friendfhip never can afpire.'

The plans of Lady Monteith would have
proved abortive, had fhe not been affifted by
two powerful coadjutors. Lord Monteith's natural difpofition was violently difpofed to the
purfuit of rural fports and athletic exercifes.
The mountains, lakes, and forefts which furrounded his caftle, promifed the diverfions of
fifhing and hunting in full perfection; and the
neighbouring gentry had endeavoured to enliven
a thinly-inhabited country by the eftablifhment
of an affembly, a bowling meeting, and a
cricket match, which returned at ftated inter-
vals. The Monteiths honoured the firft-men-
tioned amufement with their prefence very foon
after their arrival at the caftle; and, though the
company exhibited but a miniature refemblance
to the circles in which they had lately moved,
they both received pleafure from the events of
the evening. Two circumftances contributed
to his lordfhip's fatisfaction; he felt himfelf
perfectly at eafe; and, moreover, he received
information, that the neighbouring country afforded what is termed a fet of very hearty fellows, and the fineft groufe and black game in
the kingdom. His pleafure at this intelligence
was fo great, that while they returned home,
he interrupted his lady's obfervations on the female part of the company, by declaring, that
fince he found things fo agreeable, he really believed he fhould fpend a good deal of time at
Monteith. ' I think, Geraldine,' faid he,
' I cannot be very dull. What do you think?
' I fhall hunt one day, fifh another, go to the
' bowling-green a third; then there will be a
' cricket match, and fhooting, and public din-
' ners,

' ners, and private parties; and then going to
' Edinburgh. If any particular bufinefs is on
' foot, and making excurſions through the neigh-
' bouring counties. I declare I begin to think
' as your father does, that it will be a very ra-
' tional life, and quite as agreeable as ſpending
' all our time in thoſe ſtate-trappings of which
' Arabella is ſo fond. She ſaid that I ſhould
' deteſt Scotland in a month; but I will con-
' vince her that I can be happy any where. Don't
' you think ſo too, my love? You will like to
' live here, ſhall you not?'

' O! infinitely, I aſſure you; I was both
' ſurpriſed and pleaſed with the manners of ſe-
' veral of the ladies whom I met at the aſſembly.
' They ſeemed indeed a little confuſed and re-
' ſerved at firſt, and certainly they are unac-
' quainted with the more refined modifications
' of politeneſs; but many of them appeared
' well-informed, and I know they will improve
' upon acquaintance. I have projected a thou-
' ſand little ſchemes to inſpire confidence and
' cordiality. I am ſure the dear old caſtle may
' ſoon be made perfectly comfortable; and I
' hope, my lord, our reſidence among your te-
' nants and dependents will prove an eſſential
' benefit to them.'

' I ſhall, certainly, order my ſteward to give
' them the preference upon every occaſion
' which promiſes a lucrative advantage.'

' Is it impoſſible for us to extend our utility
' further? Could I not endow a ſchool, and
' introduce ſome branch of manufacture to em-
' ploy the children and the women? I am told
' that they are extremely uninformed, and in
' ſome reſpects unciviliſed. I have fancied
' that this may be owing to the narrow ſtipend
' of

' of the prefbyter, whofe poverty will not per-
' mit him to exert that influence over his flock,
' or to pay them that attention which the interefts
' of morality and religion require. A fmall ad-
' dition to his ftipend would not be felt by us,
' and would probably do more for the general
' improvement of manners in the neighbour-
' hood than would be effected by a much larger
' expenditure any other way. I fee, my lord,
' you fmile; but allow me as well as yourfelf
' to quote my rather's authority. He has fre-
' quently obferved, that by enlarging Mr.
' Evans's fphere of ufefulnefs, he did an act
' of public beneficence. " I only thought,"
' he ufed to fay, " of making one worthy man
' happy; but fince Mr. Evans has been relieved
' from the preffure of want, he has made many
' men happy, aye and worthy too."

' Why there may be fomething in what Sir
' William obferves, provided one could but be fure
' of having an Evans to deal with. But I fhall
' have no leifure for fchemes of this kind; fo
' you may amufe yourfelf with them when
' you have no other employment. You may
' fet up fchools, portion off young girls, and
' enrich old divines. But, remember, no ma-
' nufactories in my neighbourhood.—All our
' family hate the very name of them.—They
' only encourage a horde of idle infolent va-
' grants, who fly in your face upon every occa-
' fion.'—

' Not if care be taken to improve their mo-
' rals in proportion to their affluence. You fee
' how thinly your villages are peopled, and what
' extreme poverty the general appearance of the
' country befpeaks.'

VOL. I.   H   ' It

' It will be very different when I spend my
' fortune among them.   The repairs of the
' castle will employ the men.'

' But the women and children ?'

' O they shall be fed at the castle gate.'

' No; let them eat the bread of industry, and
' enjoy those delights which the active exertion
' of our native energies always inspires.   Sweet
' is the food which is earned by labour.   When
' you, my lord, pursue health and pleasure in
' the fields and woods, and return home to taste
' the repose which is procured by exertion, and
' to partake of the dainties for which you are
' indebted to your own toil, you feel this maxim
' true; and your heart will exult at the idea,
' that your provident benevolence has extended
' similar enjoyments to hundreds, who must
' long need the protecting care of their bene-
' factor, and consequently cannot affect an in-
' solent independence on his bounty.'

Perhaps Lord Monteith's principal objections
to his lady's schemes were, that he should be in-
volved in some trouble by the execution of them.
Her judicious allusion to his favourite pursuits
in the preceding speech, and the prospect of
the honour being wholly his, while he determined that the difficulties should be exclusively
hers; these reasons, added to some secret ideas
that if the plan answered it would be another
triumph over the prejudices of his obstinate
aunt, procured his acquiescence, and he uttered the words, ' You shall do as you please,
' only don't teaze me about it,' just as the chariot passed over the draw-bridge which led to
the castle.

CHAP.

CHAP. XIX.

Say, ſhould the philoſophic mind diſdain
That good which makes each humble boſom vain?
Let ſchool-taught pride diſſemble all it can,
Theſe little things are great to little man;
And wiſer he, whoſe ſympathetic mind
Exults in all the good of all mankind.

GOLDSMITH.

THE *ſang froid* with which Lord Monteith
always treated every ſcheme not immediately
connected with his own pleaſures, frequently
communicated a ſevere pang to the liberal mind
of the counteſs. Her delicacy was hurt at the
groſs character of his amuſements, and her vanity was piqued by perceiving that the tenaci-
ouſneſs of long-indulged habit would not yield
to the faſcination of her refined accompliſhments. ·
Like Deſdemona, ſhe was " an excellent muſi-
cian, and could ſing the ſavageneſs out of a
bear." Her mellifluous voice and ſweet-toned
harp ſtill retained all their exquiſite power of
transfuſing harmony and delight into her huſband's ſoul, while the early horn or the convivial appointment called him from the ſiren in
vain. But if ſhe ſought to lead his attention to
the blooming wilderneſs of ſweets planted by
her hand, or the ſcarcely leſs glowing garland
created by her pencil, he inſtantly recollected
ſome inſurmountable engagement which required every moment of his time. She was
equally unfortunate if ſhe attempted to intereſt

H 2

him

him in the history of her colony, as she termed her neat little white village; or if, opening the stores of her capacious mind, she sought to discuss some topic of literary taste, her arguments might be brilliant, but unless they were compressed within the strictest rules of Spartan brevity, her lord was either discovering the wit of his spaniel, or had fallen fast asleep.

Yet his heart was just to her merits, and his tongue so copious in her praise, that he was sometimes inclined to thrust in the agreeable subject without proper preparation. He was considered by all who visited at the castle to be a most perfect paragon of connubial merit; and Lady Monteith was as universally pronounced to be a happy woman, with which opinion I am inclined to coincide, notwithstanding that the power of Gyges' magic ring, invariably possessed by all novel writers, has enabled me to peep behind the curtain, and to see the corroding sorrow which a prudent wife will not only conceal from public observation, but even withhold from the knowlege of her bosom friend.

My young female readers, whose notions of nuptial felicity are drawn from the delusive pages of a circulating library, will start at the harsh tenet which seems to affirm, that a great number of married ladies may assign causes for discontent of a severer nature than what sometimes affected the tranquillity of the blooming Geraldine. Fearful lest they should suppose my doctrine ambiguous, or imagine that the happiness of the lady was wholly owing to the amiable constitution of her own mind, I will very plainly tell them, that, though causes for vexation occasionally occurred, lasting unhappiness in such a situation could only proceed from a discon-
                                                                    tented,

rented, ill-regulated temper, or a perverted judgment, which, instead of forming an estimate of life as it really is, erects a fallacious standard, by which it decides upon what is due to its own deserts, and how far others act as they ought. Reverse this last sentence, and let the fair scrutinizer of her husband's faults contemplate the errors of her own behaviour ; let her recollect the duties she has heedlessly omitted, and the provocations she has undesignedly given ; and let her then use the experience she derives from self-examination in her estimate of the conduct of her partner. After making some deductions for the stronger temptations to which the other sex are exposed by their more impetuous passions and blunter feelings, the early indulgence of their humours which their manners in early youth permit, and their hereditary notions of superiority derived from Adam ; I say, she will then, perhaps, justly refer the apparent neglect or cruel unkindness which had just extorted her tears, to something of business, which " had puddled his clear temper," and sent him home rather with an expectation of having his humours soothed by feminine softness, than of offering at the shrine of feminine susceptibility those attentions which fit the bridal state.

The sensibility of Lady Monteith's disposition prevented her from viewing the defects in her Lord with the indifference which a mind of common refinement would have experienced.—But to the qualities of refinement and sensibility, so generally fatal to female peace, Geraldine united a strong attachment to her husband, natural sweetness of temper, and correct notions of the human character, derived from her early intimacy with Mrs. Evans.——The precepts of

that

that excellent monitrefs, now ftrengthered by conviction of their propriety, frequently recurred to her mind, prevented her from adopting the language of complaint, opened her eyes to the agreeable part of her fituation, and transferred her attention to what her own duty required from her, till native complacency and habitual affection reftored all the fprightly energies of her mind.

Under her prefiding influence Monteith caftle realized to the idea of every beholder the delightful vifion of Spenfer's Bower of Blifs, governed by a Una inftead of an Acrafia. Magnificence was united with urbanity, hofpitality was gilded by elegance, while the prefiding enchantrefs foftened her enviable fuperiority in beauty, wealth, wit, and talents, by the moft unaffecting condefcenfion, and amiable attention to the accommodation of her guefts. If her tafte in drawing extorted admiration from thofe young ladies who were juft trying to acquire the rudiments of the fcience, the pain of that fentiment was immediately foftened by her ready offer of furnifhing them with crayons, pencils, fubjects to copy fuperior to what the country afforded, or affiftance from the mafter who occafionally attended her. Her tuneful voice and magic touch could not be impaired; but fhe had fongs and mufic books at every one's fervice, and fhe was very willing to affift in affording all the mechanical aid which that enchanting fcience admits. She had acquired a knowledge of all fafhionable works, and here again inftruction and materials only waited to be required. Her library, her confervatory, and her hot-houfe attracted general attention, and transfufed general pleafure, becaufe their refpective treafures were

not

not kept merely to gratify the oftentation of the
poffeffor, but were permitted to impart their
mental riches and odoriferous fweets to any who
wifhed to read a book or cultivate an off-fet.——
Adhering to the rule, that beauty is beft attired
when robed by fimple elegance, fhe had no
temptation to be guilty of the temerity of at-
tracting envy by the fplendor of her ornaments;
and the expence fpared from her own drefs was
employed in judicious prefents to thofe of her
young friends whofe circumftances would ill
fupport the coft of genteel appearance. To
crown this fair affemblage of complacent graces,
her exquifitely playful wit, while it dazzled by
its brilliancy, prevented by its inoffenfive fweetnefs the moft irritable mind from charging it
with farcaftic feverity.

Her village flourifhed. She had named it
James-town, in honour of her Lord, to whofe
liberality fhe properly referred every improvement of which fhe was the directing foul. The
neighbouring peafantry were emulous to become
inhabitants of a fpot which poffeffed fo many
local advantages; and a fpirit of order and improvement was gradually introduced. The melancholy highlander no longer watched his few
ftarved fheep on the bleak mountain, and for
want of occupation foothed his forrows with a
bagpipe. One of his younger boys performed
that office, while " he earned bread for his in-
fants and health for himfelf," in fhaping the
green allies of Monteith, covering the bleak
mountains with plantations of Scotch pine and
American oak, or digging the foundations of
the new buildings, which were continually added
to James-town. Befide a neat edifice appropriated to divine worfhip, it poffeffed a carpet
manufactory,

manufactory, a spinning room, a village school, and a market-house. Persons properly qualified were placed at the head of each institution, and the taste of the boys was to be consulted in their future destination, while the occupations of fishing, agriculture, and weaving, solicited their choice. The views of the girls were more circumscribed; but by being early taught the occupations of spinning and knitting, and by having a market opened for the sale of their productions, they were relieved from the burden of indolence, and the cheerless prospect of being a useless weight upon their future husbands, or dependant upon their caprice for every article of support. It was Lady Monteith's favourite amusement to take a morning excursion to James-town, and to introduce her female visitants to the young seminary which flourished under her care; and it frequently happened, that some yellow-haired lassie displayed sufficient abilities to induce one of the Countess's guests to transfer her from the task of singing at her wheel, to the enviable employment of clear-starching the lady's " kerchiefs;" and helping " to buskin her."

Yet even the exertions of liberal benevolence will not always afford a pure delight; the liberal mind must seek its surest reward in the conscious discharge of an acknowledged duty, and not in the perfect gratitude nor the complete satisfaction of the objects it labours to benefit.———— Though the inhabitants of James-town were selected from the most deserving part of Lord Monteith's tenants, it does not follow that they were quite exempt from the failings of humanity.———— The houses were all neat and comfortable; but as the Countess had amused herself by

constructing

constructing them after various models, it might happen that dame Brown would think gaffer Campbell's the more convenient, while the gaffer for a similar reason preferred that inhabited by the dame. Lady Monteith, indeed, consented to their exchanging dwellings; but then another inconvenience arose; Margery Bruce complained that a window in dame Brown's house overlooked her, and that if the said window were not walled up, she could not live; for that the dame took her station at that window, and, instead of minding her work, did nothing but watch the conduct of the aggrieved deponent. Dame Brown's rejoinder was, that Margery was suspected to be no better than she should be; that she had lately got a new plaid and kirtle, nobody knew how; and she thought it her duty to mind her goings on, lest her good lady should be imposed upon by an unworthy pretender to her favours. The fair judge found it difficult to decide in a question of such nice morality; and the more so, as the village was split into two nearly equal factions, part enlisting under the banners of the watchful Brown, and part espousing the cause of the aggrieved Margery.

Beside the perplexity which cases similar to the above often excited, Lady Monteith had to contend with other inconveniencies. The power of local attachment is very strong in people who have passed their lives on one spot, without having had much intercourse with the rest of the world; and she often found that the old Highlander preferred " the hill that lifted him to the storms," to all the advantages which, while untried, his imagination annexed to the sheltered cultivated valley. The manners of the southern

H 3

ftrangers, whom the ornamental embellifhments of Monteith had introduced among the new co-lony, did not affimilate with his pre-conceived ideas of fubmiffion, œconomy, and felf-command.——Though invited to partake of the luxuries his new neighbours introduced, his affection for four-crout and crowdy was infur-mountable, and his retired folitary humour fhrunk from the loquacious interruptions of fociety. He frequently found that he had re-nounced pleafures congenial to his habits, for comforts which he wanted the relifh to enjoy; and though refpect for his gude laird and lady checked complaint, the fmothered difcontent often made him meet the inquiries of the latter with the fombrous brow of forrow inftead of the funfhine of joy. " Ye meant it," he would fay, " aw' for the beeft, but my ain auld cot " was mair cumfurtable."

" Is virtue then only a name?" the contem-plative Geraldine would fometimes inquire, when ruminating on the untoward events which often croffed her benevolent fchemes. " I have " been taught to confider the power of beftow-" ing happinefs as the moft glorious prerogative " which wealth could enjoy. Have the means " by which I purfued this end been ill felected, " or am I particularly unfuccefsful in choofing " fit fubjects for my defign? The philofophy of one-and-twenty is not remarkably profound; the views of life are then too highly coloured to admit of the " yellow leaf," which " fober autumn" gradually introduces; and the error then prevalent even in the beft-regulated minds is, that the fcenes in which themfelves are actors furnifh exemptions to received rules as to the maxims by which they are to be governed,

or

or the forrows and difappointments which they are to encounter.——Difpaffionate experience would have taught Lady Monteith, that the very circumftances of the villagers' complaints argued comparative comfort. Pining poverty, deep affliction, and hopelefs mifery, would have adopted themes for lamentation widely different from the fuperior convenience of gaffer Campbell's houfe, the impertinence of dame Brown, the fufpicious finery of Margery Bruce, or even the remembrance of four-crout and crowdy, which haunted the " auld" Highlander. Her liberal mind would then have added to the certain fatisfaction of a pure intention the exhilarating enjoyment of that moderate fuccefs to which all fublunary fchemes can alone afpire; and fhe would have judged of the happinefs of her colony, as one of our critics has obferved of the forrows of Paftoral : " That it is a fuf- " ficient recommendation of any ftate, when " they have no greater miferies to deplore."

A full conviction of that depreffing but infallible truth, that all the good of this world muft be blended with evil, would alfo have preferved lady Monteith from the mortifications to which her love of diflinction and univerfal applaufe likewife expofed her. Againft the fhafts which, in fpite of repeated obligations, low envy and petty detraction fometimes aimed at her character, fweetnefs of temper and confcious fuperiority oppofed an inadequate defence. Lady Monteith's letters to her dear Lucy have contained a gentle complaint againft ingratitude and the hardfhips of her own lot ; for, though anxioufly folicitous to oblige and conciliate her neighbours and acquaintance, fhe often found her well-meant

endeavours

endeavours mistaken, or repaid by dislike and discontent.

If Miss Evans did not always feel the force of
her friend's complaints, it must not be ascribed
to the diminution of her affection, nor to a want
of sympathy.   I have already observed, that
her mind was of a stronger cast; it was, beside,
more intimately acquainted with real calamity.

CHAP. XX.

When thy last breath, ere nature sunk to rest,
Thy meek submission to thy God exprest's'd;
When thy last look, ere thought and feeling fled,
A mingled gleam of hope and triumph shed.
          PLEASURES OF MEMORY.

THE reader will remember that I left Mrs.
Evans struggling with the violence of a cruel
disease, whose reiterated attack seemed to leave
little hope of the preservation of her valuable
life.   She endured her allotted miseries with
exemplary patience, and after her sufferings had
almost taught her disconsolate friends to wish for
her deliverance, she meekly closed a well-spent
life, bequeathing the invaluable legacy of her
virtues to her beloved daughter.

When lady Monteith received the painful
tidings, she was in hourly expectation of her
first confinement; and the utter impossibility of
taking such a long journey alone prevented her
from exerting her personal services to sooth her
lady's forrows.   She wrote to her in the ten-
                                                derest

dereſt ſtrain of affectionate condolence. ' My
' tears,' ſaid ſhe, ' ſhall ever mingle with yours
' over the ſacred remains of my monitreſs, my
' foſter-mother, my firſt and moſt valuable
' friend! Every good action I perform, every
' evil I eſcape, every commendable ſentiment
' that riſes in my heart, is owing to her. Her
' invaluable precepts, ſanctioned by experience,
' now acquire reſiſtleſs efficacy from the painful
' reflection that her lips can repeat them no
' more. I brood over them in my memory as a
' ſacred treaſure. Come to me, my deareſt
' Lucy; my preſent ſituation, which excludes
' ſtrangers, demands your tender ſoothings, and
' will ſuit the privacy of your modeſt grief.
' Come, and tell me, while it is freſh in your
' memory, all that the dying ſaint ſaid, all that
' ſhe looked; and arm my fortitude for the trials
' which await me, by repeating how ſhe endured
' months of miſery."

" It was the ſolemn injunction of my now
' bleſſed mother," ſaid Miſs Evans, in her reply,
' that I ſhould devote myſelf to the pious office
' of ſoothing the ſorrows of my poor father, till
' time, uniting with religious reſignation, ſhould
' ſoften his griefs, divert his thoughts from one
' painful object, and enable him to occupy his
' leiſure hours, once ſo happily filled, with other
' amuſements; and ſhe enjoined this duty as the
' nobleſt method of proving my affectionate
' regard for her memory. She even added,
' that ſhe hoped her diſembodied ſpirit might be
' permitted to witneſs my perſeverance in a
' mode of conduct, the knowledge of which
' would perfect her beatitude.

' Is this the only way by which I can now prove
' my filial reverence to the beſt of mothers, and
shall

' shall I shrink from the important charge?
' Even your claims upon me, my dearest Ge-
' raldine, are annihilated by this superior tie.
' You will rejoice to hear that I am succefsful.
' My poor father was furprized into an agony of
' grief last Sunday. We attended divine fer-
' vice, though he could not attempt to perform
' the duty. The fight of my mother's prayer-
' book lying upon her vacant seat overpowered
' him. His stifled fobs were heard by feveral of
' the congregation; I knelt by his fide, I prefled
' his revered hand to my lips; I feemed at that
' moment to have a perfect control over my
' own feelings; I whispered, that his only re-
' maining Lucy would endeavour to fupply the
' place of her whom Providence had removed to
' a better world. My father viewed me with
' ferene delight, and, as we walked home, he
' told me that I was indeed his comforter, and
' worthy of my excellent mother.

' His praife is a cordial to my heart. While
' she lived, I thought my conduct as a daughter
' not blameable; but now that she is beyond the
' reach of my attention, I find infinite occafion
' for felf-reproach. The thought that we have
' paid the laft offices to a beloved object is in-
' conceivably painful. It turns the mind to a
' retrofpective view of its paft fentiments; and
' the remembrance of cafual neglects and inad-
' vertent expreffions is torture. If thou, my
' mother! couldft arife from thy earthy bed,
' how would thy Lucy feek to endear thy re-
' newed exiftence by redoubled attentions and
' more fteady virtues! Pardon, thou dear faint!
' my imperfect duty; I muft enjoy the thought
' that thou art prefent, and confcious of thefe
                                    fighs.

' fighs and tears which I generally conceal from
' every other eye.

' Do not think, my dear Geraldine, that I
' shall ever forget the particulars of her dying
' moments. The awful remembrance is en-
' graven upon my mind, and no subsequent
' events can obliterate the impreffion. I will
' defcribe it all to you when we meet; at that
' time, I truft, both the hearer and the relater
' will be more equal to the defcription.

' The exprefs which has juft arrived at the
' manor-houfe relieves my heart from many
' anxieties. You are in fafety, my Geraldine;
' you were bleffed with a daughter. Your ufe-
' ful life is fpared to your hufband, your infant,
' your father, your friends, your country. It is
' a general, a public benefit: but let your dejected
' Lucy lift her grateful voice amid the univerfal
' joy, and adore that kind Providence which has
' preferved her from further deprivations.

' We fhall meet, my beloved friend, and I
' truft foon. Sir William has juft left us. He
' is in raptures at this event, though a little in-
' clined to regret that he has not a grandfon.
' It is all for the beft, he fays; he doubts not,
' when he fees the pretty creature, he fhall be as
' fond of it as he was of his own Geraldine. ' I
' took it a little hard,' faid he, ' that my girl did
' not come to Powerfcourt at the time prefixed;
' but fhe will now bring the dear infant along
' with her, and I fhall have two pleafures inftead
' of one.'

' Dear excellent man! He has laid a fcheme,
' he fays, to make us all happy together. He
' infifts that my father and I fhall live with you
' at the manor-houfe during the time of your
' expected vifit. He fays, he can divert Mr.

' Evans

'Evans with a hit at backgammon; and that it
'will do my fpirits good to have a great deal of
'chat with you. 'Don't be fo caft down, my
'dear god-daughter,' he continued; 'we are all
'mortal you know; and your good mother is
'now much happier than it was even in your
'power to make her.'

'I know you love to hear your father's words
'repeated with all their genuine benevolence
'and fimplicity. He has truly fulfilled the pre-
'cept of frequenting the houfe of mourning.
'Scacely a day has paffed without his vifiting
'us, and his kind folicitude has been attended
'with confiderable advantage. It is fcarcely
'poffible to converfe with him without feeling a
'portion of his tranquil fpirit diffufed into our
'own bofoms.

'Adieu, dear lady Monteith! How I long to
'fee you in your matronly charaĉter, to fold
'your little babe in my arms, and in the con-
'templation of your deferved felicity to lofe for
'a time the recolleĉion of my own irremedia-
'ble forrows!'

Lady Monteith's recovery was rapid, and fhe
was foon able to introduce the young nurfery to
the eager expeĉants at Powerfcourt. Her lord,
though exceffively anxious for her fafe journey,
and doatingly fond of his little moppet, would
not accompany them. Bufinefs of the greateft
importance prevented him; his engagements at
fifhing parties, bowling meetings, and cricket
matches were fo numerous, that it was abfolutely
impoffible to break them. 'Take the greateft
'care of yourfelf, therefore, my dear Geraldine,
'till I can come and take care of you. You
'may depend upon it, that I fhall fet off to fee
'your father aĉt 'the old courtier of the
'Queen's,

' Queen's', the firft moment I am difengaged,
' for I cannot long be happy without you. By
' the bye I think your father unreafonable in
' infifting upon having fo much of your com-
' pany.'

I pafs by fir William's rapturous reception of
his daughter, the unaffected tranfport of the
countefs, and the tears of mingled pain and
pleafure which ftole filently down Lucy's faded
cheek. I fhall not dwell upon the unaffected
dignity with which Mr. Evans ftrove to prevent
his forrows from cafting a gloom over the
general joy, nor the repeated marks of grateful
veneration and affection which lady Monteith
paid to the memory of her deceafed friend. We
will fuppofe that, holding by her Lucy's arm,
fhe vifited the fpot which contained the facred
remains of her loft monitrefs; that fhe liftened
to the interefting narrative of her ficknefs and
death, and, mingling her own tears with thofe
of her amiable companion, repeated the remembered precepts of the guardian of her youth,
and enjoined upon herfelf the imitation of her
virtues. The reader will recollect, that to thefe
duties lady Monteith had added an additional
bond,—a promife given to the deceafed, ' that
' if her friendfhip could avail, her Lucy fhould
' never be unhappy.'

It will alfo be remembered, that Mr. Powerfcourt frequently wrote to his coufin, and that
lord Monteith was invited to overlook the correfpondence. He fincerely wifhed Henry well;
he would rather not have his wife make any
man miferable; and when he contrafted his own
character with the refinement and intelligence
vifible in his rival's letters, he felt a little awkward, and inclined to think that her coufin's
tafte

tafte was more congenial to lady Monteith's than his own. All thefe reafons made him very defirous that Henry fhould break Cupid's fetters; but fince he was confident that he was a very honeft fellow, and that nobody could doubt his wife's propriety, he was anxious to efcape the trouble of reading the correfpondence; for Henry's letters were generally very long, and chiefly about places which he had vifited in his travels; befide, lord Monteith was always terribly incommoded by want of leifure. The countefs was therefore left to her own obfervations, which pointed out to her that Henry's increafing vivacity augured well; and to confirm the fatisfaction which his recovered cheerfulnefs diffufed over her mind, his laft letter expreffed an intention of returning to England by the route of Lower Germany, Switzerland, and Flanders.

It was the encouraging hope which thefe circumftances fupplied, and not the ftimulation of feminine curiofity, that induced lady Monteith to develope her friend's fentiments in a point that had hitherto been guarded by the moft rigid fecrefy. She endeavoured gradually to lead her to the fubject, and began by expatiating on the beauties of Monteith. " My lord," faid fhe, ' has kindly permitted me to indulge a thoufand ' little whimfeys in embellifhing a fpot emi- ' nently indebted to nature. I have fet up tem- ' ples and alcoves out of number. Some are ' for folitary mufings, others for focial parties. ' There is one, of which I hope, Lucy, you will ' be very fond, and that we fhall fpend many ' happy hours there, when you come to ftay ' with us next autumn. It is formed upon a ' plan communicated by Henry Powerfcourt;

' he

' he took it from a beautiful ruin in Campania.
' It is open to the fouth, and fhaded by the
' loftieft beeches I ever faw. The ivy and
' woodbines which I have planted round fome
' of the columns grow very good-humouredly.
' It has befides the advantage of a profpect, to
' which even the mountain fcenery of Powerf-
' court is flat and uninterefting.'

A crimfon blufh lighted up Mifs Evans's face.
' It is,' faid fhe, ' extremely doubtful whether
' the ftate of my father's fpirits will allow me
' to fpend next autumn with you. But you
' mentioned Mr. Powerfcourt—I hope he is well.
' When did you hear of him ?'

' Very lately,' faid the countefs, drawing out
one of his letters. ' He writes in excellent fpi-
' rits, and he gives us hopes of his foon re-
' turning to England. I hope, Lucy, you will
' meet him at Monteith.'

' I meet him ?' replied Lucy, in increafing
agitation.

' Yes, my love—I am fure you will have a
' fincere pleafure in renewing your acquaintance
' with an old friend. In this very letter he ex-
' preffes a moft lively concern for your lofs, and
' a ftrong folicitude for your happinefs."

' You were always a little inclined to fib,'
replied Lucy, with a fmile, which revived the idea
of her native fignificant archnefs. ' It is *your*
' happinefs for which he feels fuch ftrong fo-
' licitude.'

' Read then, and be convinced,' faid the
' countefs, tendering her the letter.

' No,' faid Lucy, recollecting herfelf, and
affuming a ferious air ; ' I fhall preferve the
' pertinacity afcribed to my fex, and refufe con-
' viction till you, dear tempter, tell me, what
' good

‘ good would arife from my indulging a vain
‘ hope, that I excite an intereft in Mr. Powerf-
‘ court's heart. You know my fecret, Geral-
‘ dine ; and let me for ever filence your obfer-
‘ vations on this fubject, by owning that I know
‘ his. If I have not your charms to attract his
‘ affection, I have at leaft fortitude to avoid his
‘ contempt. His regret at lofing the woman of
‘ his choice fhall not be aggravated by compaf-
‘ fion for a love-lorn girl, who, betrayed by in-
‘ experience to unfolicited love, purfues him
‘ with the offer of an unaccepted heart.’

‘ I admire your lovely pride,’ faid the countefs. ‘ Yet my friend's delicacy need not be
‘ hurt when I declare, that as nothing but a pre-
‘ attachment would have made me infenfible
‘ to Henry's merits, it is my moft earneft wifh
‘ that fhe may reward them.’

‘ How reward them, lady Monteith? Can a
‘ forced alliance (and pity is compulfion to a
‘ noble mind) reward the generous, firm, felf-
‘ denying virtues of Harry Powerfcourt ? Shall
‘ the man who could renounce a blefling his
‘ whole foul was ardent to poffefs, even when
‘ by that renunciation he expofed himfelf to the
‘ anger of the friend he beft loved, be linked to
‘ a woman who found the ties of delicacy too
‘ weak to reftrain her felfifh preference ?’

‘ Can a lively fenfibility of fuperior goodnefs
‘ efface the delicacy of your character ? No, my
‘ Lucy, it gives to it a more interefting attrac-
‘ tion. Yet I perfectly agree with you, that it
‘ ought to be kept fecret from the object of your
‘ regard ; for till Henry is juft to your merits,
‘ even he is unworthy of you.’

‘ And is he not, in your fenfe of the word,
‘ unjuft ?’

‘ I own

' I own that his heart was bestowed where its
' value was less esteemed; but since that attach-
' ment is now utterly at an end———"

' Go on, my sweet flatterer, and say in plain
' terms, Now that I am married, do you, Lucy,
' come and meet the agreeable batchelor at
' Monteith; throw yourself in his way, study
' his humours, and try to persuade him to take
' a little notice of you.—No, Geraldine; the
' man who has loved you will not easily be
' caught by other lures; and dearly as I regard
' you, I shall be too tenacious of my own right
' of pre-eminence to admit of your participa-
' tion of my husband's heart.'

' His return to England," replied the coun-
' tess, ' is a clear proof that he can view me
' with indifference. Must the man who has
' been unfortunate in his first choice necessarily
' remain for ever after insensible to female merit?
' Surely, Lucy, that romantic idea was never
' inculcated by your mother's precepts.'

' Such a change is not absolutely impossible;
' but highly improbable in the present instance.
' Observe the line of conduct which I mean
' steadily to pursue; and I conjure you by our
' friendship, and your wishes for my happiness,
' do not attempt to make me deviate from it. I
' shall in the first place persist in my endeavours
' to conquer a preference which promises to be
' always irreconcilable with my peace; and as
' a means to forward this desirable end, neither
' in your letters nor your conversation do you,
' my Geraldine, introduce the painful theme.
' I will neither avoid nor seek Mr. Powerscourt;
' I will neither appear anxious to please, nor
' fearful to offend him. Whatever progress I
' make in his affections shall be all in my own
' natural

' natural character. Do you exert your pene-
' tration, and warn me when I depart from this
' line of conduct. Be as jealous of my delicacy
' as you would of your own; and if ever my
' countenance betray in his prefence the pertur-
' bation of my mind, warn me of the danger
' of exciting my own future remorse; and let
' me haften back to hide my folly in this fo-
' litude, where my mind shall foon regain its
' loft energy by the contemplation of my mo-
' ther's virtues.'

She then prefented lady Monteith with a
copy of verfes. ' Read,' faid fhe, ' this little
' tribute to filial duty, which burft from my
' heart during my lonely walk laft night. It is
' not finifhed, but it will convince you that I
' am capable of more worthy feelings than the
' weak regrets of unrequited love.' So faying,
fhe fuddenly left the countefs, who with mingled
admiration and regret perufed the following
fragment:

Still will I wander through thefe mofs-grown bowers,
And fcent the grateful fragrance of thefe flowers;
Still will I pace the path her footfteps prefs'd,
Still watch the favour'd plants her culture blefs'd;
While the loud throttle warbling fills the grove,
Mix'd with the murmurs of the melting dove.
    Here, when the fun's declining car allows
A deeper fhade to hover o'er the boughs,
Sweet Philomel, who fhunn'd the " garifh day,"
Awakes th' enamour'd echoes with her lay;
O Bird! beft darling of the houfe, again
Pour on my penfive ear that thrilling ftrain;
Again repeat it!—Fancy fhall prolong
Thy notes, and give expreffion to thy fong;

Tell what deep fwells defcribe parental woe,
For fever'd love what fofter defcants flow ;
Sing on—the tender fympathy I feel,
For, as around me night's dun fhadows fteal,
Keen retrofpection every fenfe employs,
And gives a fubftance to departed joys.
I fee thy form, my honour'd mother ! glide
Wrapt in a filmy mift, and fcarce defcried ;
I turn delighted, and again rejoice
In the known cadence of thy filver voice.
O ! ever-lov'd, rever'd, lamented, fay,
From what far region haft thou wing'd thy way ?
Charg'd with what kind injunction art thou come
To turn my footfteps from the path-worn tomb ?
Appear'ft thou in difpleafure, to upbraid
Some broken promife, or fome right unpaid ;
Or haft thou journey'd to this dark terrene
To tell the fecrets of the world unfeen ? —
'Tis filence all—Light zephyrs wave the trees,—
'Twas but the glancing boughs, and rifing breeze ;
The faint impreffion fades upon my brain,
The vifion clofes, but my griefs remain !

CHAP.

CHAP. XXI.

Still to ourselves in every place confign'd,
Our own felicity we make or find :
With fecret courfe, while no loud ftorms annoy,
Glides the fmooth current of domeftic joy.

GOLDSMITH.

AMONG the various means employed by
Providence to foften human calamity, none are
more eminently beneficial than the opiates
which time adminifters to grief. It was finely
obferved by a novelift (not one of the prefent
fchool), that none but the guilty are long and
completely miferable. In vain does the foul,
while labouring under the ftrong paroxyfms of
calamity or difappointment, renounce all acquaintance with terreftrial pleafures, and, like
the Hebrew patriarch, refolve to ' go down to
the grave mourning.' Time will foften the
poignancy of regret ; a Benjamin may arife to
divert affection from the grave of Jofeph, and
the tears of anguifh may be converted to thofe
of joy. This fuppofition, however, premifes
that the grief did not originate in the depravity
of the fufferer. Intervening years may render vice
callous or penitent ; but the impenetrability of
one ftate, and the apprehenfivenefs of the other,
are alike irreconcilable with the idea of happinefs. It has been long acknowledged, that,
though the lofs of a beloved friend feems at
firft the moft infupportable of all calamities,
even affectionate minds fooner acquiefce in fuch

deprivations,

deprivations, than they do in many other kinds
of diftrefs. This may fometimes be accounted
for upon religious principles; but even when it
does not own fuch exalted motives, it feems
fevere to afcribe it to levity of difpofition. Ex-
ifting in the midft of a dying world, we fhould
rather employ our faculties in extracting improvement from fcenes of mortality, than wafte
them in unavailing regret. The bond of friendfhip is not, indeed, diffolved by death; yet it
does not impofe inceffant woe on the furvivor,
who muft foon journey through the fame dark
valley which the lamented object has juft explored.

Strengthened by fuch confiderations, ftill further enforced by the precepts and example of
her father, Mifs Evans's grief gradually fubfided into the tranquil cheerfulnefs which naturally belonged to her character. Her affection for her mother fhewed itfelf in a tender
attachment to her memory, and to every fubject connected with it; in a fteady imitation of
her virtues, and a faithful obfervance of her
precepts The high heroic tone of her mind
would have been wounded by a fuppofition, that
love was more invulnerable than filial grief; and
fhe certainly fo far fubdued her early preference,
as to render it very little troublefome either to
herfelf or her friends. It did not incapacitate
her for any duties, nor did it abforb any of her
agreeable properties. She vifited Monteith in a
few months after her mother's death, and delighted all who faw her with her good fenfe and
agreeable vivacity. She even met Mr. Powerfcourt without betraying her fecret emotion to
the moft fcrutinizing eye. She received him
without either difcovering ftrong tranfport or

adopting an artificial referve : and fhe bade him adieu with a voice fo little tremulous, that even Lady Monteith could fcarcely detect her latent emotion.

It may be for the advantage of all love fick young ladies, who fit under woodbine bowers or fhady beeches, or who walk by moonlight to hear nightingales and waterfalls, to learn by what means Mifs Evans was enabled to make fo refpectable a defence againft the purblind archer. In the firft place, fhe was conftantly employed ; in the fecond, fhe never indulged in the dangerous pleafure of dwelling on the name and merits of her beloved, either in her converfation or in her letters, nor did fhe ever allow herfelf to complain of her hard lot. To prevent fuch repinings, fhe often vifited the abodes of real mifery, and her attention was directed to that courfe of ftudy which is the reverfe of fentimental refinement.

Mr. Powerfcourt's fhort refidence at Monteith did not indicate a revival of that ftrong attachment to his lovely coufin which had given him fo much unhappinefs. He had found abfence a grand fpecific. Change of fcene, and interefting objects of purfuit, had counteracted the effect of love upon a mind, which, though naturally calm and contemplative, was remarkably fufceptible of deep impreffions, and addicted to a penfive caft of thought. He had derived ftill further advantages from his travels. His capacious underftanding was eminently difpofed to receive all the improvement which an extenfive view of men and things could afford. Habits of fociety wore off his natural referve ; and, as his youthful awkwardnefs was owing to uncommon diffidence, the fame circumftances which infpired a modeft confcioufnefs in his

own

own powers, gave grace to his perfon and elegance to his addrefs. Thus improved, Mifs
Evans might have found her determined fto-
icifm an ineffectual defence, if it had been long
expofed to fo powerful an affailant. It may,
on the other hand, be afked, if Mifs Evans's
merit was not equally calculated to convince
Henry, that female attractions may fafcinate in
more than one form. I readily affent to the
fuggeftion; but the prefence of Lady Monteith
did not admit the fair difplay of Lucy's powers;
and that young lady contributed to her own defeat, by continually fufpecting that her friend
led the difcourfe to fuch a topic purpofely to call
her out, and that fuch or fuch an amufement
was projected with a defign to leave her tête-à-
tête with Mr. Powerfcourt. Her indignation at
thefe ideas was fo warm, that inftead of being
peculiarly brilliant, her determination to avoid
being fingular could not prevent her from being uncommonly referved.

Henry, on the other hand, confcious of the
fragility of new-formed refolutions, was prevented from attending to the attractions of Mifs
Evans by a fcrupulous watchfulnefs over his
own heart, left it fhould deviate from thofe limits which he had prefcribed, in order to prevent Lady Monteith from occupying more of his
thoughts than common admiration juftified.
He found, upon this vifit, that her wit and
beauty were her leaft attractions. As a wife,
as a mother, how admirable!—how enchanting
as the prefiding directrefs of a large family!—
how intelligent in her pleafures!—how prudent
in her benevolence! Lord Monteith was uncommonly attentive to him, and fhewed a ftrong
defire to contract a friendly intimacy. He

talked

talked of the pleasures of the chace, of the
agreeable society of many gay careless souls with
whom he spent several happy hours. Good
heavens! could the husband of Geraldine re-
lish such low amusements, and be worthy of
her? This thought kept Henry awake one
whole night, and the next morning he determined to set off on a tour to the Hebrides.
Lord Monteith earnestly pressed him to take his
castle in his return, and tempted him by offering
to introduce him to a party who proposed spending a month in hunting the red deer among the
Grampian hills. Mr. Powerscourt determined
to avoid every opportunity of drawing com-
parisons dangerous to his integrity, and proposed going to Ireland in his way back, with
an intention of paying a long-intended visit to
a particular friend.

The attachment of the Monteiths to their
northern residence seemed to increase. My lord
was sometimes reluctantly forced by the unavoidable pressure of parliamentary business to
visit London, and the countess generally em-
braced that opportunity of paying her duty at
Powerscourt. She once accompanied her lord
to London, where lady Arabella, who was still
aspiring to the character of a first rate toast,
was terrified at the appearance of rivalry with
which the undiminished charms of her lovely
sister threatened her, even in her own domain.
Probably this visit would have proved fatal to all
the fond terms of affection which lady Arabella's letters had constantly expressed, had not
family harmony been preserved by the alarming
illness of Lady Monteith's eldest daughter who
was left in Scotland, which summoned the affrighted mother from the haunts of pleasure to
the

the bed of pain. The child foon recovered under her watchful eye, and, though not infenfible to the blandifhments of adulation and the fedudions of pleafure, the grateful heart of Geraldine forgot the difappointment of lofing the promifed amufement in the tranfporting idea of the reftoration of her darling.

She was by this time the mother of three daughters, all promifing and lovely. The repeated difappointment of having male iffue fomewhat difconcerted her lord, yet the chagrin was not fo predominant as to caufe any diminution in his attachment to his lady. Experience taught him that her unvaried fweetnefs was neceffary to his happinefs; and it never occurred to him, that his peculiar pleafures and purfuits were any impediments to her's. With too little refledion ever to attend to his own defedts, and too little judgment to appreciate Geraldine's refined excellence, he gave an unqualified affent to the affertions of his acquaintance, and believed himfelf not only a very happy, but alfo a very excellent hufband: and who among the lords of the creation will controvert that opinion, when they hear that his lady never contradicted him, and never found fault?

I fhall leave to the fentimental part of my readers the tafk of commenting on the felfifhnefs and inelegance of Lord Monteith's charadter; for, doubtlefs, they have long ago obferved, that his mind was caft in too grofs a mould to form the proper counterpart of Geraldine's; and I am ready to allow, that the diffimilarity muft be fatal to that pure felicity, the refult of a perfedt congeniality in tafte and fentiment, which is always the reward of he-

roes and heroines, and is sometimes realised on
the stage of life. Such marked disproportion
affords an unanswerable argument to dissuade a
young lady of strong feeling from accepting an
otherwise unexceptionable offer; but since no
law, either human or divine, permits it to dissolve
the marriage bond, it cannot be urged as an excuse for married wretchedness, unless some moral defect or painful peculiarity in temper be
superadded.   Sensibility may wish that the
stock of mutual happiness may receive every
agreeable addition; but judgment will look
abroad, and, estimating its own real situation
by adverting to the lot of others, will find reasons for content, particularly if humility whisper somewhat of its own conscious deficiencies.
I speak of general wretchedness, not of a mo-
mentary pang; of a confirmed train of thinking, not of a sudden reflection which reason
examines and rejects.

Long before the period of which I am now
treating, Lady Monteith had abandoned the impracticable scheme of arraying Acteon in the
vestments of Apollo.   The discovery was painful to her vanity, which had taught her credu-
lity to believe, that love and beauty are the true
alchymists that can transmute the basest metals
into the purest gold.   But the sanguine hopes
of youth do not sink under one disappointment.
Her lord possessed many good qualities, and the
uncontrolled power which he gave her over his
fortune allowed her to execute every scheme that
her liberality suggested, and pursue her own
taste in its fullest extent, provided she spared
him the irksome task of being obliged to pay
attention to her plans.   As to any idea of being
impeded in the execution of his own, the yielding

ing gentlenefs of Lady Monteith preferved her
from making the mad attempt, which could
only have been compared to "drinking up
Eifel, or eating a crocodile."

If the fuggeftions of latent pride, or, to call
it by its fofter name, confcious fuperiority,
fometimes led her to think that fhe might have
made a more congenial choice, returning tendernefs bade her ftart from the injurious fuggeftion, and fly to her colony or her plantations, which, prefenting the idea of her lord's
indulgence, never failed to infpire complacency.
The future was an ample field for hope, and fhe
filled it with the moft agreeable images. She
determined, by ftrictly attending to the education of her daughters, to bend their ductile
minds to fuch purfuits as would enable her to
find thofe colloquial pleafures in her maternal
character, which had been withheld from her
connubial portion.

Her thoughts were fometimes diverted from
her favourite employment of framing fuch a
plan of education as fhould infure fuccefs, to
the contemplation of her Lucy's approaching
happinefs, which every day rendered more probable. Henry now generally refided at Powerfcourt. His filial attentions and agreeable manners enlivened Sir William's declining years;
and his frequent opportunities of obferving
Mifs Evans convinced the countefs that her beloved friend would gradually make the conqueft
fo important to her repofe, in the manner which
her ftrict fenfe of delicacy and propriety required.

Bending under the enfeebling load of time,
but ftill tranquil, focial, and benevolent, the
vifits of his beloved daughter feemed to renew

Sir

Sir William Powerfcourt's frail exiftence. Her countenance always befpoke happinefs, and he forgave the negligent inadvertencies vifible in Lord Monteith's behaviour to himfelf. " Old men and young lords," faid he, " can't be ex- " pected to fuit one another ; but he is kind to " my child, and that is fufficient."

I have now defcribed thofe fcenes of Lady Monteith's life, in which, judging by the proper eftimate of terreftrial good, fhe might be termed innocent and happy. An artful feducer com- bining with her mafter-paffion reverfed the pleafing profpects, and produced fcenes which the following pages will develope. While I profecute my arduous, and perhaps unpopular tafk, I rely on the lenity of thofe who fincerely regret the alarming relaxation of principle that too furely difcriminates a declining age ; and I anticipate the candid allowances which they will make for any incidental defects in a well- meant endeavour to point out the tendency of feveral opinions now too generally diffufed through every rank in fociety.

CHAP. XXII.

When Florio speaks, what virgin could withstand,
If gentle Damon did not squeeze her hand?
With varying vanities, from every part,
They shift the moving toyshop of their heart;
Where wigs with wigs, with swordknots swordknots
  strive,
Beaus banish beaus, and coaches coaches drive.

POPE.

WHILE Lady Monteith exerted all the powers of her mind to enjoy fame and to diffuse happiness, and her beloved Lucy Evans pursued the humbler but surer path of conscientiously endeavouring to discharge her duty to God and man, Lady Arabella Macdonald, already embarked on the sea of gaiety and dissipation, applied all her thoughts to the attainment of two doubtful blessings, a husband and a coronet.

Disinterested love is always a very favourite topic with youth and beauty. After a sly observation, that pretty little Geraldine might owe some attractions to Powerscourt manor, she entreated that her aunt would cautiously suppress the communication of her intended liberality; and, by hinting that jointures always reverted to the family from which they were granted, leave her to depend upon her own radiant eyes for procuring a splendid establishment. Oroondates himself must feel some increase of rapture, if, while his bride curtesied to him after the per-

I 3

formance

formance of the marriage ceremony, she at the same time whispered to him, that she was the acknowledged heiress of four thousand a year. But if Lady Arabella's husband had any spark of Oroondates' gallantry, his rapture would solely result from the delicate reserve of the lady, and he would undoubtedly reply, " Wealth cannot " add to the transport I feel in calling you mine. " Employ the gaudy toys you mention in what- " ever way you please ; they will be no other- " wise welcome to me, than as they promote " your satisfaction ; for your heart is the only " treasure which I wish to retain."

In ages of very remote antiquity lovers might talk in this style ; but as all authentic memorials of these periods are unhappily lost, sceptics are inclined to doubt the actual existence of such very disinterested heroism. Poor Lady Arabella found that the swains who flourished in the close of the eighteenth century were of a very different order of beings. Perceiving that the first London winter produced more starers than adorers, she set out for Bath. Here Cupid in vain continued to shoot his arrows from her eyes ; the apathy of dissipation, more invulnerable than the shield of Minerva, defended the intended victims.——Idleness is said to be the mother of Love ; but not the idleness of public places. The lounging beaus, as they sauntered arm in arm along the rooms, occasionally cheered her spirits with a passing " How d'ye do," and then joined in protesting, " that she was an im- " mense fine girl, and that it was a shame her " father had not left her a fortune." The con- versation generally concluded with a laugh at the repulsive state of Lady Madelina, which nobody seemed willing to infringe.

Lady

Lady Arabella now determined to try the effect of rural fcenes; and; having chofen the then fafhionable retirement of Brighton as the probable refidence of the vagrant loves, fhe perfuaded Lady Madelina, who went to Bath to fix a flying gout, that her complaint was certainly fcorbutic, for which fea-bathing was the only fpecific ; and there at laft the expected lover appeared in the form of Sir Phelim O'Connaught, a very perfonable and very affiduous Irifh gentleman of good family, and unqueftionable honour. Though Lady Arabella had protefted that fhe never would furrender to any thing beneath a coronet, Sir Phelim's addreffes were fo perfectly rhapfodical, that her heart feemed to flutter, when at this critical period its tranquillity was re-eftablifhed by the appearance of fome very ungenteel company,—I mean, a couple of fheriff's officers. Sir Phelim was fo fhocked at the audacity of fuch low villains intruding upon the haunts of gentlemen, that he was never feen abroad after their arrival. It afterwards appeared, that his attachment was not fo perfectly difinterefted as had been fuppofed ; for that he had acquired fome knowledge of the difpofal of Lady Madelina's jointure.

Lady Arabella joined in the laugh againft her quondam adorer, and declared, that though certainly he was very fpecious, fhe had found him out in an inftant, and was determined to divert herfelf with the fellow's ridiculous ways. She alfo added, that this was another proof how prudent it was in ladies of fortune to *conceal* their expectations, for *avowed* wealth was always expofed to degrading folicitations.

The·

The winter campaign opened with eclat.—
A noble Earl, whofe affairs were a little de-
ranged, laid fiege in form, and the conteft
feemed to predict a happy iffue, had not Lady
Madelina put the young general prematurely to
the rout by inquiring after his rent-roll. Poor
Arabella felt a little piqued; but no matter;—
thefe were her happieft days; fhe loved liberty,.
detefted reftraint, and danced, laughed, and
vifited more than ever.

The defection of the noble Earl was repaired
by the attendance. of two admirers, a Vifcount
and a private gentleman, who ftarted in the
career of honourable love at the fame inftant.—
Hitherto her ladyfhip had been rather unfortunate in the character of her adorers; but her
indecifion in the prefent inftance proved that fhe
was actuated by motives widely different from
the defire of connubial happinefs. Lord Fitzofborne was an emaciated victim to licentious
purfuits; Mr. Stanley was a youth of great
promife, educated under the aufpices of a worthy
father. The aim of the former was to. repair
his fhattered fortune, and to gratify his felfifh
vanity by exhibiting to the world a fine young
woman in the character of his wife. The latter
fought domeftic tranquillity: the beauty of
Lady Arabella had caught his eye; her reported
expectations far exceeded what his father would
require in pecuniary affairs; and, fuppofing that
a young woman muft imbibe every virtue under
the aufpices of a perfon of Lady. Madelina's
ftrict decorum, he called her levity innocent
gaiety, her affectation, fprightlinefs of manner;
and, fincerely worfhipping the image he had fet
up, he ardently folicited his charmer's heart.—
Though my difcoveries have enabled my fagacious

ous readers to conclude, that the unfortunate Stanley was in purfuit of a non-entity, an impaffioned lover could not perceive that nothing but the adverfe weight of a coronet prevented the nodding fcale from preponderating in his favour. True to the firft object of her youthful defires, even the unworthinefs of the giver could not in her idea invalidate the gift. But the progrefs of my hiftory now calls me from the portraiture of fafhionable love to the definition of polite friendfhip.

Though Lady Arabella had very little of the fentimental in her character, fhe enjoyed the bleffing of a bofom friend. Her acquaintance with Mifs Campley commenced at her firft arrival in London. They dreffed in the fame uniform, went to the fame parties, laughed at the fame quizzes, and flirted with the fame beaus. But Mifs Campley being the uncontrolled miftrefs of her own actions, foared to a character which fome reftrictions of Lady Madelina's prevented her niece from adopting; I mean, that of a dafher. She drove four in hand, laid wagers, ran in debt, played at Pharo, and, though infinitely inferior to her friend in beauty, certainly laid claim to greater tafte and fpirit.

As the ladies had never interfered in each other's conquefts, their friendfhip was fixed as adamant. To own the truth, conqueft and Harriet Campley were no longer fynonimous terms. The gentlemen had long been more defirous of winning her money than her heart; and even few knight-errants would have poffeffed fufficient courage and difinterefted generofity, to refcue a diftreffed damfel from the

harpy

harpy talons of the law at the rifk of their own
certain ruin.

As the profpect of a fplendid eftablifhment
became lefs probable, Mifs Campley's creditors
were more clamorous ; and, though fhe profeffed herfelf highly delighted with the expected
eclat of an execution, her haggard countenance
betrayed an agonized mind. The period of
Lady Arabella's double triumph proved the crifis
of her fate ; and the unexpected death of an
only brother changed her profpects from the
gloom of a prifon to pleafure and affluence.

Lord Fitzofborne had known Mifs Campley
from her earlieft youth ; he had often been at
her parties, and had won her money without
wifhing for a further connexion ; but fhe now
ftruck him in a much more interefting point of
view. I do not mean to infinuate, that he
thought her mourning was particularly becoming, and fuited to her complexion ; his lordfhip's tafte led him to purfue more folid advantages than a fet of features can promife. He
was an excellent calculator ; and, though he too
well underftood the character of his prefent
miftrefs, to fear the ultimate fuccefs of his rival,
he laid fo much ftrefs upon the attractions of
old dowagers, and the frailty of vows of widow-
hood, that he confidered three thoufand a year
in immediate poffeffion as better than four thoufand in reverfion. But while he continued
rather unrefolved, the gout fixed in lady Madelina's foot, and her phyfician congratulated her
upon an event which would infallibly add at leaft
twenty years to her life. His lordfhip waited
for no other inducement to pay his devoirs at
the fhrine of the other divinity. Mifs Campley's yielding gentlenefs forgave paft flights ; and

in

in less than a month lady Arabella received bride-cake and favours from the viscountess Fitzosborne.

This certainly was provoking; but the faithful Stanley was a sure resource. Here again lady Arabella's evil genius met her to blast her projects. Mr. Stanley was not quite so much in love as to lose all his powers of observation. His charmer's conduct had been at least doubtful. The encouraging smiles which had beamed full upon him ever since the viscount's dereliction, were too suspicious to be completely fascinating; and he thought a journey into the country would at least show his mistress, that he was not one of Cupid's tame votaries. In his take-leave visit he made some further discoveries into her ladyship's character; and while he made his final bow, his regret at his disappointment was softened by the consciousness of escaping that worst of evils, a dissipated unprincipled wife.

Lady Arabella had charming spirits. She laughed at the vanity of the men, creatures who supposed themselves of consequence; and, intimating that though she had private reasons for rejecting Lord Fitzosborne, they were not of a nature to influence her dearest Harriet's choice, she waited with impatience for the return of the bride and bridegroom to town. She flew to make the wedding visit, gave in her card, was admitted, and congratulated the happy pair in terms equally sincere with the professions of esteem and friendship which she received in return. The viscountess now insisted that she should be her constant visitor, and strongly urged her not to mope herself at home during her aunt's confinement. Lady Arabella declared, that her ladyship was the only good Christian

that

that fhe had talked to for a long time; and that it really would be charity to take her out of the fphere of flannels and fomentations. They agreed to go to every place where there was any thing to be feen. Lady Fitzofborne declared with a fmile, that even if her lord were fometimes of the party fhe had a foul too capacious for jealoufy; and her equally liberal friend, with a loud laugh, obferved, that fhe was not yet arrived at the age of envy and her laft prayers. Lady Fitzofborne's fpeech needs no explanation; but the wit of lady Arabella's retort confifted in an allufion to the circumftance of her dear friend's being ten years older than herfelf.

The friends were conftantly together, except when the myfteries of Pharo impofed a temporary feparation. I have already faid, that lady Madelina's fevere notions reftricted fome of her niece's propenfities; but this was not the only thing that prevented Arabella from being caught in that ruinous vortex from whofe fatal contact peace and honour muft never hope to efcape. Lord Fitzofborne was, fince his marriage, become a man of character, a lover of decorum, and a confiderable obferver of pecuniary advantages. Fortune feldom beftows her gifts fingly, and, fince her acceffion to her brother's eftate, his lady had an amazing run of luck. She was not only able to difcharge her own debts of honour, but to pay fome of his; and this was the only circumftance which could at all reconcile his notions of propriety with her infraction of the laws of her country. His thoughts were now turned to the advantageous eftablifhment of his brother Edward Fitzofborne, who had refided many years abroad upon the limited portion of a younger fon. His lordfhip had been affured by many

many refpectable travellers, that this young gentleman was an honour to his name, poffeffed of
elegant manners, uncommon erudition, and an
irreproachable character: that he appeared in
the firft circles, correfponded with the firft literary characters of the age, and was fitted to
move in the moft exalted fphere. The noble
vifcount's fraternal tendernefs yearned at the recital. He determined to fend for him to England, to get him into parliament, to pufh him in
the world, and to marry him to a fortune. It
was with a reference to this defign that he prohibited the vifcountefs from initiating her friend
in her private myfteries.

Mr. Fitzofborne received his brother's fummons to England with regret, and begged that he
might be permitted to remain at Paris, where he
was juft then contemplating the fublime fpectacle
of a great nation emancipating itfelf from the
fetters of tyranny and fuperftition. It was, he
faid, his wifh to continue abroad, to watch the
progrefs of events that would enlarge his mind,
and render him ftill worthier of the office of a
Britifh legiflator. The peer, whofe ideas were
equally liberal, granted the requeft; and, depending upon his own watchfulnefs, and the
chicanery of his lady, to prevent the glittering
gold-fifh that he wifhed to entrap from efcaping
their net, he permitted Mr. Fitzofborne to profecute his ftudies, till the coercive meafures which
democracy was compelled to adopt obliged even
the lovers of freedom to take fhelter in the legal
defpotifm of Old England.

CHAP.

CHAP. XXIII.

——'Tis not impoffible
But one, the wicked'ft caitiff on the ground,
May feem as fhy, as grave, as juft, as abfolute,
As Angelo ; even fo may Angelo
In all his dreffings, characts, titles, forms,
Be an arch villain.

SHAKESPEARE.

LADY ARABELLA was with her dear Harriet when Mr. Fitzofborne unexpectedly arrived.
He had narrowly efcaped the guillotine, had
paffed the fea in a fifhing-boat, and had en-
countered fo many perils, that his admiration of
that meretricious liberty whofe diftinguifhing
code is equality of wretchednefs, was rather
abated. " Hair-breadth 'fcapes" are very interefting to moft ladies, and Mr. Fitzofborne's
powers of recitation were unrivalled. His perfon had every charm, his manner every advantage. Lady Arabella looked, liftened, admired,
and went home vaftly rejoiced, that fuch a delightful young man had efcaped the odious de-
mocrats.

The next morning, at an early hour, lady
Fitzofborne rufhed into her friend's dreffing-
room. ' Enchanting news! my deareft Bella,'
faid fhe ; ' we fhall never more be diftreffed for
' want of a cicifbeo. My lord has afked Ed-
' ward to live with us till he forms an eftablifh-
' ment of his own. Is not he a divine fellow ?'
' And this morning he looks more reftlefs than
' ever.

' ever. Such fpirit! fuch information! It
' would have been a fhame to have had him
' confounded with a parcel of emigrant defpe-
' radoes. He fpoke very fine things of you,
' my dear; he feems quite ftruck, I affure you.
' If you were but a little more Greek in your
' drapery, he declared, you would have put him
' in mind of La Liberté on the day of deifica-
' tion, who was the handfomeft courtefan in all
' Paris.

' But, blefs me!' continued the Britifh peer-
efs, looking at her watch, ' how I trifle. I vow
' I have fifty vifits to make this morning. Good
' bye! I fhall call upon you for the opera this
' evening. I long to fhow Edward the new
' houfe. O, I declare I have not had the huma-
' nity to inquire after *aunty*; but I can't ftay to
' hear now. You'll tell me to-night all the
' procefs of the foot, and the doctor. Sparkle,
' my love: Edward is amazingly fond of
' wit.'

Pity is faid to be near akin to Love: and
when blended with admiration, and infpired by
the idea of awakening reciprocal fentiments in
the bofom of another, it may certainly be ftyled
the parent of the foft infatuation. Though
philofophy was Mr. Fitzofborne's chief forte,
he did not belong to the fchool of Diogenes.
One prime article in his creed was, that an adept
did not ftudy to lefs advantage for poffeffing the
good things of this life. Indeed, as his views
were not very clear on the fubject of a future
ftate, he confidered it to be his bounden duty
to embrace all the advantages which the prefent
afforded. Gentlemen of his principles do not
mean by their general declamations in favour of
liberality, honour, and philofophical equanimity,

to

to convey the precife idea, that fuch qualities are indifpenfab'y requifite in their own characters: for they know, that the exterior refemblance exactly anfwers the fame end. Superficial obfervers (and the major part of mankind belong to this clafs) will give you credit for poffeffing a virtue, provided you are loud in your cenfures of an oppofite vice. Good notions of public liberty give the licence which permits you to be a private tyrant. The daring atheift and fophifticating fceptic may alike fhelter under the veil of religious moderation: and provided the words honour, fentiment, and philanthropy be upon your tongue, you may difturb the repofe of mankind, either individually or collectively, with impunity.

To illuftrate the analogy in the prefent inftance: Could the enlarged foul of Edward Fitzofborne have heard the fhameful tale of mercenary indigence concealing difguft under the mafk of admiration to entrap the wealth of inanity into a degrading connexion, without expreffing the moft generous emotion? How would his ftrong feelings have revolted at the fight of thofe fordid fhackles which militated againft the natural liberty of man, and the idea of that *confirmed habit* of diffimulation which annihilated his fuppofed inherent perfection. He could certainly have been very eloquent upon thefe themes, if they referred to the conduct of a methodift or a formalift; but when applied to his own concerns it was foon adjufted. The girl wanted a hufband, the gentleman a fortune; ths balance, therefore, was as nicely trimmed as the moft equalizing fpirit could defire. This confideration might have been further ufeful, as it neceffarily diffolved all ties of gratitude; but

Mr.

Mr. Fitzofborne had long before difcovered, that private gratitude is inconfiftent with public virtue.

Lady Arabella had no doubt that her wit and beauty held out fufficient attractions to a gentleman fo profeffedly difinterefted as her new admirer (for he affumed that character in a few days); and fhe did not even attempt to mifconftrue his behaviour, or to difguife the pleafure which fhe received from his addreffes. Fitzofborne was not a fenfualift. Beauty was to him a mere abftract quality, particularly when affociated to the idea of a wife. He had been too long accuftomed to the corufcations of real genius, to beftow more than a languid fmile on lady Arabella's jejune *bons mots.* Even that languid fmile was foon converted into faturnine filence. Her character was too fuperficial even to intereft his attention. He difcovered her foibles, detected her artifices, and defpifed her underftanding, in the firft month of his courtfhip. She was too eafy a conqueft for his ambition; and nothing but the reluctance which he felt at the thought of being dependent upon his brother could have reconciled him to the idea of an alliance.

Perceiving her heart irredeemably enthralled, (though in this opinion he was fomewhat duped by his own vanity,) he began to act the preconcerted part. He was now no longer the affiduous lover, but the man of firm honour and inviolable integrity, incapable of betraying unfufpicious innocence, or of feducing a young lady from the duty which fhe owed to the protecting kindnefs of a venerable relation. Lady Arabella unwarily acknowledged, that her aunt was inclined to fufpect a mercenary motive for
his

his addresses, and this drew from him an exordium on the purity and disinterestedness of his attachment, with a declaration, that though it would glow in his breast with unabated fervour, yet he had rather perish the untimely victim of despair, than justify lady Madelina's sentiments by a departure from that strict honour which had ever been the ruling principle of his life. ' No! lady Arabella,' continued he, while the astonished lady was incapable of interrupting him, ' the enlightened mind needs no other
' incentive than conscious rectitude to enable it
' always to act as it ought. I can support penury,
' exile, or even the loss of you ; but I cannot
' support disgrace. Lady Madelina has injured
' me by her unjust suspicions. She has cruelly
' striven to infuse her own narrow prejudices
' into a mind which I hoped was incapable of
' an illiberal doubt. How can I be sure that she
' has not succeeded ? Your eyes, your manner,
' evince less confidence than they were wont :
' and my alarmed heart anticipates the gloomy
' period, when reserve and suspicion shall chill
' the sentiments of pure, ingenuous, disinterested
' love. Sooner than such mischiefs shall fall
' upon me, I will resign you, madam, and even
' at this moment tear myself from you for
' ever.'

' I cannot see for what reason,' returned the lady, whom this vehement oratory had driven from her usual resource of playing with her fan or adjusting her dress ; ' I declare, Mr. Fitz-
' osborne, I can't bear to hear you talk so.' If the declamation of the gentleman was pathetic, the silence of the lady was no less so ; for it proceeded from a flood of tears.

After

After a few forced compliments to this trait of feeling, Edward resumed the discourse on the subject of the claims of duty, which were, he said, often incompatible with those of the heart. In the conclusion he seemed a little softened on the harsh subject of eternal separation: but then lady Madelina must come forward, unsay her former cruel aspersions, and with her own hand lead her niece to the altar.

Reveal then, ye immortal Muses! who inspire great designs, what means achieved the glorious task of subjugating lady Madelina's narrow suspicions, and restoring to her mind the beautiful simplicity of nature. Neither the resplendent character nor the exalted birth of a Fitzosborne could have gained the arduous victory, if powers supernal had not intervened. First, Venus, queen of gentle devices! taught her prototype, lady Arabella, the use of feigned sighs, artificial tears, and studied faintings: while Esculapius descended from Olympus, and, assuming the form of a smart physician, stepped out of an elegant chariot, and on viewing the patient, after three sagacious nods, whispered to the trembling aunt, that the young lady's disorder, being purely mental, was beyond the power of the healing art. Reduced to the dire alternative of resigning the fair sufferer to a husband or to the grave, the relenting lady Madelina did not long hesitate. The resentment of injured honour was appeased by expressions which more nearly resembled concessions than any that her ladyship had ever uttered; and Arabella soon appeared again in public with very little diminution of her charms, notwithstanding her late alarming illness.

It

It muft now be obferved, that Mr. Fitzofborne
was entirely paffive through the whole of this
affair.   Young ladies are apt to miftake general
politenefs for fignificant attentions, and gentlemen are not blamable for the tinder-like fufceptibility of their hearts.   As foon as lady Arabella's preference was vifible, he became more
referved in his conduct, as all his friends could
witnefs.   Nay, he had even gone fo far as to
recall to her mind thofe principles of action,
which he gloried in avowing to be the acknowledged energies of his foul.   Her unhappy predilection filenced his obfervations.   What then!
could he be blamed, or ought he to have fuppreffed that flow of liberal benevolence which a
full heart prompted him to pour forth, and
which undoubtedly captivated the amiable fair
one ?   Recollecting the motives which an illiberal world might affign to his behaviour, he believed he ought to have done fo, but it was now
too late.   The public knew the reft. He trufted
that the lady had fufficiently confulted her own
happinefs to ftudy the peculiarities of his character.   It was above difguife and abhorrent of
reftriction.   If fhe had been miftaken, he de-
plored the confequences.   But as the ftrong
characteriftics of nature were engraven on his
mind with indelible force, he could not be expected to change.
The claffical embellifhments of the heroic ages
gave infinite advantages to defcriptive narrations,
to which the cold copyift of modern manners
can never afpire.   How animating is the perfo-
nification of winged loves, and choral graces,
white-armed nymphs ftrewing flowers, and fpor-
tive fawns chanting an epithalamium, Juno on
her radiant car, and Hymen in his faffron
mantle !

mantle! What can the brightest imagination do
with such uncouth figures as lawyers in tie-wigs,
with their green bags and parchments, or even
a little painted French milliner with her band-
box? The British like the Grecian bride offers
sacrifices, but not to the deities of Complacence
and nuptial Harmony—Her devoirs are too frequently directed to the shrine of Fashion and
Vanity; and the merits of the villa, the town-
house, the jewels, and the nuptial paraphernalia
are discussed with all imaginable scrupulosity,
while the lover's character is overlooked. He
on the other hand is too busy in balancing the
chances of the lady's fortune against her father's
demand of settlement, and the possibility of
privately clearing off his most pressing incumbrances, to consider his destined wife in any
other light than as a necessary appendage, which
entitles him to take possession.

Every scheme preparatory to lady Arabella's
intended nuptials was conducted with the
greatest decorum. Lady Madelina herself undertook the business of directing the settlements;
and Mr. Fitzosborne, contenting himself with
the power of putting a negative upon her deter-
minations should the terms be unreasonable,
showed little of the alacrity and rapture which
a destined bridegroom is expected to assume.
Various delays arose to retard the concluding
ceremony; and the good-natured world began
to doubt, whether the gentleman was most unwilling to part with his liberty, or lady Madelina
with her fortune.

Lady Arabella enjoyed, in its fullest extent,
the consequence which her present situation gave
her. Some mornings she went a shopping to
cheap ware-houses; at others she was waited

upon by different tradefmen at home: fl e ordered and counter-ordered; bought and returned; thought this monftrous pretty, and that monftrous frightful; gave as much trouble as her rank would poffibly enable her to impofe, and then complained of the impertinence and impofition of trades people.

During one of the delays, which, as I have already obferved, retarded the lighting of the Hymeneal torch, Lady Arabella recollected, that her conqueft over fcience, philofophy, and genius, was infinitely more arduous than Geraldine's eafy fafcination of fuch a thoughtlefs random youth as her brother. It next cccurred to her, that fhe fhould prodigioufly like to mortify her fifter's pretended fuperiority in fenfe and talents, by exhibiting a Fitzofborne in her chains. The thought of an excurfion to Scotland as foon as fhe was married, muft be attended with many inconveniencies; and what was ftill more repugnant to her feelings, with the renunciation of much eclat and fplendor. Befide, it was moft defirable that the exhibition fhould be made while fhe was invefted with full plenitude of power. An exprefs was, therefore, difpatched to Scotland to requeft, that a brother's hand would confign her's to a hufband every way worthy of his alliance. The letter concluded with an acknowlegement of tender trepidations, which nothing but the prefence of her Geraldine could allay. Lady Madelina's increafing infirmities rendered her unfit to be the depofitory of her forrows; and her dear Lady Fitzofborne, her only friend, was infinitely too much in the interefts of her happy brother, as fhe ftyled him, to treat her apprehenfive heart with fufficient delicacy.

The

The Monteiths readily complied with a fummons which indicated a perfect renewal of domeftic harmony. Though the yellow teint of early autumn had juft diffufed a more picturefque appearance over the romantic banks of Loch Lomond, and announced the joyous feafon of the " hound and horn," a dangerous fall from his horfe had given the earl a tranfient difguft to field fports: and though the blooming countefs was by no means weary of her rural enjoyments and occupations, fhe was too young, and to lovely, to reject an invitation to partake of the elegant varieties which London afforded. She intended to act in this, as fhe had done at her preceding vifits; to tafte the Circean cup with moderation, and then to retire with dignity from the fafcinating banquet. But there are periods, when, if left to its own ftability, the firmeft foot would fail; and the beft regulated mind, deprived of fuperior guidance, may often deplore its own depravity.

C H A P. XXIV.

—— He reads much,
He is a great obferver, and he looks
Quite through the deeds of men.

SHAKESPEARE.

LADY ARABELLA prepared her lover for the arrival of the expected ftrangers. " I " would not fay fo to other people," faid fhe, " becaufe one ought to fhew refpect to one's " relations. But to be fure the Monteiths are " the very oddeft creatures in the world. My

K 2 " brother

" brother is well enough for one of your fox-
" hunters, as they call them; but the lady,
" O! she is so fine and so sensible, and so cau-
" tious, and so——I don't know how—vastly
" disagreeable; I assure you, you will be high-
" ly diverted with her: pray observe her, and
" tell me all you think of her; for I shall not
" take any thing ill that you say. She is pro-
" digiously wise, you must know. I hate wise
" people, at least such wise people as she is.
" Play her off; I shall be vastly entertained."

Developing characters was Mr. Fitzofborne's
favourite amusement; and it was one of his topics of complaint, that he had never since his
return to England met with any person that was
worth studying. But after he had seen the
Monteiths, he did not repeat that opinion.
The interesting beauty of the countess, her apparent happiness, and visible influence over her
lord's affections, which even his careless manners could not disguise, excited in the philosophic mind of Fitzofborne nearly the same emotions as those which the arch Apostate felt on
viewing Adam and Eve in Paradise: and, like
him,

> ——" Aside he turn'd
> " For envy; yet with jealous leer malign
> " Ey'd them askance."

In one particular the resemblance was certainly
incomplete. The superior intelligence of the
fallen angel knew, that the happiness which he
intended to destroy was real. Habitually scep-
tical, Fitzofborne doubted. He watched the
varying turns of Geraldine's animated countenance, analyzed her manner and her expressions

fions with the hope of difcovering fomething
to convince him that fhe was only a polifhed
diffembler.   For it was utterly repugnant to all
his received ideas, that affection could really
fubfift between perfons of difcordant habits,
or that principle could fupply the place of
attachment, and give equal uniformity to the
conduct.

The joyous occafion which had fummoned
him to town gave Lord Monteith a prodigious
flow of fpirits; and he certainly always appeared to leaft advantage when moft inclined to
take the lead in converfation.   When he was
difpofed to talk, he never confidered how far
the indulgence of his own humour was agreeable to the company.   His difcourfe could only
be interefting to himfelf and Lady Madelina;
for it related to his own caftle; how much he
and Geraldine had improved it; how popular
they were among their neighbours; and how
they fpent their time.   He faid many ridiculous
things, and uttered many expreffions indicative
of good-nature and benevolence; yet, though
he certainly did not intend it, retirement had
transformed the gallant Monteith; and his wife
and his little girls were ftill the heroines of his
tale.   Meantime the countefs appeared to be
engaged by Lady Arabella's frivolity.   Her eye
indeed frequently reverted to her lord.   But
whether her attention proceeded from anxiety
or affection even Fitzofborne could not difcover.

His lordfhip at length grew tired; his fifter
had exhaufted her hyperbolical rapture at this
happy interview; and the converfation chang-
ing to places of public amufement allowed fome
opening to the countefs.   The opera was mentioned.

tioned. Lady Arabella declared, that the new grand ballet was so charming, that it absolutely threw her into hysterics. "I protest," continued she, "I don't think I shall dare to go " again, for it makes me downright nervous " the next day."

" I congratulate you," said Lady Monteith, " on the acquisition of a new pleasure. You " had used to express yourself an enemy to " music."

" O! I hate it still in a room, or where " there is but one performer. But the opera " is so different. There the lights and the com-" pany, and the scenes, and the dresses, do so " increase the effect! And the dances are so " fine, and every body is so overcome, and " one feels so fascinated !"

" The music I have been lately accustomed " to," resumed Geraldine, " is in a very dif-" ferent style. An old Highlander playing " upon his bagpipe, and the voices of two or " three Scotch girls chaunting one of their " simple ditties, which reverberates among our " rocks, convey to me a more perfect idea of " the powers of melody, than the scenes you " describe. And though I hope frequently to " visit the opera while in London, I much " doubt whether my sensibility can be so " strongly affected there, as it has frequently " been during my evening rambles about " James-town."

" I hope, madam," said Madelina, " that " your ladyship never *walks* beyond the limits " of your own park."

" James-town is but a little way from the " castle," replied the countess, not immediately entering

entering into the force of this obfervation; " I go there moſt days, and the walk is much " pleaſanter than the drive."

" It is very right, niece," obſerved Lady Madelina, in a tone of ſtricter authority, " that you ſhould aſſiſt your dependants; " but you ſhould do it like a gentlewoman ; " and too frequent intercourſe breeds fami- " liarity and contempt"

" I have fortunately not found familiarity " and contempt ſynonimous," reſumed Lady Monteith, who, though generally ſilently acqui- eſcent, ſeemed on the preſent occaſion diſpoſed to defend her own conduct. " I appear to my " colony in one uniform character; and how- " ever frequent my viſits, or in whatever ſtyle " I make them, a friend is not unwelcome, " and a benefactreſs need not fear contempt. " Continual intercourſe creates a mutual in- " tereſt. I thoroughly enter into their cha- " racters. Beſide, I acquire much knowlege in " various particulars, which thoſe who are not " perſonally acquainted with humble life can " never accurately poſſeſs."

" And of what uſe is that knowlege?" in- quired Lady Madelina.

" It may be applied to various purpoſes. It " teaches me the value of time. Becauſe while " we are ſtudying amuſements to get rid of " what we feel to be an incumbrance, the po- " verty of the labourer makes him conſcious of " its importance. He knows that he cannot " waſte an hour without finding his daily food " abridged. And when I ſee the œconomical " contrivances which neceſſity teaches, the " humble comforts which ſtand inſtead of " luxuries, and the cheerful patience with " which real inconveniencies are borne by " thoſe

" thofe who know no happier lot, I cannot (at
" leaft immediately) become faftidious and ex-
" travagant."

" The unfortunate fenfibility of my temper,"
faid Lady Arabella, " would never permit me to
" frequent fuch places. You certainly muft
" have very ftrong nerves, fifter. I-proteft,
" when I have feen feveral little dirty, ftarved,
" naked children, peeping out of thofe fmoky
" hovels which ftand by the road fide, I have
" often thought that it would be great mercy
" to fhoot them, as one does worn-out
" horfes."

" To fhoot them !" exclaimed moft of the
company.

" Yes !" refumed lady Arabella; " for only
" think what a miferable life their's muft be."

" Did you never fee any of thefe poor little
" creatures merry ?" inquired the countefs.

" O yes! the little favages grinned fome-
" times, and jumped about like monkeys ; and
" with juft as much fenfe; for if they thought
" at all, they muft be miferable."

Geraldine recollected the fentiment, that
" where ignorance is blifs," it is both cruel and
foolifh to impart a knowledge which difcovers
wretchednefs. But while fhe was confidering
how beft to point out thofe comforts which
opulence and intelligence might impart to the
poor, without creating defires unfuitable to
their ftations, her reflections were interrupted
by an harangue of Mr. Fitzofborne.

' Nature, madam,' faid he, addreffing himfelf to Lady Arabella, ' is not a niggard ;
' though the imbecillity of political inftitutions
' and the corrupt ftate of fociety frequently
' confine her beneficent views. Thefe infant
favages

' favages enjoy bleffings to which perhaps their
' oppreffors are ftrangers.   Health, natural li-
' berty, exemption from care, and a happy
' ignorance of all the reftraints which cuftom
' impofes, and all the falfe indulgencies which
' affluence requires. Their manners are unde-
' praved, their inclinations unfophifticated.—I
' fhould think thefe obfcure cots the chofen
' abodes of innocence and virtue.'

' That is rather too liberal a conjecture,' returned Lady Monteith, beaming upon the fuppofed champion of the equal dealings of Providence a complacent fmile. ' My long refidence
' in retirement allows me pofitively to contradict
' the popular notion, that the country is the feat
' of Arcadian happinefs and purity, though
' much may be done to ameliorate the condition
' of the lower claffes of fociety ; and I am con-
' vinced, that refiding among them is one of
' the moft probable means of effecting that im-
' portant defign.'

' I perfectly agree with your Ladyfhip's fenti-
' ments, particularly when the poor, like the
' fortunate vaffals of Monteith, may contem-
' plate exalted rank without fear of imbibing
' exotic vices.' The Countefs blufhed, and
bowed at this compliment, without recollecting,
that it might be intended for her Lord. Fitzofborne watched the fudden emotion. ' Can
' vanity,' faid he to himfelf, ' be the ruling
' foible? If it be, the fmothered flame fhall
' blaze.'

Lord Monteith now took part in the converfation. ' I hope, Sir, you mean to put your
' own principles in practice, and that we fhall
' be very good friends when you come to refide
' at Kinloch Caftle. It is within eighty miles

' of us, and we may frequently join in parties
' upon the lakes and the moors. I was there
' once. I thought it a horrid place with its
' canopied state beds, and worm-eaten tapeftry;
' but you will give it a more agreeable air when
' you live there.'

' Live there!' fhrieked Lady Arabella.——
' What! live at Kinloch caftle? What a bar-
' barous idea!'

' O you are thinking of times of old, poor
' Bella. Yes, they were barbarous, I'll grant.
' But it will be very different when you fhall be
' living there with a good hufband, from what
' it was when you wanted to fet off from it in
' fearch of one. Poor Bella! I remember your
' peeping through the painted glafs between the
' huge ftone window-frames, and wondering,
' whether the object that looked black at a great
' diftance was a cow or a gentleman. Poor
' Bella! If you are any thing of a knight-
' errant, Fitzofborne, you would have liked to
' have feen her fhut up in that caftle, like an
' enchan'ed lady, waiting for fome gallant
' Longfword to fet her at liberty. But I fuppofe
' Longfword was benighted, or fet upon by
' Saracens, for he never found his way to the
' caftle—Did he, Bella?'

My Lord had now recovered the converfation; and no common effort could get it out of
his hands, till Lady Arabella very gravely told
him, that his raillery was mifplaced. His Lordfhip then, ftarting up, gave his fifter a good-
humoured kifs, declared that he did not mean
to difpleafe her, promifed to fay no more about
the caftle that nobody could get out of, or the
knight that never could get in; and whifpering
her, that he then thought her the prettieft pri-

foner he ever faw in his life, he fummoned the
Countefs and hurried her back to Portland-
place.

Lady Arabella fcarcely waited till they were
out of fight, to afk if they were not ftrange
creatures.

' The Countefs,' faid Fitzofborne, ' is moft
' amazingly beautiful.'

' She muft be very much improved then,' returned Lady Arabella; ' for it ufed to be
' doubted whether fhe was even pretty. But I
' believe gentlemen who have lived much abroad
' have a *fingular* tafte in beauty.'

' There are fome forms,' faid Fitzofborne,
bowing with a fignificant air, ' which would
' be efteemed lovely in every region. Lady
' Monteith's chief beauty is the fparkling intel-
' ligence of her countenance ; for certainly her
' features are not regular.'

' No,' rejoined her Ladyfhip a little ap-
peafed, ' her features are not regular ; and
' fome people will call that intelligence in her
' countenance conceit."

' Is fhe counted vain ?'

' Infufferably fo. It is her ruling foible.—
' Every body who is acquainted with her knows
' it. I wonder you did not difcover it.'

Fitzofborne promifed to confider her character
with deeper attention at the next opportunity.
' If vanity,' faid he to himfelf, ' be indeed her
' predominant fault, it is impoffible that her
' apparent happinefs can be fincere. The vanity
' of a fuperior mind is not gratified by common
' incenfe; and Monteith feems too thoughtlefs
' to difcern her peculiar excellencies, and too
' felf-engroffed to give them their appropriate
' praife. I fufpect, that his perfonal advan-
' tages

' tages attracted her inexperience, and that her
' judgment now secretly reprobates the prema-
' ture choice.'

Lord Monteith's opinion of the intended
disposal of his sister was, that it was a very
well-schemed thing. ' She was just a fit match,'
said he, ' for a younger brother. Fitzosborne
' seems to have a great deal of sense, and we
' all know that Arabella is not one of king So-
' lomon's family. She will, perhaps, prove a
' little refractory at first ; but he will conduct
' himself cleverly, and soon convince her that
' the husband is the superior character. You
' think so, Geraldine, don't you ?"

' O, undoubtedly !" But, with whatever
certainty the Countess could speak of her own
situation, she felt extremely doubtful as to the
happy issue of Lady Arabella's prospects.—In
spite of the reserve of her lover's character,
their dissimilarity was evident. She was trifling,
superficial, selfish, and unguarded : with respect
to Fitzosborne, whenever the thick veil with
which he chose to obscure himself admitted a
casual discovery, superior intelligence and liberality of sentiment were apparent. ' I know,'
said Geraldine to herself, " that Arabella's tem-
' per is impetuous, her prejudices are rooted,
' and her views of connubial happiness are too
' superficial to make her even wish to assimilate
' her taste to that of her husband's, or to assign
' any merit to complacent acquiescence. His
' enlarged understanding must discover her
' foolish pertinacity ; and the generous feeling
' that always accompanies a liberal mind will be
' perpetually wounded by the contracted ideas of
' a selfish heart. Her ridiculous opinion of the
' constant incense which beauty demands pre-
                                    ' cludes

' cludes all hope of her improvement. She
' will be continually requiring a flatterer, and
' he a companion. I am certain, that even now
' he strongly feels the disproportion of their
' minds. What harsh expressions did he utter
' against the oppressors of the poor. They
' were, doubtless, pointed at her extravagant
' notions, which seemed to degrade them from
' the rank of rational creatures. Indeed, though
' his mercenary design somewhat debases his
' character, I pity Mr. Fitzosborne. He appears
' to be well worthy of a happier fate.'

The chain of her reflections was here broken
by his Lordship's observing, that she was as dull
and as bad company as his future brother-in-law.

CHAP. XXV.

Calm thinking villains, whom no faith can fix,
Of crooked councils and dark politics.

POPE.

FITZOSBORNE called to return the honour
of Lord Monteith's visit just at the time when
his Lordship was gone out on some important
business. This engagement had been discussed
the preceding evening, but philosophers are very
apt to be absent. He inquired if the Countess
were at home, and on sending in his name he
was admitted. There could be no impropriety
in receiving a visit from a gentleman who was
soon to become a relation ; and Geraldine had
been

been sufficiently interested by his appearance to
be anxious to know if the estimate that she had
formed of his character were just.

Previous to his arrival, she had been amusing
herself with a harp which had lain silent for
some years. It had been new strung by an emi-
nent hand, and was become capable of producing the most ravishing harmony. Fitzosborne
was an idolator of music. The skill of the
countess was too well known to admit of dif-
qualifying speeches. She readily complied with
his request to exhibit the powers of her instru-
ment, and after a graceful prelude accompanied it with her voice in the following
sonnet :

SONNET TO MAY.

Come May, the empire of the earth assume,
   Be crown'd with flowers as universal queen ;
  Take from fresh budded groves their tender
    green,
Bespangled with Pomona's richest bloom,
And form thy vesture. Let the sun illume
   The dew-drops glittering in the blue serene,
  And let them hang, like orient pearls, between
Thy locks besprent with Flora's best perfume.
Attend your sovereign's steps, ye balmy gales !
  O'er her ambrosial floods of fragrance pour ;
Let livelier verdure animate the vales,
  And brighter hues embellish every flower ;
And hark, the concert of the woodland hails,
  All gracious May ! thy presence, and thy power.

She enforced the last line with the whole com-
pass of her melodious voice. The apartment
reverberated with the magic sounds. She paused.
Fitzosborne seemed lost in speechless ecstasy.
                           He

He raifed his eyes, fuffufed with tears, and they met thofe of the countefs —He retired to the window to recover from his emotion, while fhe formed the ineffectual wifh, that Arabella had poffeffed a mind capable of eftimating and rewarding fuch refined fenfibility.

It was fome moments before Fitzofborne was able to renew the converfation. At length he hefitatingly articulated, ‘ You devote many hours ‘ every day to this charming fcience ?’

‘ No, indeed ! I very feldom play, unlefs to ‘ perfect myfelf in a new tune, or to amufe lord ‘ Monteith.’

‘ Is lord Monteith fond of mufic ?’

‘ Paffionately fo.’

‘ I did not fufpect fo. Of what kind ?’

‘ Every kind : from the loftieft compofitions ‘ of Handel to the fimpleft ftrains of ruftic har- ‘ mony. But I prefume, fir, your tafte is more ‘ difcriminating ; and being formed upon the ‘ refined Italian model, it requires artful com- ‘ bination and ftriking contraft.’

‘ It requires, madam, fuch an exalted grati- ‘ fication as it has juft enjoyed.’ He then rofe, as if intending to take leave, when a miniature of Lucy Evans, which hung over the chimney glafs, appeared firft to attract his eye ; and he exclaimed, ‘ You paint, I know ; do you take ‘ likeneffes ?’

‘ Very bad ones,’ faid the countefs, handing to him the picture. ‘ And when you view that ‘ juvenile performance with attention, you will ‘ fay fo. But it is highly valuable to me, fince ‘ it gives me a faint refemblance of a very efti- ‘ mable friend.’

‘ I know,’ faid Fitzofborne, fixing his eyes upon her with a moft penetrating glance, ‘ that ‘ your

‘ your foul was really formed for friendfhip.   I
‘ am a phyfiognomift, madam.’

‘ I do not fufpect you of magical fkill,’ replied
‘ Geraldine laughing, for I am very much in-
‘ clined to controvert your opinion.   I never
‘ had but one intimate friendfhip ; and I meet
‘ with my Lucy too feldom, and our epiftolary
‘ communications are too limited, to admit of
‘ our attachment imprinting any ftrong lines
‘ upon my countenance ; even allowing, what
‘ I am not inclined to admit, that mental habits
‘ imprefs indelible marks upon the mufcular
‘ organs.’

‘ I muft enter upon a defence of my art,
‘ madam ; and if I am betrayed into any impro-
‘ prieties, remember yourfelf only can be to
‘ blame.   You have long been attached to this
‘ lady, and fhe is fenfible, animated, and pe-
‘ netrating.’

‘ If you go on with fuch fortunate guefles, I
‘ fhall begin to retract, and believe you poffefled
‘ of the power of divination.’

‘ I only wifh to conceive you, that a conftant
‘ perfeverance in one train of thought muft give
‘ a correct habit to the mind, and diffufe a ferene
‘ dignity over the countenance.   And certainly
‘ the collifion of two ingenuous minds will
‘ brighten the qualities of each.   The foul ever
‘ feeks its counterpart, and tries to affimilate
‘ itfelf to what it admires.   Your correfpon-
‘ dence with a perfon fuch as you allow this lady
‘ to be, accounts for the fparkling intelligence
‘ of your manner, and all the lively emanations
‘ of your fafcinating wit.’

The countefs replied with a blufhing fmile,
‘ I believe you are labouring under a little illufi-
‘ on.   You certainly miftake me for lady Ara-
‘ bella ;

‘ bella; or are you fo accuftomed to compli-
‘ ment, that you involuntarily adopt that ftrain
‘ to every body ?’

‘ You may miftake my character, madam,’
faid Fitzofborne ; ‘ but it is impoffible that I can
‘ fuppofe you are lady Arabella.’ A deep figh
efcaped at thofe words. He hefitated, and then
proceeded : ‘ I can, however, entreat your pardon
‘ with a better grace, as I did not feek an op-
‘ portunity of expreffing the fentiments which I
‘ ftrongly feel. If there be any indecorum in
‘ admiring you and requefting your friendfhip,
‘ recollect, madam, I fhare that guilt with the
‘ original of this charming portrait.’

The countefs immediately replied : ‘ Every
‘ branch of lord Monteith’s family has indubi-
‘ table claims on my attention. Give me leave
‘ to affure you, that his lordfhip regards you
‘ with the fincereft efteem, and that he is im-
‘ patient for an event to take place which will
‘ cement his friendfhip by the bond of alli-
‘ ance.”

‘ If it be in my power to make lady Arabella
‘ happy——,’ faid Fitzofborne, fixing his eyes
upon the ground, and feeming to plunge into a
gloomy choas of doubt ; ‘ but I will hope for
‘ the beft. We know, that ‘ whatever is is
‘ right.’ As the world is now conftituted, events
‘ are not in our own hands.’ He then rofe, and took
leave with a more profound figh than any he
had before uttered. ‘ Poor man !’ ejaculated
lady Monteith, ‘ his feelings are too acute for
‘ happinefs. He will become a prey to the moft
‘ morbid melancholy, and his inattentive wife
‘ will confider his dejection as a fufficient ex-
‘ cufe for her diffipation. I fee he is forced
‘ into this fatal connexion by his friends. Why
‘ does

' does he not exert the natural independence of
' his energetic character, and contemn the mer-
' cenary bond ? How happy would he be with
' such a partner as my Lucy !'

Could lady Monteith have penetrated the
dark disguises of premeditating villany, how different would have been the conclusion of her
mental soliloquy ! She would as soon have pointed
out an alliance between the meek dignified
Octavia, and the insidious, cruel, impenetrable
Tiberius. And now let me for a few moments
exercise that digressive privilege which I have
claimed for moral purposes.

I would ask the accurate judges of mankind,
what striking traits of superior eminence are yet
visible in Fitzosborne's conduct ? What generous sentiment falling spontaneously from the
tongue ? what artless discovery of the genuine
emotions of an upright worthy heart ? Are they
charmed with the morals of a man, whose ambiguous expressions, can only be interpreted by
supposing that he secretly despises the woman
whom he avowedly pursues ? Contempt for such
mercenary treachery must be the natural sentiment in unsophisticated minds ; and contempt
must rise into abhorrence in every breast that is
uncorrupted by the laxity of modern principles,
if they suppose that his ardent commendations
of a *married* lady were intended to convey to her
heart the audacious idea, that they proceeded
from the warm emotions of preference.

The mind of Geraldine was unsophisticated
and incorrupt. She saw his reluctance to his
intended marriage, and interpreted his praises as
he designed she should. Yet neither contempt
nor abhorrence arose in her breast. On the contrary, though steadily determined to prevent any
insinuation.

infinuation to lady Arabella's difadvantage, and
to reprefs every expreffion inconfiftent with
the pure dignity of a matron, fhe felt for
the wiley Fitzofborne a mixture of pity and
efteem.

———— O Flattery!
How foon thy foft infinuating oil
Supples the toughest fouls!

What better method can I adopt to convince the
younger part of my readers of the neceffity of
fhutting their ears to the firen fong, than placing the example of lady Monteith full in their
view? Adorned with every natural and acquired
accomplifhment; ' chafte as the icicle on Dian's
temple;' attached to her hufband; the fondeft
of mothers; domeftic, prudent, and religious.
What profanation even to *fuppofe* fuch confummate excellence open to an illicit attack! Yet
Fitzofborne, deeply verfed in the fcience of
human frailty, no fooner perceived that her
vanity liftened to his blandifhments, than he not
only determined to *affail* her principles, but felt
a firm conviction that his enterprize would
fucceed.

Her delicacy required, and his duplicity meditated, a covert affault. He perceived on recollection, that he had been too unguarded in the
preceding converfation, and he refolved to follow
the path which fhe had pointed out, by affecting
great refpect for lady Arabella, and cultivating
the friendfhip of lord Monteith. He defpifed
his lordfhip's abilities too much to fear that his
obfervation would be any impediment to his
views; and his own affumption of the title of a
hufband would only give an unprincipled feducer

more

more unfufpected opportunities of forwarding his
infidious defigns.

His vifits were now generally made when he
knew that lord Monteith was at home; and if
his lordfhip was abroad, he only left a card for
the countefs. His behaviour to her, when they
met in company, was pointedly refpectful and
referved. But care was always taken to fhow
that fuch referve was the effect of painful effort.
By ftudioufly avoiding every opportunity of
engaging her in converfation, and by a marked
neglect of thofe offices of general civility which
the laws of politenefs prefcribed, he appeared
fearful of trufting to the fufceptibility of his
own heart. He feemed only anxious to guard
his mind from the intrufion of every image inconfiftent with his fidelity to lady Arabella.
His eyes were fixed upon her, as if he hoped
to difcover fomething worthy of his attention.
Sometimes, indeed, they wandered to lady
Monteith; but if fhe obferved him, they were
inftantly withdrawn, with an expreffion of regret
for the involuntary dereliction.

His aim was to exhibit a fuperior mind, in-
flexible in principle, but tenderly fufceptible,
maintaining a fevere ftruggle, and determined
to be victorious. Lady Monteith was fo far the
dupe of his artifices, as to view his conduct in
the light that he defired. But fhe alfo drew from
it a confequence which he did not intend. She
fancied his apparent efforts were fuccefsful, and
fhe now only regretted, that Arabella wanted
both the inclination and the capacity to improve
her delicate fituation to her own advantage.

It has been obferved, that the feducer feveral
times conquers his unwarrantable defires in the
courfe of his guilty purfuit. Compelled to
adopt

adopt difguifes, to confult opportunities, to avoid
premature difcoveries, the pain of repeated reftrictions, impofed for the purpofes of vice, is
greater than would attend the virtuous refolution of abandoning the infidious project. This
obfervation was eminently juft in the inftance of
Fitzofborne. His foul was not whirled along
by the tempeft of paffion. Beauty did not excite violent emotion. Senfe and fweetnefs carried with them no irrefiftible charm. His frigid
heart was too cold and felfifh to prompt his dia-
bolical invention, or to extenuate his crimes.
His vices were fyftematic, the refult of defign,
guided by method, fanctioned by fophiftry, and
originating from the covert war which he waged,
not merely againft the chaftity, but alfo againft
the principles of his victims : not folely againft
their reputation, their peace of mind, and their
temporal profpects, but againft their notions of
rectitude and religion, againft thofe immortal
hopes which fuftain the afflicted and footh the
corroding pangs of repentant guilt.

To lady Arabella, unconfcious of his defigns,
Fitzofborne's increafed attention gave a livelier
pleafure, from the idea that he intended by that
means to convey a marked contempt of the
countefs. Her elation would have been more
complete, if he would have cordially joined in
thofe remarks on the perfon and behaviour of
Geraldine which fupplied lady Madelina's domeftic party with an agreeable topic for converfation. She recollected, however, with fatisfaction, that if he did not *join* in thefe cenfures, he
did not contradict them, and the extenuating apologies which he fometimes urged might rather be
termed an attempt to ' damn with faint praife,'
than a friendly defence. She was confirmed in her
opinion

opinion, that her admirer secretly despised lady Monteith's pretensions to mental superiority, by observing that her *bons mots* and remarks passed equally unregarded, while her own were sure of having in him one attentive listener. Lady Arabella's views of life were neither very accurate nor extensive. Yet she had some suspicion, that the connubial bond operated as a powerful soporific upon the deference, observance, and tenderness, which lovers sometimes, even in this refined age, think proper to assume. Her dear viscountess had assured her, that if Edward's behaviour as a husband equalled his attentions as an admirer, they would certainly be pointed at as an *exemplary* couple; for that at present all the world knew him by the title of lady Arabella Macdonald's slave. No one more strongly felt those passions which Pope affirms to be the predominate features in the mind of women, 'the love of pleasure,' and 'the love of sway,' than her ladyship. But since it was at least doubtful, whether she could continue to be 'queen for life,' she was desirous to protract the period which acknowledged her right of government; and as the gentleman was not very urgent for an early day, the lady's sensibility was not hurt by repeated denials.

Another unexpected cause of delay at this time intervened. Lady Madelina had often declared, that as soon as she had settled her dear niece to her satisfaction she should have entirely done with a world of which she repeatedly assured her friends she was quite weary. Twenty years before, on her first marriage with her ever-lamented Sir Simon Frazer, she had used similar expressions. She then said that she only lived for his sake; and if she were so unfortunate as to lose him, her 'oc-

cupation

cupation would be gone,' and exiflence would become an infupportable burden. But as that deprecated event did happen without any lafting change in her ladyfhip's apparent relifh for the good things of this life, it was fufpected, that twenty years hence her affectionate heart might find fome pretext for the ftrong attachment to her perfon, which her exceffive attention to her own health and fafety rendered vifible to all who knew her. When the reader, therefore, confiders the infinite fucceffion of laft plans, and final engagements, which fhe would probably have pleaded, his fenfibility will be lefs hurt to find, that death dealt by her, as he did by 'the fair lady in coftly robes,' mentioned in the good old fong, by compelling her to truft future events to that Providence whofe fuperintendence had not been her favourite fpeculation.

I have obferved, that the fettlements were drawn up under lady Madel'na's eye, who feemed defirous of extending the fupremacy which fhe had uniformly exercifed over every perfon with whom fhe was connected (except her niece) beyond the grave. She had multiplied entails, and confidered every poffible event of contention, feparation, divorce and fecond marriage. She had explored the family pedigree, picked out the moft fonorous hereditary chriftian names, and ftringing three or four together, which were capable of liquid pronunciation, fhe ordered, that they fhould be adopted by the fucceffive fons and daughters of this intended marriage, on pain of forfeiting all right to inheritance. Jointure, pin-money, and alimony took up feveral pages, and the finifhed deed had more the appearance of a truce between two inveterate enemies than a recognition of mutual confidence and esteem. The very sight of these formidable parchments must have annihilated the whole court of Cytherea; but fortunately the modern Hymen never brings his causes before that tribunal, which is now exclusively employed in trying affairs of libertinism, or, as it is politely termed, gallantry.

Lady Madelina perused the stupendous performance with delight; weighed the technical meaning of every word which the useful tautology of the law had introduced; and, trusting, that the united names of Fitzosborne, Frazer, and Macdonald might found in courts and castles a thousand years hence, declared that she was *perfectly satisfied.* It is supposed that the pronunciation of those words, which she had never before been known to use, occasioned a mortal revulsion in her oracular organs, for she was found speechless next morning. Lady Arabella's determined resolution of enjoying the pleasures of a public breakfast prevented her from attending to the assurances of her aunt's woman, that such a change must be inevitably followed by mortal consequences. She contented herself with leaving positive orders to be immediately sent for if lady Madelina grew worse, and drove off with lady Fitzosborne, who convinced her that she was perfectly right; for, as the patient could not speak, company could do her no service. The office of smoothing the bed of death devolved on Geraldine, who hastened to the house of mourning at the first intimation of what had happened, and arrived a few moments before lady Madelina expired.

CHAP. XXVI.

Let then the fair one beautifully cry,
In Magdalene's loofe hair and lifted eye.

POPE.

THE melancholy event related in my laft
Chapter was fpeedily conveyed to the gay groupe
whom the elegant *dejeuné* of the duchefs of A.
had affembled on the flowery banks of Thames.
It was announced to lady Arabella with very
little preparation; for as, in compliance with
the wifhes of the company, though declaredly
out of fpirits, fhe had juft confented to exhibit
her own fine perfon and her lover's to the beft
advantage by ftanding up in a reel, no one fuppofed but that fhe might hear the fad tale with
decent compofure. It was, however, quite the
reverfe, and her fenfibility now became as remarkable, as her fortitude had been before.
She fainted, fell into hyfterics, wept, recovered,
and was at laft conveyed apparently lifelefs to her
carriage. Every creature prefent partook in her
concern for lady Madelina's death, for it certainly fpoiled a moft delightful party. Though
the company endeavoured to recover their fpirits
after the fair mourner was removed, all attempt
at brilliancy was prevented by the unavoidable
intrufion of ferious ideas. The ladies grew as
ftupid as if they were at church. Death's heads
and phyficians intruded into every fubject;
and the laft topic of converfation that was ftarted

by the gentlemen was a difcuffion of the merits of the patent coffin.

Lady Arabella was accompanied home by the Fitzofbornes. The vifcountefs engaged in the friendly tafk of confolation, while Edward, leaning back with his arms folded, and his eyes fixed upon the lovely fufferer, (I fuppofe) more deeply fympathized in her forrow; for the harangues of the comforter were only interrupted by lady Arabella's fobs and fighs, which did not abate in violence, though lady Fitzofborne was diffufe on the folly of grieving for what was fure to happen, and therefore what nobody could prevent. The carriage at length ftopped. Lady Arabella was fupported up ftairs, fwallowed more hartfhorn, and at length became fufficient- ly compofed to make inquiries after the particulars of an event of which fhe had only yet received a general account.

Lady Madelina's firft gentlewoman, a Macdonald by an an indirect defcent, entered on the fad recital. Nothing could be more capable of being compreffed into a fmall compafs; but Mrs. Margaret was eminently gifted with that fpecies of oratory which may be termed expanfion. Her poor dear lady's merits, her poor dear lady's fufferings, the confidence her poor dear lady placed in her faithful fervices, and a firm conviction that fhe never fhould furvive her poor dear lady: thefe topics were expatiated upon, till Arabella became a little difpleafed that any one fhould take up grief juft at the inftant herfelf had laid it down. It came out in the courfe of the narration, that from fome peculiar circumftances lady Monteith had adopted an opinion, that the fpark of life was not actually extinguifhed but that the fpeedy exertion of proper means might

might revive the fufpended animation. To this opinion the phyficians who had been fummoned, lent fome countenance; and the humanity of the countefs prompted her not only to command thefe applications, but by her prefence to prevent the proceedings which are fometimes injudicioufly adopted at the firft moment of apparent diffolution.

Mrs. Margaret was not only convinced of the inefficacy of the attempt, but confcientioufly believing it to be very prefumptuous, had refufed her fervices with fome little fenfe of indignity at having had them required, and keen fufceptibility at the fuppofition that fhe could bear to ftay in the room where her poor dear lady lay. Arabella joined in her opinion; and the difcourfe changed from the virtues of Mrs. Margaret and the deceafed, to the wickednefs of difturbing the dead, and the concern which the affectionate niece now felt, that her dear aunt had none of her *own* family to attend her in her laft moments.

The failure of lady Monteith's efforts relieved Arabella from what might more properly be called a vexation than a diftrefs; and her fofter feelings, freed from difagreeable embarraffments, had leifure to flow in the delicate channels which etiquette prefcribes to grief. She mourned for one fortnight in the fweeteft manner imaginable, dreffed in a clofe cap, with her bouquet ftuck on one fide, her robe loofely faftened, and her arms hanging negligently. All her vifitauts agreed, that fhe looked prettier than ever, and Fitzofborne was continually reminded of thofe well known lines which characterife the fair fex, as defigned to ' be adorned

L 2

by diftrefs,' and ' dreffed moft amiably in tears.'

But it was not over the unconfcious tomb that this fair fiowret drooped. The increafed fenfibility of the prefent age, grown too fragile to encounter the morbid contagion of death, declines all intimate acquaintance with fpecta-cles of mortality, and deputes hireling hands to perform thofe offices which the fterner fortitude of former times claimed as the peculiar privilege of affection and kindred. My attachment to obfolete manners inclines me to refer the uni-verfal cuftom of flying from the bed of death and its melancholy appendages, to fome other caufe than exceffive tendernefs. I fufpect the faftidioufnefs of indulgence, accuftomed to bafk in the funfhine of life, and bereft of fufficient energy even to wifh to procure a defence againft the ftorm. I difcover the enervating habits of diffipation, the cant of flattery, and the fophifms of felf-delufion. Beauty will not contemplate the fixed raylefs eye, left the recollection fhould obfcure the brilliancy of its own : youth and health refufe to be acquainted with the livid cheek, which preaches the importance of the paffing hours ; and gaiety abjures all knowledge of the clay-cold reliques of the human form, left the fearful fentence of ' fuch fhalt thou be' fhould palfy the graceful ftep, arreft the fwift ca-reer of levity, and render the whifper of adu-lation uninterefting.

Lady Arabella's firft tears flowed beneath her brother's roof; but her extreme fufceptibility foon required a frefh afylum. Lady Monteith was the worft comforter in the world; and fhe was convinced that her poor fpirits would be quite overcome,

overcome, if she did not get amongst people a little
more like other folks. Geraldine indeed had performed the office of a consoler to her Lucy with
tolerable success; but the retired daughter of a
country clergyman, and a fashionable belle, are
different characters: and either the simplicity
of the countess did not discriminate, or some
secret spark of ill-nature prevented her from
adopting the proper method of treating her present guest. She permitted lady Arabella's tears
to stream without any admonition that they
might dim her eyes or injure her complexion;
and in the most violent paroxysms of grief she strove
to soften her emotions by leading the discourse
to her dear-aunt's affection for her, and anxious
solicitude to promote her happiness. She had
once the inhumanity to suggest the idea, that the
separated spirit would be afflicted by witnessing
the sorrow of surviving friends; and that the
violent indulgence of extreme regret might be
construed to proceed from a want of due submission to the Supreme Disposer of events. She
had indeed successively expatiated on these topics
to Miss Evans. The countenance of that artless
girl assumed an angelic composure whilst listen-
ing to the solemn sentiments; and her hands
and eyes uplifted in meek resignation seemed to
say, ' I will not impede the beatitude of my
' mother, nor murmur at the dispensations of
' my God.'

But in the present instance the awful allusion
produced very horrific effects. Lady Arabella's
ideas of ' things unseen' were extremely con-
fused. She had never had time to investigate
the subject herself; and, from some arguments
which Mr. Fitzosborne had used, she was inclined to hope, that the vague notions which she

had

had picked up in her early years were purely
chimerical terrors, the effect of low prejudices.
She, therefore, replied to the confolatory arguments of the countefs with a fhriek of apprehenfion; befought her in future to avoid fuch
fhocking expreffions; and, looking round her,
as if in expectation of feeing lady Madelina's
ghoft, fhe became fo fearful of having a vifion-
ary attendant, that fhe durft not move from one
room to another without being accompanied by
a corporeal guard.

At Mr. Fitzofborne's next vifit fhe expatiated
on the premeditated cruelty of lady Monteith,
who chofe the very period of her being fo low
that fhe could hardly fupport herfelf, to afflict
her by naming fubjects that fhe never could
bear. She was perfectly innocent, fhe faid;
had never hurt any body, nor committed any
crime in her life; and why need fhe be talked to
about feparated fpirits, and religion, as if fhe
were the greateft finner in the world? Lady
Monteith had even hinted, that there would be
an indecorum in her going into public immediately after the interment of an aunt, who had to
her fupplied the tendernefs and protection of
the maternal character; and fhe was certain
that the funeral was delayed, not fo much out of
refpect, as to keep her immured, and to make
her break her heart, which was much too refined
and tender to endure thofe forms of woe to
which ftronger minds might fubmit. In fine,
fhe enjoined Fitzofborne to ftate to lady Monteith the impropriety of her conduct, and to
convince her how wrong it was to talk about
difagreeable things which fhe could not be fure
were true. Edward undertook the office, but
advifed lady Arabella not to be too fanguine of
fuccefs.

succefs.   Prejudices, he faid, were ftubborn
things to contend with, and lady Monteith had
unfortunately imbibed feveral.   He compli-
mented lady Arabella on her more enlarged
notions, but conjured her to conceal a fuperiority
which might probably excite envy ; and in cafe
of any future attempts to infpire her with fuper-
ftitious terrors, he wifhed her either to give a
fudden turn to the converfation, or to enjoy the
triumph of reafon over bigotry in a dignified
filence.

Fitzofborne entered on the tafk enjoined,
with the cruel avidity of a fanguinary mind,
bent on deftroying what it was neceffitated to
revere.   His obfervations on lady Monteith's
behaviour enabled him clearly to devolope her
character ; and as he founded his hopes of fuccefs on her evident love of praife, he was fenfible that the unaffected fincerity of her religious
principles would prove a fteady bulwark too
powerful to be affailed by open attacks, and
which he muft either undermine or abandon his
purfuit.   He perceived, that though her vivacity
at times tranfcended the limits of rigid prudence,
even in the wildeft flights of gaiety the moft
guarded ridicule on facred fubjects was unpala-
table ; and though the engroffing amufements
of polite life afforded lefs leifure for reflection
and devotional exercifes during her ftay in town,
fhe ever paffed a diffipated Sunday with evident
regret, and appeared to feel every omiffion of
duty with the felf-reproach of confcious error,
rather than to avow her neglect with the bold
air of one who expects to be applauded for liberality and exemption from prefcribed forms.   The
footing on which he was received in the family
gave him frequent occafions of perceiving, that,

though

though she did not burst out into frequent censures against immorality, she never treated a gross
deviation from morality and decorum with that
levity of remark which warrants the conclusion,
that the observer's principles are too relaxed to
view flagitious conduct with proper abhorrence.
Though no one knew better how to wing the
shaft of raillery, and to encourage 'sport that
'wrinkled care derides,' wit was with her the
companion of unreproved pleasure, not the child
of unrestrained liberty. Its frolic hand was
ever taught to respect the palladium of virtue
and religion.

The event which Geraldine had lately wit-
nessed confirmed her habitual reverence for
serious subjects. Without professing to feel any
marked attachment to lady Madelina, or affecting sorrow for her loss, she had contemplated an
object of mortality with the sympathetic thought-
fulness of one who felt conscious that she was
a fellow-pilgrim, journeying to the same bourne.
A conviction of the instability of temporal possessions, and the inefficiency of human aid,
would naturally direct a considerate mind to
firmer supports, and to recur to the idea of a
traveller, than which nothing can be more
analogous to human life. The certainty of a
limited residence amongst the objects of sense
excited a strong solicitude to extend her knowledge of things invisible, and to secure an
interest in that undiscovered world of which she
must one day become an inhabitant.

A state of mind like that which I have de-
scribed appears at the first glance to be unfavourable to the designs of a Fitzosborne. He thought
it otherwise. It was a disposition which naturally led to the discussion of moral and religious
truths.

truths.   The decent forms which the cuftom of the world ftill fanctions prefcribed to the Monteiths the neceffity of avoiding promifcuous vifitors, and abfenting from public amufements. And though the fair Arabella feemed to caft a longing look from her folitude upon forbidden pleafure, the countefs liftened to the narrative of the day with a more languid attention, and imperceptibly led back the converfation to fome improving fubject.   Her attempts generally frightened lady Arabella, and compelled her to take refuge in her own apartments; where fhe found occupation in confulting with her maid on the changes of ornament which the alterations in her mourning would admit.   Lord Monteith, though at firft doubtful how he fhould kill time during this melancholy period of confinement, found fo much amufement in ringing the dumb bell and learning to play on the violin, that he relapfed into his old misfortune of want of leifure ; and Fitzofborne would have found it more difficult to avoid than to felect opportunities for private converfation with Geraldine.

CHAP. XXVII.

—— In difcourfe more fwcet—
Others apart fat on a hill retir'd,
In thoughts more elevate, and reafon'd high
Of Providence, fo.e-knowledge, will, and fate,
Fix'd fate, free will, fore-knowledge abfolute,
And found no end, in wandering mazes loft.
Of good and evil much they argued, then,
Of happinefs and final mifery,
Paffion and apathy, glory and fhame,
Vain wifdom all, and falfe philofophy.

MILTON.

READING was one of lady Monteith's conftant amufements; and among her favourite
writers the moral pages of Johnfon held a diftinguifhed pre-eminence.   His inftructive romance of Raffelas occupied her one morning.
She ftopped at the part which feemed to intimate
the author's belief in the poffibility of fpectral
appearances.   The idea ftrongly engrofied her
imagination.   She ruminated on the arguments
which might be adduced on either fide, and continued in a profound reverie when Fitzofborne
entered the room.

After a paufe, in which lady Monteith was
trying to difengage her ideas from the train of
reflection which they had purfued, Edward politely expreffed his fears that he had interrupted
an agreeable ftudy; and, with an intimation that
he would immediately withdraw, inquired what
fubject occupied her attention.   She delivered
to him the unclofed volume without any com-
ment.   He read the paffage to which her finger
referred,

referred, and reftored it with an obfervation,. that the Britifh cenfor was perfectly confiftent. Geraldine, miftaking this remark for approba- tion, replied, that fhe had ever thought him fo, and therefore ftrove to form her mind by the exalted ftandard his works prefcribed.

"I agree with you," faid Fitzofborne. "His writings do indeed prefcribe an exalted "ftandard of morality. A gigantic one, I "fhould rather fay, utterly inadequate to the "prefent ftate of the world. His views and "writings are, however, all uniform. An "enemy to levity and fimplicity, a lover of "difcipline and fyftem, averfe to thofe rights "which man inherently poffeffes, tenacious of "thofe bulwarks which fociety forms, he is re- "pulfive in his politics, uncomplying in his. "morality, and auftere in his religion."

It was only the laft obfervation which con- vinced the countefs that this exordium was de- figned to cenfure her favourite author, and fhe began his defence by making fome preliminary conceffions. In extenuation of that air of dif- content and depreffion which ever pervades his works when he refers to the fituation of a pro- feffed writer, fhe maintained, that large allow- ances ought to be made for the fenfibility of unpatronifed merit, confcious of defert and ftruggling under calamity. She added, that the fituation of the moralift in his early years pre- cluded him from entering into thofe more re- fined claffes of fociety, whofe amiable polifh might have foftened the afperities of his natural character. But fince the world already poffeffed many elegant inftructors, who knew how to aim the lighter fhafts of fatire, and to blend im- provement with amufement, perhaps the lover

of

of literature would not regret the circumstances that gave him one less urbane moralist, whose austere sense exhibited the noblest model of energetic composition and exalted principle.

" Your justification, madam," said Fitzosborne, " is conclusive. The page of Johnson " will ever be resorted to by the lover of va- " riety, and will claim the appropriate com- " mendations which you have given it, from " minds capable of appreciating his real worth. " He is too profound to be the idol of the " million : and as his beauties can only be relish- " ed by an understanding as vigorous as his own, " so his precepts seem calculated for disposi- " tions that resemble him in firmness. On " such strong minds his tendency to superstition " can produce no bad effects."

" My acquaintance is too limited," rejoined the countess, " for me to know a person to " whom I could not safely recommend the " works of Johnson."

" I beg your pardon," interrupted Edward. " I should have many objections to Lady Ara- " bella's seeing the passage which has wrought " your mind into its present state of *high* en- " thusiasm. The uncommon susceptibility and " delicacy of her character would make her " feel painful alarms, while I see you only in- " dulge a ' fine frenzy.' In a conversation you " lately had with her, even some of your " guarded expressions have caused her the most " distressing agitation."

Lady Monteith recollected that she was talking to a lover, and determined to endure a little puerility. She acknowleged, that it was natural for Arabella to seem depressed immediately after the loss of a friend who had acted the part

of

of a foster-mother to her, and she promised to
be very cautious in future. " But," continued
she, " I must own that the invisible agency of
" separated spirits is a very favourite theme
" with me; and though, contrary to the opi-
" nion of the Abyssinian sage, I could affirm,
" that we never have any certain evidence that
" the dead are permitted to become objects of
" our senses, I have long rejoiced in the hope,
" that our departed friends are the agents em-
" ployed by over-ruling Providence to perform
" offices of care and tenderness to their surviv-
" ing connexions. This thought has most fre-
" quently occurred to me, as I have bent over
" my sleeping children, and have fancied glo-
" rified beings watched our unconscious hours
" with similar attention. When I was once
" threatened with the loss of my eldest darling,
" I found sensible consolation in the idea of
" its becoming a guardian cherub to sustain the
" innocence of its sisters through a dangerous
" world, and to receive my parting spirit at the
" hour of my dissolution."

While the countess spoke, her radiant eyes
were suffused with tears. Fitzosborne, check-
ing some unsubdued struggles of conscience,
which almost tempted him to wish he could enjoy such visionary delights, coolly replied to her
energetic speech : " I should be very sorry, ma-
" dam, to interrupt those agreeable reveries
" which in minds of your temperature can
" *rarely* be prejudicial. I shall only state the
" dangerous consequences of such illusions be-
" coming general. What a tremendous super-
" structure of imposition might priest-craft
" erect upon such a visionary basis ! You do
" not pretend, madam, to say, that your hopes
rest

" reſt upon any real foundation. The nature
" of the ſoul has hitherto eluded inquiry. It
" may in time become capable of abſolute de-
" finition ; and though the age is not at pre-
" ſent ſufficiently enlightened to afford abſolute
" proof of this ſuppoſed immaterial ſubſtance
" being only a more exquiſite configuration of
" periſhable atoms, incapable of diſtinct ex-
" iſtence, the glorious epocha of truth and
" reaſon is too near to aliow us to believe the
" poſſibility of ſpectral appearances, or even of
" ſpiritual agency, in the manner your imagi-
" nation prompts you to wiſh."

Though Lady Monteith was no deep theolo-
gian, ſhe had heard of the millennium, and the
ſuſpenſion of conſciouſneſs in the diſembodied
ſoul; and ſhe concluded that Fitzoſborne was a
convert to thoſe doctrines. She was by no
means aware of the deeper tendency of his views;
yet, as ſhe thought there was ſomething peculiar
in his opinions, ſhe wiſhed to fathom him upon
theſe ſubjects. She knew enough of the world to
be convinced, that divinity was not the favourite
ſtudy of young men of faſhion : but ſhe knew
too, that deep learning was equally excluded
from polite circles. Fitzoſborne had been announced to her as the " mirror of information;"
and ſhe ſaw nothing ridiculous in the idea, that
a man of reading ſhould devote part of his attention to the ſtudy of the nobleſt truths. Indifference on ſerious ſubjects was, as far as her
obſervations extended, combined with ignorance
and a general relaxation of mind. Fitzoſborne's manner evinced energy and attention.
She had often felt indignant at hearing the wit-
ling attempt to ridicule what he did not under-
ſtand, or the libertine ſeek to invalidate what he
feared to believe. But Fitzoſborne poſſeſſed too
much

much real talent to envy the wreath that fades
upon the coxcomb's brow, and his conduct
feemed too correct to fupply him with a motive for taking fhelter in infidelity. His fentiments on every fubject were moral and liberal.
His felf-command was exemplary; his information
tion general; his reafoning, though flowery,
ingenious, and, in Lady Monteith's opinion,
judicious. I have already obferved, that her
parts were rather brilliant than profound. It
will not therefore be furprifing, that fhe fhould
be eafily entangled in the fnare of a fyllogifm,
or that the unfufpecting fincerity of her heart
fhould render her a dupe to any one who took
the trouble to play the fpecious confummate
hypocrite.

   In forming her opinion of the dangerous character which was now expofed to her obfervation, fhe had fallen into the fame error of pre-
cipitate judgment which fhe had been formerly
guilty of in the cafe of Lord Monteith. She
now fupplied talents with as much liberality as
fhe formerly created virtues. Experience had
convinced her, that love is apt to look through
magnifying optics; yet, though one pleafing
phantom faded after another, fomething really
eftimable ftill remained; and on her comparing
her own lot with that of others, fhe found
abundant reafon to acquiefce in a ftate of refigned content. Recalling fome of Mrs. Evans's
early precepts, fhe had laboured to fubdue
thofe more exquifite refinements of fenfibility,
which vainly look for confummate enjoyment
in this world; and, without feeling too lively
regrets for the want of unattainable good, fhe
enjoyed the cup of bleffing which Providence
tendered to her acceptance. She was in this

state of mind when her acquaintance with Fitzofborne commenced. The peculiarity of his character drew her attention. The evident infelicity of his connubial profpects attracted pity. His conduct awakened esteem, and his intellectual fuperiority excited admiration. Neither did she difcover from what fecret failing in herfelf that admiration fprung, nor that Vanity is as great a magnifier as Love.

Fitzofborne had been fo careful to veil his fcepticifm in ambiguous phrafes, that Lady Monteith's folicitude to difcover his principles really arofe from an idea that their fingularity chiefly proceeded from their excellence, and that by converfing with him she should strengthen her own convictions. She had often lamented, that Lord Monteith's volatile temper deprived her of that fupporting judgment and directing care which the conjugal institution was intended to afford to the fofter fex. Though not doubtful of the propriety of her own conduct, she naturally wished it should receive the approbation of an obferving eye; and a confcioufnefs of her own abilities was attended with fome repugnance to their " wafting their fweetnefs in the defert air." The friend, the advifer she had long wished for, feemed now to prefent himfelf to her view in the perfon of an accomplished intelligent gentleman of irreproachable worth, who would foon become a near relation.——— Every idea of impropriety was removed by this latter confideration ; and, with the ufual imbecillity of short-fighted mortals, she fancied her character might acquire additional luftre by im-

bibing the fplendor of fo fair an archetype.—
She had not difcovered, that

> All was falfe, and hollow ; though his tongue
> Dropp'd manna, and could make the worfe appear
> The better reafon, to perplex and dafh
> Matureft councils; for his thoughts were low ;
> To vice induftrious, but to nobler deeds
> Tim'rous and flothful ; yet he pleas'd the ear.

Her endeavours to diveft this " Demon of
fentiment" of his cherubic veil were, however,
ineffectual. Wrapped in his darling myfticifm,
he defied her fcrutiny. His knowledge of the
human heart convinced him how powerful an
engine fecrefy becomes when wielded by a fkill-
ful hand, and oppofed to the reftlefs fpirit of
female curiofity. But while he eluded her inquiries, and avoided a full difcovery of his own
opinions, he threw out enough to convince her,
that they were not only extraordinary but permanent ; and by complimenting the fagacious
avidity with which fhe feized every fentiment
he feemed unwarily to difclofe, he roufed the
mingled folicitude of inquifitivenefs and vanity,
and formed an intereft which he determined to
improve.

The converfation ended on his part with a
panegyric on morality, which he loaded with
oftentatious ornaments ; and a philippic againft
the illiberality of fuppofing that exalted minds
needed any other inducement to act rightly than
the abftract lovelinefs of virtue. His laft obfervation was prefaced by a folemn avowal of
his own refpect for religion, which he acknowledged

ledged to be a moſt uſeful invention, and a neceſſary reſtriction upon the untutored part of
mankind.   He left Lady Monteith in a ſort of
maze, regretting that he had not been more explicit on thoſe points in which he had confeſſed
his opinions differed from hers, delighted with
his pure morality, and enchanted with his converſation.

Her reverie was interrupted by Lady Arabella's requeſting the favour of her opinion,
whether tiffany, jeſſamine, or crape roſes, would
make the moſt elegant feſtoon.   She liſtened
with perplexed attention to a recapitulation of
the light airineſs of the former ornament, and
the quiet accommodation of the latter ; and
ſhe felt mortified at being obliged to witneſs the
effect of their alternate diſplay on her Ladyſhip's court dreſs.   While her eyes were fixed
upon vacancy, and her thoughts were regretting
the wilful negligence, which would give to
Fitzoſborne a frivolous unintelligent partner,
ſhe, with the indifference of Swift's Vaneſſa,
pronounced an unconſcious preference of the
crape roſes.   This fiat was deciſive, and Lady
Arabella returned to her own apartment with
her maid and her milliner ; a happy groupe, till
the diſcovery, that a lady whom Lady Arabella
hated wore crape roſes, drew from the diſtreſſed
fair one ſeveral pathetic ejaculations on the peculiar unhappineſs of her own lot, in being
thus prevented from having the prettieſt trim-
ming in the world.   Some tender tears were
dropped, which were placed to the account of
her aunt ; and after a few expreſſions, which
from a perſon of leſs delicacy might be termed
ſcolding, ſhe diſmiſſed her terrified auditors with
a declaration,

a declaration, that fhe was very low, and could not bear contradiction and difappointment.

Meantime Lady Monteith had refumed her ftudies, and began to difcover fome of thofe faults in her beloved Johnfon which Fitzofborne had pointed out, when Lord Monteith entered the room, highly elated that he had juft made himfelf complete mafter of " Britons " ftrike home," and entreating her to accompany him upon the harp. She complied ; but the fmile of acquiefcence was more of the penfive than of the exhilarating kind; and her thoughts wandered to the prohibited haunts of ufelefs regrets for the paft, and vain anticipations of the future. But while, in her career of impoffibilities, fhe was beginning to wifh that Monteith poffeffed the intelligent mind of Fitzofborne, her carelefs hand ftruck a falfe chord, and a mechanical impulfe aroufed her attention time enough to anfwer her Lord's inquiries, if fhe was well, and if any thing made her unhappy. His affectionate folicitude reftored her mind to its ufual temperament, and fhe chided herfelf for indulging a thought inconfiftent with the gratitude and efteem which fhe owed to her plighted confort. She recollected that different excellencies belong to different characters ; and that it is the abufe, not the want, of a talent which ftamps criminality upon any one. She made allowances for the force of habit confpiring with ftrong paffions, unreftrained by an expenfive, yet defective, education, and inflamed by the feductions of affluence and uncontrolled freedom of action.—— While thefe reflections fucceffively occupied her

mind,

mind, a tender fweetnefs diffufed itfelf over her countenance, and her hand executed " Britons " ftrike home" entirely to his Lordfhip's fatisfaction.

END OF THE FIRST VOLUME.